Welcome to *Wildling...*

DOWNLOAD YOUR FREE NOVELLA WHISKEY RIDGE NOW!

Two people vanish deep in the Australian Alps. Only one comes back.

When ranger Mia Thomas and her border collie Koda are called to search Wildling National Park, they find a campsite abandoned and a terrified young woman stumbling from the bush. Issy Inglewood insists her lover disappeared after his drone captured something it shouldn't have - but when her story starts to unravel suspicion turns on her.

As Mia fights to uncover the truth, she finds herself caught between loyalty, fear, and the rules she's sworn tofollow. In a community where everyone has something to hide, she must decide who to trust - and how far she'll go to uncover the truth.

A taut, emotional prequel to the Wildling K9 Mystery Series, this novella introduces search and rescue officer Mia Thomas and her dog Koda - a team driven by instinct, haunted by the past, and about to discover that in the mountains, nothing stays lost forever.

DOWNLOAD
FREE AT

nikkileetaylor.com

NIKKI LEE
TAYLOR

WILDLING
ROAD

Published by Magpie Creative Media

ISBN   978-0-6484406-9-7

WILDLING ROAD

BOOK ONE
WILDLING K9 MYSTERY SERIES

Trigger Warning

This book contains references to sexual abuse and self-harm. While no scenes contain active descriptions of abuse or self-harm taking place, there are backstory references to historic instances of these types of issues. Aboriginal and Torres Strait Islander persons should be aware that this book contains the names of fictional deceased people.

Should any of these references raise any concerns, please contact your nearest mental health provider.

Acknowledgement of Country

I acknowledge the Traditional Custodians of the land and pay my respects to Elders past, present, and emerging. I recognise their enduring connection to the land, waters, and culture, and extend that respect to all Aboriginal and Torres Strait Islander Peoples. While this book is set in a fictional place, it is representative of a land we now know as the NSW Snowy Mountains. It is not my intention to represent the Traditional Land Owners of this region, but to touch on the various cultures of this country and the importance of preserving the land. I also thank and acknowledge Australian author and proud Wiradjuri woman Ruth Wkyes for carrying out a sensitivity read on this work prior to publication.

Author's Note

In recent years, I have begun to uncover and explore my own First Nations heritage. It's something I was not fully aware of growing up, and is a journey I approach with deep humility.

I do not claim to fully understand the complexity, strength, or lived experience of Aboriginal and Torres Strait Islander Peoples

What I do carry is a desire to listen, to learn, and to do better.

If I have fallen short in any portrayal of First Nations characters, beliefs, traditions, or heritage, I sincerely apologise. It is never my intention to cause harm. Rather, my hope is to contribute to a greater awareness and appreciation of the stories that have long belonged to this land – stories far older than mine.

Nikki Lee Taylor

Dedication

Max and Sam, you taught me unconditional love.
Saxon, without you there would be no me.
There are people out there who may say, *it's just a dog,* but
we know better, don't we?
Those of us fortunate enough to have been loved by a dog.
Who've cried into their fur, come home to a joyful wagging
tail, and felt the pain of saying the hardest goodbye of all.

To all the dogs who've loved us... this is for you.

Chapter One

THE scent of damp earth and eucalyptus hangs in the air – a stark reminder that we are in the thick of Wildling National Park. Behind us, the mountain range stretches out across the horizon, dawn's first light washing its peaks in gold.

I shiver and glance at my watch. It's been thirteen hours since local teenager Lilly Daniels was reported missing. I've checked the time so often it's started to feel like a reflex, as though it might tell me something new if I look hard enough. But nothing is going to change the fact that we're on the clock and that every second counts.

Over my shoulder, a cluster of bright orange vests stands out against the muted greens of the bush. New South Wales Parks Rangers, police, SES officers, and community volunteers. Their huddle is tight, their faces a mix of hope and grim resolve as they wait for my signal to move out. Most are men I've known my whole life. Men who still stare through me, then look again when they realise I'm the one in charge.

I zip my jacket and remind myself to stand up straight. The breeze has already pulled strands of dark hair from my beanie. They hang loose around my face, and I think to myself that I probably look more like one of the volunteers' daughters than the canine search and rescue officer in charge. I let the thought pass. Doubt is a luxury I can't afford out here. Not when everyone is counting on me – especially Lilly.

At my feet, my border collie shifts his weight from one paw to the other. Dew beads on his coat, his warm breath visible in the cold air. He barks and nuzzles his head against my leg. Koda never questions me. Some days it's the only thing that keeps me going.

'You ready to work?' I ask, running a hand over his thick chocolate and white fur. 'You ready to find someone?'

At full speed, Koda can run in bursts of up to fifty kilometres an hour and traverse this rugged landscape better than any of us. He prances on the spot, reminding me of a boxer ready to enter the ring. All muscle and focus, with no fear of what might come next.

'All right, everyone,' I call out, willing my voice not to break, 'once we head out, stay in your groups and keep in constant communication. We're reaching a critical window for finding Lilly Daniels safe and well. Every minute counts. If you think you've found something, no matter how small or seemingly insignificant, blow your whistle.'

Aside from police and rangers, most of the SES and

other searchers are volunteers. Local farmers, horsemen, and members of the community. They know this land like the back of their hands. There's a few women in the group, including Bett Hastings, a red-headed, outspoken, third-generation cattle farmer known for her ability to wrangle a herd and slip curse words into every sentence, but most are men - the self-proclaimed pillars of the community. They are the sturdy hardwood that forms the structure of the town. Gnarly, weathered, and unwavering, Wildling's patriarchy has always called the shots. Generation after generation of men standing tall and barking orders, disguising themselves as strong when, in truth, their rotten roots have been poisoning this place for decades.

I take out the Ziploc bag containing Lilly's cotton nightgown and crouch beside Koda. His incredible nose can detect scent molecules on the ground and in the atmosphere, even rising from a person trapped beneath snow. It makes him the perfect search-and-rescue dog for an alpine area like Wildling National Park, which can see dozens of skiers and snowboarders become lost in white-out conditions and avalanches every winter.

I open the bag and exchange a glance with the park's head ranger, and my boss, Kevin Daley. He watches closely but doesn't say anything. He doesn't need to. I know he trusts me, and it's not something I take lightly.

Koda sniffs at the opening, and his posture shifts, a shiver of excitement travelling along his spine. He barks and pulls against his harness.

I take a deep breath, shake out the tremor in my hands, and nod. It's time. One way or another, we're going to find Lilly Daniels.

'Okay, Koda,' I tell him. 'Search!'

As we head out along the mountain track, I breathe in the crisp morning air. I catch myself counting steps and shake my head. It was something I did as a kid to make sure I never got lost. I guess old habits die hard, but at least the conditions are perfect. In the cold, scent molecules move closer together, creating a higher concentration of smell per square metre. At training, we were taught to think of them as individual football players spread out across the field.

Now imagine the weather turns bad and all the stinky men run in and huddle together in one locker room, our trainer had said. *That's how much easier it is for dogs to locate scent in cold weather.*

I'd laughed back then, but as we head deeper into the park, it doesn't seem so funny anymore.

Beside me, Koda's feet brush against twigs and brittle autumn leaves. In a few days, the first snowfall of winter will arrive in the park, bringing with it an entirely new landscape. The world will be blanketed in white, the skeletal branches of gum trees laden with snow, and trails and tracks will disappear – along with any clues of what happened to Lilly.

Behind us, the team of searchers spreads out across the land like a human chain. Lilly's phone last pinged in this location. In her statement, seventeen-year-old Britt Davis assured Wildling's chief of police that her best friend would never be caught dead without her phone. That's what I'm afraid of – that we'll find the phone discarded in a rock pile or crevice somewhere near a cold and lifeless Lilly.

Out in front, Koda pushes ahead. 'You're doing great, mate,' I tell him, keeping my voice light. 'Good job, good job.'

A gentle breeze stirs the silence, rustling through the alpine scrub and catching the strands of hair that slipped from my beanie. I adjust my pack and follow Koda as he weaves over rocks and through narrow clearings, his ears flicking with each subtle shift in the wind.

He keeps his nose to the ground as he brackets left and right across the trail, searching for the scent cone – an invisible but pungent triangle that will point him in Lilly's direction. I train my focus on his shoulders, his tail, all the small tells I've learned to read like a second language.

The breeze lifts again, and I glance upslope, following the line toward Mount Saxby. At this time of the morning, the park's highest peak remains blanketed in cloud. Even though I can't see it, I know it's there, teasing and taunting, beckoning people to try and reach the summit. For the unprepared, the national park is like a giant Venus flytrap, drawing you in and then suddenly closing its jaws around you.

Suddenly, the high-pitched sound of a whistle causes my stomach to sink.

'Stop!' Daley's voice bellows across the valley, and the chain of searchers comes to a halt.

'Koda, wait,' I command, then look over my shoulder to see what's happening.

About fifty metres away, Daley is marching toward one of the SES searchers who's crouched with his hand up. They've found something. Relief and dread instantly tangle in my gut.

Even as a pup, Koda could read my face, deciphering the slightest twitch of my lip or pull of my brow. As he gazes up at me, I know he doesn't understand why we've stopped when he hasn't located the scent source.

'You're good, mate,' I tell him. 'We'll start again in a minute.'

His lack of interest in the direction of the searchers tells me they haven't found Lilly – but perhaps they've located her phone.

Daley is quickly joined by a police officer, and together they crouch and point at something on the ground. I squint, trying to see what's happening, but they're too far away. A couple of minutes later, my walkie-talkie crackles and Daley's voice booms against my shoulder.

'Thomas, it's Daley. Come in.'

'Thomas,' I reply.

'We've got the phone. Battery's dead. Keep pushing forward with Koda.'

'Understood.'

'And Mia...'

I swallow hard. Daley only ever calls me by my first name when something bad is about to happen. 'Yeah, boss?'

'Looks like there's blood on the phone.'

Shit.

I nod but forget to speak as if he can see me.

'You good?'

'Good, boss. Resuming search.'

I glance down and meet Koda's eye. There's every chance today will be the day we locate our first body, and I wonder how that might affect him. Will Koda understand death, or think only that he's done his job by finding the scent source? I scratch him behind the ear and remind myself that I'm projecting my human emotions onto him. He'll be fine. I, on the other hand, have never found a body – not to mention that of a young woman I know.

Lilly is a teenager, and a wild one at that. At twenty-nine, I'm twelve years older than she is. I don't know her well, but she and Britt Davis are known around Wildling as the kind of girls nice boys don't bring home for barbecues or Christmas dinners. They're promiscuous and rebellious. It's hard to know if they're bad girls or whether their poor choices are just the result of boredom. Around here, the line between the two is razor-thin. In a town of just 3,203 people, there isn't a whole lot to do – and what you actually do can't be kept secret.

Suddenly, Koda barks. Once, twice, three times. He's found the scent cone.

'In scent!' I call into the walkie-talkie. 'Letting my canine off lead.'

Once Koda is locked onto a scent, keeping pace is a challenge. There's no way I can maintain his speed, so I unclip the leash from his harness and let him go. If Lilly's on the move, Koda will catch up to her a lot faster than I can. He'll find her, confirm visual contact, and then come back to me.

As he sprints into the bush, I pick up the pace, my lungs already burning. By the time Koda confirms a visual, I'll be about halfway there. Hopefully, seeing my dog with his fluorescent orange K9 Search and Rescue vest will be enough to let Lilly know she's safe.

'Lilly Daniels!' I call out as I run after him. 'If you can hear me, stay where you are. My name is Mia Thomas. I'm a NSW Canine Search and Rescue Officer. My dog Koda is coming to you.'

But when only Koda's frenzied bark echoes back, my stomach drops.

'Lilly Daniels, can you hear me?' I call again.

Once again, my walkie-talkie crackles, and Daley's voice fills the air. 'Thomas, come in.'

'Thomas,' I manage, gasping for air.

'You got anything?'

'No… visual… as yet,' I huff. 'Koda's… got something. En route now.'

'Confirm when you have a visual.'

'Will… do.'

I push myself to run harder, wincing as branches catch my sleeve and scratch at my face. A few seconds later, Koda bounds back through the bush toward me, barking, then spinning in a tight circle. He has visual confirmation.

'Good job, buddy,' I tell him. 'Show me.'

He turns and takes off. Once again, I call out, 'Li… ll… y! Can you hear me?'

At this range, and with Koda's visual confirmation, if she were alive, she'd have heard me.

Goddamn it.

I follow the sound of Koda's short, sharp barks until he comes into view, perched in a small clearing up ahead. He's led us back toward the farming properties that border the edge of the national park. Just beyond where Koda is standing, the land drops into a small ravine about six metres deep. Beyond that is Willow's Crossing, a sprawling cattle farm owned by Wildling's most influential family, the Stantons.

As I draw closer, three crows burst out, the beat of their wings matching my heart. They land on the branch of a nearby snow gum, their macabre wails echoing against the eerie silence. The bush knows before we do.

'Shit,' I whisper on a long breath. 'That's not good.'

I remind myself to stay calm. To do my job. Not to panic.

Koda runs back to me and spins in another tight circle before dashing to the edge, where he plants himself and continues barking. Every few seconds, he glances back, his eyes pleading for me to come and see what he's found. The sound of his incessant barking spikes my anxiety even further, but reluctantly, I take another step forward.

'Easy, mate,' I tell him. 'I know. Quiet now.'

I say it even though I know there's no point. I need to let him show me what he's found. I need to reward him for doing his job.

One more step. Koda moves to the side, and I look over the edge.

Immediately, her dead eyes stare back at me. There's a gash across her face, the skin flayed open where crows have started to feed. Strawberry-blonde hair is matted with congealed blood that's turned black during the night. She's fully clothed, the collar of her peach parka riding up around her neck. Bright purple nail polish looks garish against pale, lifeless skin, and beside her, one sneaker has come off, the laces still tied in a perfect bow.

I gasp and turn away, desperate to push her milky skin and stunned eyes out of my mind.

'Jesus,' I manage, as bile climbs the back of my throat.

'Shit.'

I hunch over, resting my arms on my knees. I count my breaths. One. Two. Then blow my whistle – three short, sharp blasts to indicate we've found the scent source.

Beside me, Koda barks, and I know I have to get my shit together. He's done his job. He deserves to be rewarded.

I slowly stand and slide the pack off my back. 'You did so good, buddy, so good.'

I force myself to sound excited and joyful. He deserves that. Koda might have fur, four legs, and a tail, but I'm still his mum, and a mum's job is to always put her child's needs before her own.

His eyes light up as I take the chew rope from my pack. I swing it, and he hangs on, his entire body swaying side to side like a pendulum, counting down the minutes until the space around us becomes an official crime scene.

This is how I was trained, to reward Koda for a successful find, but it feels wrong to play with him while Lilly's lifeless body lies just metres away. Turning away, pretending she isn't down there, feels wrong too. So instead, I ruffle the fur around Koda's neck, tell him he's a good boy, then put the rope away. I've done everything by the book. There's just nothing in the manual about what to do while I wait – how to quiet the ache in my chest, or quash the desperate need to say something, anything.

If Mimi were here, she'd know what to do. I close my eyes and try to picture her beside me. I imagine her kneeling at the edge of the ravine, dress flowing out behind her, palms pressed to the earth. She'd tell me Lilly's spirit had become one with the land - that as she left this world, the mountain wrapped its arms around her, held her tight, and whispered, *welcome, child, you are home.*

But Mimi's beliefs about the land mean nothing to me, even if she is my grandmother. So instead, I quiet Koda and lead him a few metres back from the edge of the ravine. I close my eyes, draw in a slow breath, and do the only thing left. I whisper to Lilly's body that I will do everything in my power to find out what happened to her.

Chapter Two

THE scene is an ant's nest, crawling with police and crime scene investigators. It's the kind of organised chaos that makes you feel like you're in the way even when you're not. Anyone who isn't a cop or medic has been relegated to the sidelines and told in no uncertain terms not to interfere. As Daley and I watch them work, I shove my hands deeper into my pockets so no one can see they're still shaking.

'You did good today, kid,' he tells me. 'Real good.' He doesn't go into any detail. That's not who he is. If he did, I wouldn't even know what to say.

'Koda did all the work,' I reply. 'I just tried to keep up.'

'You did good.'

I nod and glance up at him. Standing at least a head taller than me, Daley is a hulking bear of a man. His shoulders are thick and square. Time has streaked his hair with grey and it's cut short – practical, like him. A scruff of stubble perpetually covers his chin, and every time I look at it, I wonder if he's taking proper care of himself. But his uniform is always perfectly ironed, his boots polished to a shine. I often joke that it must be easy to keep them that way when you sit behind a desk all day instead of being out in the field, but he never bites. Daley's never been much for jokes.

'Thanks,' I manage. 'I... well, thanks.'

'Yep.'

He isn't much for emotion either.

When Wildling's local cop, Herm Drinkwater, makes his way toward us, Daley's body shifts a fraction, like he's bracing for impact. 'Let me deal with him,' he tells me out of the corner of his mouth. 'And don't get angry.'

'I'm not going to get angry.'

He glances down at me, a knowing look in his eyes. 'What? I'm not.'

'Just let me do the talking.'

Known by teenagers as Herm the Worm, Herm Drinkwater is a paunchy man in his mid-fifties. A beer belly strains the buttons of his police shirt, and on top of his head is a slice of devon – a round bald spot he tries to cover with wispy strands of hair. The only son of parents who never amounted to much, Herm grew up on the outskirts of town and, from what I can gather, was always known as a creepy boy who hung around the farms, trying to befriend the rich kids.

Now, as the local cop, he loves to throw his weight around. Most days, he strolls down Main Street with a deliberate swagger, thumbs tucked into his belt, eyes narrowed, and giving slow nods to anyone who passes. Really, he's nothing more than a lackey for Jack Stanton. Whatever Jack says, Herm does – just like everyone else. That's the unofficial law of Wildling. Always was. Always will be.

'Kevin.' Herm greets Daley, then, as an afterthought, adds, '…Mia.'

I nod and remind myself not to say anything I might regret later.

'Not a good way to start the day.'

'Nope, it's not.'

'These girls…' He trails off.

'What's that supposed to—'

Daley silences me with a look, and I stop mid-sentence. Herm turns and looks me over like he's just remembered I'm standing here.

'It was you who found the body?'

I shake my head in quiet frustration. 'You know we did.'

'You and the dog, right?'

'Koda, yes.'

He glances at Koda, who looks back at him and barks. Good, I think. At least one of us isn't bothering to pretend.

'And you didn't contaminate the scene in any way?'

'No.' I quickly replay every step, every breath, I took as I drew nearer to the edge.

'How can you be so sure?'

'Because I'm trained to deal with crime scenes.'

'But you've never actually been to a crime scene, have you?'

'Have you?' I snap.

'All right, that's enough,' Daley interjects, stepping forward. 'If you have any questions for Mia, let's make a time to come into headquarters and debrief. I think she's been through enough this morning.'

Herm clicks his tongue and adjusts his hat, a black felt Stetson that looks like it belongs on a sheriff somewhere in Texas.

'Fine. Just one last thing...'

I sigh. There's always one last thing with men like him.

'I trust you know your place in all this, Mia.'

'My place?'

Daley stiffens. I feel it in the space between us.

'Yes, your *place*, which is nowhere near this investigation.' His eyes dart toward the boundary of Willow's Crossing.

'If you say so.'

Herm nods and turns his attention back to Daley. 'Just keep her away from the Stanton property, Kevin. We clear?'

'Mia's done her job. She and Koda located the body. What else would there be to do?'

'I'm just saying...'

The rustle of footsteps cuts him off.

'Oh, Jack. Good morning.'

Together, Daley and I turn to see Jack Stanton coming up behind us, his looming figure almost blocking the sun. Dressed in a red check shirt, jeans, and aviator sunglasses, he looks like Clint Eastwood. And I'm pretty sure he knows it.

'Jack,' Daley says with a nod.

'Daley,' he replies, removing his sunglasses. 'Hell of a morning.'

'Sure is.'

'What do they know?'

'Not much. It's the Daniels girl. My guess is she's been here at least twelve hours, maybe more. Definite signs of—'

'I'm expecting a full report from the medical examiner this afternoon,' Herm interjects, stepping in closer to Jack. 'My contacts will let me know everything, and rest assured, you'll be the first call I make, Jack.'

Jack Stanton studies Herm, and it's hard to read his thoughts. Contempt, pity, annoyance. I can't say for sure, but the weaselly look on Herm's face leaves no doubt about how far he would go to please him.

'You be sure to do that,' Jack says eventually. 'This circus is almost on my damned boundary line. What if Sarah had found her?'

I glance over my shoulder toward the sprawling homestead and wonder if Jack's wife, Sarah, is up at the window. It's too far to see, but I can almost feel her there – fingertips of one hand pressed against the glass, pearls clutched nervously in the other.

It's no secret that Sarah struggled after the death of her sister. They were just teenagers when Missy drowned herself in the lake on their family farm next door to Willow's Crossing. Sarah had been the one to find her.

'I couldn't agree more,' Herm is saying. 'Whatever happened here, you can rest assured I'll get to the bottom of it.'

Jack peers over my head toward the medics pulling Lilly's body out on a stretcher. 'Can't say I'm all that surprised. That girl was headed down a dangerous path. We all knew it.'

I glance at Herm, expecting him to at least take out his notepad, but instead, he shoves his hands into his pockets.

'A lot of people in town, including my wife, tried to help her,' Jack continues. 'The other girl too, but they wouldn't listen. Thought it was a waste of time myself. Told Sarah as much. You know what womenfolk are like, though, always meddling and trying to fix things.'

He sighs and shakes his head. 'You'll probably find it was drugs or some kind of misadventure. Was bound to happen eventually. Maybe the other one will learn her lesson now. Pull her head in.'

I look at Daley, waiting to see if he'll tell Jack how inappropriate this is. When, instead, he turns and gazes out at the mountains, I drop my head. Sometimes silence is its own kind of response.

'You know what I'm talking about, Mia,' Jack adds, turning his attention to me. 'Wasn't so long ago you were just like them, but look at you now, out here with that mutt of yours. It's commendable, really.'

I bite my lip to stop from screaming. Everyone in Wildling knows I have a past. In a small town reliant on farming to stay afloat, growing up with an eccentric grand-mother who claimed she could hear the land weeping every time a tractor ploughed its way across a paddock made me a target. And unlike my brother, I didn't always react well.

'I think we're done here,' Daley says at last. 'Great job today, Thomas. Let's head back to headquarters. We'll do a debrief and then get you and Koda some breakfast. What do you say?'

My eyes linger on Jack as I decide whether to acknowl-edge his attempt to insult me, but in the end, just like everyone else in town, I keep my mouth shut.

'Sure, Daley,' I say with a nod. 'Sounds good.'

'Jack, is it okay with you if we cut across your boundary? It's a lot quicker than heading back over the mountain track.'

Jack stiffens and, for a moment, just stares out over the field. Then he spits on the ground and nods. 'Fine, but I don't want that dog spooking my livestock.' He looks right at me when he adds, 'So keep it on a short leash.'

Chapter Three

AS we make our way across the paddocks toward the Willow's Crossing homestead, morning sun falls across the kangaroo grass in a pale sweep.

I try my best to push Jack's comments out of my mind, but with every step, they needle me, like burrs digging into my skin. I try telling myself I don't care, but my body refuses to believe it. I hate that, again, I've let him get to me. Despite his multimillion-dollar cattle farm, Jack is a red-neck arsehole who, for the life of him, will never crawl out from under the past, and yet in some sick way, I still crave his respect. It's embarrassing, wanting approval from a man I can't stand. A better version of me would have told him to mind his own business, but I can never find the nerve. Instead, I imagine all the words I'd like to shout at him, then clamp them down behind my teeth and try not to implode.

When the land dips into a shallow fold, I notice a shift in Koda's energy. An electric current hums its way up the lead, coursing through my fingers and along my arm. I glance down, quickly cataloguing my dog's every move. The flicker of his ears. The change in his tail, moving from relaxed to straight out behind him. The way he pulls against his harness.

'Koda, what is it?' I whisper, quiet enough that Jack doesn't hear me. 'What have you got?'

I glance around the property, my pulse counting ahead, like it wants to get there before I do. Only cattle, as far as the eye can see. But Koda's not looking at cattle. He's looking past them.

'You good?' Daley asks over his shoulder.

'Yep, we're all good back here.'

Jack's property is pristine farmland nestled at the base of the mountains. The ground undulates here and there, but for the most part, it's flat. I squint and stare out across the land, determined to see whatever Koda can smell.

'Do you have any workers out here who tend to the property?' I ask Jack.

'It's five thousand acres,' he answers without stopping or looking back.

Apparently, that's supposed to be an answer, because he doesn't elaborate. Daley turns and looks at me, clearly confused.

I nod toward Koda, widening my eyes to signal he's onto something. It takes a moment, but as Daley follows my line of sight, he picks up on Koda's cues as well. Somewhere out here is another person. Koda is never wrong.

Like clockwork, he begins to bark. Once, twice, three times. The sound cuts straight through my ribs. Jack glances back and scowls.

'Shut that dog up,' he growls. 'I told you I don't want it spooking my cattle.'

Daley and I immediately exchange a glance. I can't see as far as Koda can smell, but something doesn't feel right. I pull my phone from my pocket and open the GPS app. I want to note the exact coordinates. A breadcrumb trail for later. When Daley sees what I'm doing, he shoots me a quick look that can only be read as *don't start trouble.*

Since losing his daughter to cancer nine years ago, I've become the closest thing to family Daley has. Likewise, growing up without a father, Daley's gruff voice and tough love have undeniably shaped who I am. He's a constant. Someone I can rely on. So, when Daley shoots me a look that says *don't start trouble*, I know it's probably in my best interest to follow his lead.

I tuck my phone away, and we push on until eventually the homestead rises up before us like a mirage. Hamptons white, tennis court, inground pool, manicured gardens, and inside, a floor rumoured to be made from exotic timber Jack had flown in from West Africa. It's a house that screams money, even when the world around it falls silent.

Mimi calls it *Infaustus* – cursed. It's typical of her to choose a Latin name, the same way she labels jars of herbs and names sketches of plants with words that no one else can read.

She calls it that because decades ago, Jack's great-grandfather Edgar Stanton convinced the Traditional Elders to sell him the land for a pittance. She says he cast a spell on them. Tricked them into selling. She believes that in return, the mountain spirits put a curse on Willow's Crossing and everyone who lives there. In my opinion, there's nothing supernatural about Willow's Crossing or the Stanton family. I don't believe any spells were cast or that anyone was punished for what Old Edgar did. The only magic surrounding that family is their ability to make other people's money disappear before pulling it out from behind their ear like a novelty gold coin.

'You need a ride into town?' Jack grumbles as we stop beside the tennis court. 'I can have one of the farmhands take you. Dog has to ride in the back, obviously.'

By *in the back* he means in the open tray of a farm ute. I've no doubt Koda would be fine, but it's not happening.

'We're good,' Daley tells him. 'Appreciate the offer, though. I'll be in touch with any updates.'

As we walk across the lush green lawn, past the glistening pool and Sarah's perfectly tended rose garden, I spot Herm's police car parked out front.

When he catches me looking, he clears his throat. 'It was just easier than taking the mountain track on foot. And faster. I... uh, can give you guys a ride if you like. The dog can sit in the back seat. I don't mind.'

Daley and I exchange a glance. It's at least ten kilometres back to where Daley and I left our vehicles, and Herm's car will be a lot quicker.

'If it's no trouble, Herm. Thanks,' Daley says. 'Got a lot of paperwork to get through after this morning's… situation.'

Daley folds himself into the front seat, and I climb into the back, Koda pressed up against my leg. The car reeks of sweat and cigarettes, and I quickly wind down the window.

'Don't think badly of Jack,' Herm says, glancing at me in the rear-view mirror. 'He's old school. Still thinks dogs belong outdoors and all.'

Sometimes I can't help but wonder about the difference between being old school and just plain cruel, but I give him my best tight smile and nod. Whatever I say will be relayed back to Jack the moment we step out of the car. Best to keep my mouth shut.

When we eventually pull up beside Daley's white Toyota LandCruiser, the NSW National Parks and Wildlife logo emblazoned along the side, I gather Koda's leash and slip my fingers through the door latch. I've got one leg out when, once again, Herm clears his throat.

'I, uh, couldn't help but notice your dog got a bit excited on the walk back.'

Only the back of Daley's head is visible through the gap in the headrest, but I don't miss the way his shoulders stiffen.

'It was nothing unusual, Herm,' I reply. 'He gets excited by the smell of cow shit in a field. Kangaroo poo. Possum dung. You name the crap, Koda gets excited by it.'

Herm nods, and I catch him stealing another glance at me. 'Just seemed like maybe...'

'...like maybe what?'

'Like maybe he caught wind of something back there.'

Without meaning to, I swallow hard and immediately hope he doesn't notice. 'Nope. Not that I saw. Like I said, he's a dog. He barks and gets excited at the strangest things. In fact, there was this one time my neighbour's cat had the most disgusting diarrhoea and he actually—'

'That's... that's okay, Mia,' Herm says, holding up his hand. 'I just wanted to be clear that Willow's Crossing is private property. You can't go traipsing around without Jack's permission and without letting me know. So don't go getting any ideas about heading back out there. Understood?'

'There's nothing to worry about, Herm. She knows,' Daley tells him. 'Right, Mia?'

Daley turns his head just far enough for me to see the profile of his face. Tight jaw. Stern chin.

'Right,' I reply. 'Like I said, Koda's Koda. I'd know if he alerted to a scent. He didn't.'

Herm's shoulders visibly relax, and he twists around to face me. 'Well, all right then. And good job today, Mia. You and Koda did right by Lilly out there. Really well done.'

His words of praise shock me, and for a moment, I almost forget all the times he hauled me into the station as a teenager. The time Mrs Henry reported me for drinking down by the basketball courts. The time I walked out of the supermarket with a Snickers bar tucked down my pants. The time he cruised by as I spray-painted my initials on the concrete curve of the skate park. But just as quickly, memories of his cold, bony fingers and flabby white skin come rushing back, and I squeeze my eyes shut. Herm is a lecher. An opportunist who shields himself behind Jack Stanton's knees, his tentacled arms wrapped tight around the legs of a giant. It's his way of making sure no one ever holds him accountable for the way he treats the young women of Wildling, should they be unfortunate enough to find themselves in his company.

'That's what we're trained for,' I tell him, moving closer to Koda. 'It's our job.'

'Well, it was impressive. But like I said, just stick to procedure. No searches unless the police officially request your presence. They're the rules.'

'I know the rules, Herm.'

'Good to hear,' he says with a click of his tongue. 'No doubt I'll see you both soon.'

Chapter Four

THE Gold Rush Inn is buzzing. The smell of stale beer and fried food is thick in the air. Cigarette smoke seeps in from the small outdoor area, where three men and a woman huddle against an icy wind blowing in off the mountains. As Wildling's only pub, the Goldie is where everything happens. Meetings, dinners, catch-ups, celebrations, and commiserations. Not that there's often much to celebrate or commiserate in Wildling. It's the kind of town where most days and weeks are the same, and everyone seems to like it that way.

As I squeeze past a group of rowdy farmhands, I catch snippets of their banter. It's mostly friendly teasing and exaggerated tales of glory from last weekend's footy game, harmless fun between mates. In the background, glasses clink, people laugh, and I take a deep breath to try and steady myself. I hate being around this many people at once. I can see in their eyes that most of them don't like me, that they think I don't measure up. I've learned to read the micro-expressions – a flicker of judgement here, the quick look-away there, but it's more than that. The space feels tight, claustrophobic, and a familiar knot of anxiety twists in my chest. The therapist in Sydney told me it was normal. That after what I went through, there would be situations that triggered me. That it was to be expected.

That's one of the things I love most about the national park – all that open space. Most days out there, the only sounds I hear are the calls of currawongs, chirping frogs, and water whispering over rocks. Other days, it's so quiet I can hear the rise and fall of my own breath. Those are the days I feel stitched back together. The moments that remind me how small I am in the scheme of things. That I am a tiny blade of grass beneath a sky that saw the start of time. Despite being seven thousand square kilometres of rugged mountains, glacial lakes, and dense alpine forest, I feel safe out there. I know how to survive. To the untrained eye, nature seems unpredictable, but that's not completely true. There are always signs, and once you know how to read them, they'll keep you safe. Sudden temperature drops. A shift in the breeze. A change in the clouds. The park doesn't want to hurt you. If you pay attention, it will tell you when it wants you out. People aren't like that. Nature works off balance. People work by tipping the scales in their favour – no matter the cost.

And they have short memories.

Grief has always had a shelf life in Wildling, and it's shorter than the milk at Leslie Harrigan's IGA. Less than twenty-four hours ago, Koda and I discovered the body of a seventeen-year-old girl just metres from the Willow's Crossing boundary line, but no one is here tonight to talk about that. People have already decided she took drugs, got drunk, maybe both, then wandered into the park and froze to death. At this time of year, the temperature drops to minus four at night. It wouldn't be the first time someone died out there from the cold.

Such a shame. She was so young.

That's what I overheard Sarah Stanton saying to one of the other Country Women's Association ladies a few minutes ago, and she probably meant it. Sarah has always seemed nice, despite being married to Jack. She's forever trying to mend the divide between farmers, townies, and the First Nations community through talks, bake sales, and library meetings, but none of it works. Jack would never allow real change in his town. He lets her play at it because it keeps her happy and quiet, but everyone knows it's futile. Wildling is Wildling, and not Sarah, or anyone, is ever going to change that.

I excuse myself as I push through the crowd and find a seat at the back. Around me, the last stragglers file in. Chairs scrape against the wooden floor. Handbags drop to the ground. A woman laughs awkwardly, probably for sitting in a seat that was being held for someone else.

'Thank you so much for coming out on a Thursday night,' my brother announces as he steps onto a small platform that passes for a stage. 'If everyone wouldn't mind finding a seat, we can get started. I don't want to keep you long.'

Jason lets his arm drop to his side and gives everyone a moment to get settled. He's always had the knack of knowing when to wait. When it's better to let something come to him rather than to go chasing after it.

He catches my eye and gives me a quick wink. Despite the dark denim jeans, crisp white shirt, and navy blazer, he carries the outdoors with him wherever he goes. His sun-darkened skin, perpetually wind-roughed hair, and muscular build are all proof of a life balanced perfectly between meeting rooms and the mountains.

When the room falls silent, he raises the microphone. 'Now, given the circumstances, before we begin, I think it's fitting that we take a moment of silence and pay our respects to young Lilly Daniels. What happened is a tragedy, and I know you must all be feeling her loss in your own way.'

The room falls quiet, save for the scrunch of a lolly wrapper somewhere near the front and the sharp hiss of a mother telling her kid to *stop it*.

After a moment, Jason nods and raises the mic again. 'Seeing all of you brave the cold to be here tonight certainly warms my heart,' he begins, 'even more than a double shot of Old Jimmy's finest whisky. And I'm not talking about the one on the shelf, if you know what I mean.'

As always, my brother knows how to shift the tone of a room. On cue, everyone laughs, and not for the first time, I envy how easily he can make them like him.

'But seriously,' he continues, 'what I'm going to talk about tonight is important, so thank you for being here.'

He pauses, giving everyone time to shake off the joke, then drops his gaze and exhales. Seeing him up there, in complete control, is a far cry from the childhood we shared. Being packed up and shipped off to live with Mimi, his sticky hand squeezing mine in the dark when I'd cry because Mum didn't want us anymore. His whispered promises that one day we'd run away from Wildling and live in Antarctica with the penguins. As a little girl, I couldn't think of anything worse, but if he'd asked, I would have gone. That's the power of Jason, and I have no doubt he'll find a way to get the town on board with what he's about to propose.

'Some of you may have heard whispers about what my company, EnviroTech, has been working on,' he begins. 'I know you've heard it's something big, and you're right. It is.'

Jason paces slowly across the stage, making eye contact with everyone, drawing them in. I glance across the room in amazement as he pulls everyone under his spell. It's as if an invisible thread runs from his hand to every person in the room, leading them wherever he wants them to go. As much as I try to deny it, as I watch him, there's a tiny part of me, a stubborn, jealous part, that wants to leap out of my seat and violently yank at it.

'Our company plans to launch a state-of-the-art geothermal drilling project in the national park before the snow gets too heavy. Now, I can already see some curious faces, so let me explain what this means and how it benefits us all.

'Geothermal drilling is an innovative technology that allows us to harness energy efficiently and sustainably. Unlike traditional methods, this approach is environmentally friendly and minimally invasive, especially through winter when most of the park's flora is dormant. I assure you, we've put everything into ensuring our technique respects and preserves the natural beauty of our park.'

I scan the room as people lean in, whispering. It's hard to catch their words, but more than once, I see eyes flick toward Jack, gauging his reaction.

'Now, let's talk benefits. First, this project will create numerous jobs, bringing new people to town and boosting our local economy. We all know how the construction of the bypass has impacted Wildling. It didn't just redirect traffic – it redirected money. Ted, Laura... you'd know that better than anyone. How much business have you lost at Sweet Sips Café in the past eighteen months?'

Everyone turns as the couple glance at each other. Laura nods at Ted, and he gets to his feet. 'Business is down seventy-five percent,' he says. 'Haven't turned a profit in the past six months. Makes trying to break even damned near impossible, doesn't it love?' He turns to Laura, and she nods and dabs at her eyes with a tissue.

Jason looks back out over the room. 'Seventy-five per cent. That's a catastrophic number, and I know Ted and Laura aren't the only ones doing it tough. This project is a chance to bring people back to Wildling. Construction workers, staff to work on the rig, and researchers to make sure we're doing everything right. Those people will go to the café, the pub, the IGA. They'll spend money locally. It's not the answer, but it's a start. Now… second, the energy produced will be clean, renewable, and reliable. That means lower costs for our homes and businesses. Imagine reducing your heating bills through winter while securing a sustainable energy source for generations.'

In front of me, Mary Johnson nods and then quickly checks that her husband, Bert, is doing the same.

'Third, we're committed to giving back to the community. A portion of the revenue will be reinvested in town improvements. New classrooms at Wildling Public School. A water slide at the swimming pool. That kind of thing. Now, I know for the most part, Jack has held the title of town benefactor,' he adds, pausing as the room laughs, 'but this isn't just about energy. It's about enhancing our quality of life.'

He pauses and looks people square in the eye.

'I understand change can be daunting, and you'll have

questions. That's why I'm here tonight. To listen, provide answers, and ensure this project benefits everyone. I believe this is an incredible opportunity. It's a chance to lead the way in sustainable energy, boost our economy, and preserve the natural beauty we all cherish. I'm excited about what we can achieve together, and I'm grateful for your support.'

Jason smiles and lowers the mic. He's clearly expecting a barrage of questions, but instead, the room holds its breath as everyone turns to Jack, waiting to see what he'll say.

Chapter Five

I SIP my coffee and tilt my head back. At this time of year, when the sky is usually washed-out and grey, the sun warming my face feels like a tiny gift. Koda is flopped down beside me, basking in a sun puddle. His eyes are closed, and it would be easy to think he's asleep, but I know better. The occasional flick of his ear tells me he's alert. The subtle twitch of his nose, proof that he's still reading the world around him.

For a town as small as Wildling, the coffee at Sweet Sips Café is unbelievably good. Creamy milk, perfectly blended with robust espresso. It's the best coffee I've ever had anywhere. Not that I've been to many places, but I know a good coffee when I taste it.

'Morning, Mia. You ready to order?' Amelia asks, appearing with a stack of dirty plates balanced in the crook of her elbow.

I shield my eyes and look up. Amelia is Jason's girlfriend. Growing up, I thought no one would ever be good enough for my brother. After what we went through as kids, it comforted me to think he and I would always be a team, but the day she appeared, I knew I was wrong. My brother adores her and, if I'm honest, sometimes it bothers me just how much. It's not jealousy. For me, it feels more like displacement.

'I'll wait for Will,' I tell her. 'He should be here in a minute. He got stuck on the phone again.'

'Okay, no problem.' She flashes her perfect white teeth, and I return a tight-lipped smile.

One table over, a tiny sparrow flits about collecting crumbs. I focus on it, distracting myself, until a few minutes later, Will slides into the seat across from me.

'Sorry. Usual bureaucratic bullshit.'

'You're worth waiting for,' I say, smiling.

Even after all these years, every time I look at him, my stomach flip-flops. Will, Jason, and I – the three musketeers. We spent our childhood together out in the park, pretending the mountains and rivers were kingdoms. *Narnia* one day, *Neverland* the next. Out there, our imaginations ran wild. We could be anything we wanted. Pirates, warriors, and sorcerers. But amid all the cloaks and changing characters, the role I always longed to play most was being his.

Will's clothes have changed since then. Baggy shorts and loose tees have been replaced by sharp suits and neat ties but his pillowy top lip, the angle of his jaw, and those dark eyes and the way they pull me in haven't changed at all. Lately, though, he's been different. Distant. Like he's already halfway somewhere else. I know it's work. The constant back-and-forth travel to Canberra must be exhausting, but it feels like more than that.

'What's the issue this time?' I ask.

He scoffs and bats my question away. 'Just political shit. Nothing you'd be interested in, Mi. Anyway, let's order. I've got to be in Canberra by nine, and it's already seven. I've got twenty minutes tops.'

I swallow the urge to ask why it suddenly feels like he's always running away instead of toward me the way he used to.

'How did it go last night at the pub?' he continues. 'I was out cold by the time you got home. Was Jason happy with the turnout?'

I nod and reach for the menu. I know it by heart but holding it will stop me from fidgeting. 'Jack didn't push back. You know how it is. If he's on board, the town's on board.'

'Good,' he says, as he punches out a text on his phone. 'I'm meeting with the Minister this afternoon. We're getting close to an approval for the drilling rig. Shouldn't be long now.'

'Sounds like it's going well. Jason will be happy.'

He nods, then puts his phone down and looks over the menu at me. 'Do you know what you want?'

'We should get the Eggs Benedict,' I suggest, hoping

it might be something new we can try together. A small marker of us moving forward. 'Amelia says they're really good and—'

'Babe, I just said I've got twenty minutes. Can you just order toast or something quick? I don't have time for Eggs Benedict today.'

I drop my gaze to the menu. 'Sure. Sorry. Maybe on the weekend.'

'Oh, shit,' he mutters, shaking his head. 'I didn't tell you. I've got to stay down in Canberra this weekend.'

My head snaps up and the café tilts, just slightly. 'No, we're going up to Crystal Lake. You promised.'

Will puts down the menu and rubs his chin. I don't miss the clench of his jaw as he looks at me. 'Don't make me feel worse than I already do, Mia. You know I've got a shitload on my plate. Do you think I like this? Driving back and forth to Canberra all the time?'

'Will, it's our anniversary. I understand, but—'

'But nothing,' he snaps. 'Unless you want to move to Canberra, this is how it has to be. You want to leave the mountains? Pack up Koda and move him to the city?'

I glance down at Koda, and he looks back at me, his tongue lolling sideways like it's too big for his mouth. 'No. He'd hate that.'

'Right, so that's your choice. Don't put it back on me. We've been through this.'

'I know, Will, but it just feels like... I don't know. Something's different. You haven't even asked if I'm all right after what happened the other day. Finding Lilly like that... it was hard.'

He shakes his head. 'I'm sorry, really, but it was inevitable that you'd find a body. Does it suck that it was a teenager? Of course, but that's what you're trained to do – find people who get themselves into shit. You've had a good run so far, but you had to know it was going to happen at some point?' He sighs and glances away for a moment. 'And I know things probably feel different now. Christ, I'm one step away from being the Prime Minister's executive advisor. You know how hard I've worked for this. So, cut me some slack, would you? It's not like I can spend my days playing with Koda and hiking in the mountains with you and your brother anymore.'

The way he says it instantly shrinks my greatest accomplishments down to a hobby. 'Right. Because that's all I do?'

'I didn't mean it like that.'

'Well, I'm sorry I'm not some political big shot, or a genius like my brother.' My eyes burn, and I blink back my tears. 'I thought I was enough for you just how I am.'

'Oh, for Christ's sake. I don't have time for this.' He pushes back in his seat, the scrape of the chair legs sealing my fate. 'You're being ridiculous, Mia. Seriously.'

I don't want to fight. If he leaves angry, I'll spend the entire day wondering what he's thinking and hating myself for always being so stupid. I reach across the table for his hand, but he pulls away and the space between us widens. 'I'm sorry. I'll order the raisin toast. Just don't go, please. Not like this.'

But he's already on his feet. 'I don't know why you behave this way. I have almost no free time, but I still try to fit you in wherever I can. We could have had a nice breakfast together.' He glares at me, and my mouth goes dry. 'Just... don't answer. I'll see you tonight.'

'Will—' The look in his eyes silences me, and I drop my gaze so he won't see the tear slipping over my cheek.

'Try to have a good day, all right?'

'Yep,' I murmur. 'You too.'

After he leaves, Amelia hovers at the table. 'You okay?'

She means well, but knowing how much Jason loves her and how happy they are only makes me feel worse. Comparison can be a merciless thief. 'Yep, I'm fine,' I lie.

'Can I get you something?'

I exhale and let my hand fall to Koda's head. I scratch behind his ear, and he leans into my touch, no conditions attached. 'Sure,' I say, pushing the menu away. 'I'll have the raisin toast.'

Chapter Six
Britt

I TAKE one last drag of my smoke, hold it longer than I should, then flick the butt out toward the river. It arcs through the air and lands with a gentle plop on the surface. For a moment, it just floats there, bobbing like it might stay forever, but the current is stronger than it looks. My eyes follow along as it's carried off, further and further, until it's barely a speck, and then nothing at all. A reminder that everything disappears eventually. Even the things you swear won't.

I shouldn't be out here by myself. Not after what happened to Lilly. I'm so freaking tired I could pass out, but no matter how hard I try, I can't sleep. She was my best friend, and now she's just... gone. *How can that be?*

Not for the first time, I pull at my hair and twist it tight around my finger until the tip turns white.

This whole town is a joke. And everyone in it.

Lilly was the only thing that made living here bearable. No matter what anyone says, she's the best person I know... *knew*. Shit, I'll never get used to saying things like that. She can't be gone. She just can't.

I let go of my hair and consider pushing up to my feet, then hesitate. Standing will set the day in motion, and I don't think I can face that. Not today. Maybe not ever.

The whole thing feels like a dream, and a freaking bad one at that. I knew something was wrong when she never answered my messages. She always answers, and I always answer hers. It's what we do.

Like muscle memory, I pull out my phone and glance at the screen. No matter how many times I check, it still feels like a punch in the gut when there's no message from her staring back at me. Usually, we text all day. About nothing. About everything. Like, I get it. I know she can't. But it just feels wrong. Like in those movies where astronauts come unhooked from the rope thing that ties them to the ship, then float off into oblivion. That's what it's like. Untethered, doomed, claustrophobic and completely lonely all at once, and just like space, there's no end to it. It'll last forever, and there's not a damned thing I can do to change it.

God, Lilly. This sucks.

A twig snaps behind me, and I spin around. The clearing is empty, but I remind myself that just because I can't see someone, it doesn't mean they're not there.

'Hello?' I peer toward the tree line, searching for any sign of movement.

Met only with the murmur of water running over rocks,

I swallow and stare harder into the bush.

'If you think you can hurt me, arsehole, you've got no idea who you're dealing with.' The words tumble out before I can stop them. 'I know what really happened to Lilly!'

I take a step back, and my left boot sinks into the mud. I glance down at my soaking wet foot now covered in shit. Of course. 'Well, that's just frickin' great.'

Another twig snaps, and the hairs along the back of my neck prickle. I snap my head back toward the tree line.

'I know what you're doing. You're not scaring me.'

I hold my breath and wait to see if he's got the balls to show himself. The thing is, if he does, I've got no idea what I'll do. *Shit, what was I thinking coming out here alone?*

I reach around and pull a small silver switchblade from the back pocket of my jeans. In a town like Wildling, a seventeen-year-old girl shouldn't need to carry a knife, but this is no ordinary town. Everyone thinks it is. They think it's boring. Predictable. They don't see the cracks because they don't fall through them. They've got no idea what really goes on here. I do. So did Lilly. Now she's dead.

I wait a few minutes, and when nothing happens, I slowly slide the knife back into my pocket.

What was it like for her? I wonder for the hundredth time.

It's the thought that's kept me awake every night since it happened. No one will tell me the details, so I've got no choice but to imagine how she died. Was it fast? Was she lying there alone, knowing she was going to die? Did she call out for me?

It's a never-ending list of questions, with answers that don't make a damn bit of difference, but I need to know. And I should know. Not out of morbid curiosity, but because I was her person. I've shared every moment of her life since kindergarten. No matter how many people in this town thought she didn't matter, she did. At least to me. And that has to count for something.

I pull up the collar of my denim jacket and shove my hands deep into the pockets. Getting home means walking back through the bush. I remind myself that if someone was in there, they just had every chance to kill me and dump my body in the river. No one would ever know, but they didn't. I should be relieved, but thought doesn't comfort me the way it should.

My wet foot squelches as I take a step forward toward the tree line. Another step, and just in case, I reach for the knife.

One more step.

A crow wails and launches from the trees. Something spooked it.

I freeze, swallowing the lump in my throat. My legs are jelly.

'Shit. Screw this for a joke.'

I take out my phone and hover my thumb over the

screen. I want to dial but the list of potential names feels painfully short. My mother? She won't know what to do. My father? He can't answer at work. My sister? She's in Sydney, and I don't have any other friends, not anyone who gives a rat's arse.

The only person I want to call is Lilly.

'Hey!'

The male voice pulls my eyes from the screen, and I see Luke Mittigan stepping out from the trees.

'Luke, are you touched in the head?' I sigh and feel my shoulders unclench. 'What are you even doing out here?'

He jogs toward me, all lanky limbs and awkwardness. His face is still boyish, a mix of angles and acne. Freckles scatter the bridge of his nose, but the sharp line of his jaw hints at the man he's becoming. We've been in a situationship for a few months, probably more from a lack of options than genuine interest.

His grin widens, and I know it was him being stupid in the bush. He's such a wanker like that sometimes.

'Gotcha,' he laughs. 'Was just out for a run. Clearing my head. Who did you think it was?'

I glare and punch his shoulder, harder than if we were just messing around. 'I don't know, and why would you scare me like that? Lilly just died.'

'Dunno,' he says with a shrug. 'Just trying to make you laugh, I s'pose. Was stupid. My bad.' He moves in closer and loops an arm around my shoulder. I stiffen before I can stop myself. 'Everything feels weird since she died, hey?'

I study his face for a moment. He's been acting different since Lilly. Like he's trying to fill a space that isn't his or wanting too much from me, or something.

'Of course it's weird,' I say, wishing he'd get his arm off me. I don't want his lame attempts to comfort me. I just want Lilly back.

He nods, waits a beat, then asks, 'What were you shouting about before? You reckon someone killed her?'

Like me, Luke never quite measured up. His older brother was recruited by the Canberra Raiders NRL team, and by comparison, everything Luke does is shit, at least that's what he thinks. So, instead of proving his parents wrong, he proves them right by not trying at all.

'I don't know,' I reply quickly. 'I'm probably just tired.'

'You need something?'

He's also Wildling's unofficial chemist. His dad runs the local pharmacy, and badly, given Luke always has a stash of prescription drugs he'll hand out for the right price – which isn't always money.

'I'd love a few Vals if you've got any. Might help me sleep.'

'Not on me, but I can hook you up with some later.'

'Thanks.'

'What do I get in return?' he asks, nudging me with his shoulder.

'My best friend just died. As if I feel like doing that.'

'Fair enough,' he says, squeezing my bottom. 'You've still got me, though.'

Instead of answering, I sidestep, creating space between us. There's no right way to tell him that it's not the same. That if I could, I'd swap him for Lilly in a second.

As we walk back through the bush, I try to calm myself but subconsciously catalogue every sound. Today it was just Luke being stupid, but after what happened to Lilly, I know I'm not safe. Eventually, the person responsible for her death will want to make sure I stay quiet.

The only question is when.

Chapter Seven

I ABSENTLY push away my plate and stare into the empty hours ahead. Fridays are the one weekday I have off work, and I told Daley that under no circumstances was he to put me on call over the weekend because I'd be spending it with Will. Now I have nothing to do, and that's a recipe for disaster.

The quiet is not my friend. Will's always asking why I can't just sit down and relax. Why I'm always off in my head about something. *I can feel you thinking, Mia. Why are you like this? Just go to sleep.*

I don't have an answer for why I'm like this. Sometimes I think maybe I just came into the world thinking and worrying. *Am I on time? Am I crying too loud? Am I all you'd hoped for?* Jason's the same, except when his mind ticks over, the outcome is always some kind of world-changing concept or idea. All I come up with are more things to worry about.

On cue, visions of Lilly's blank, staring eyes flash through my mind.

Daley wants me to have a counselling session just to debrief, but the thought of sitting in another room with muted walls and a chair pointed at me sends my palms clammy. I can't do that again. Not for any reason.

But her skin was so pale. My mind drifts up to the gash on her cheek, and I squeeze my eyes closed, desperate to stop seeing it. Going over it again and again isn't going to change the fact that she's dead. All I'm doing is tormenting myself. I need to stop, so instead I let my thoughts turn to Will, and the way he looked at me when he got up from the table. It wasn't anger in his eyes. It was pity, and you can't be in love with someone you pity. That much I know for sure. Maybe that's why he's being different. Maybe compared to the people in Canberra, I seem pathetic and sad.

My thumb hunts for the ragged edge of a nail, finds it, and pulls until the familiar tear makes me wince. Will hates it when I pull at my nails. *Stop it, Mia, your fingers are going to look like frayed rope if you keep doing that.* I never say anything back, but it always makes me wonder if, despite all the past counselling sessions, my fingernails are a reflection of my slowly unravelling mind.

He's miles away and can't shout at me, but I stop and glance down at my left hand. Sure enough, it's bleeding. Now I'll never be able to leave it alone. I'll pull at it and pull at it until... my mind flashes back to the ravine and Lilly's hands. Her nails. They were perfect.

My body stiffens, and I close my eyes, quickly thinking back. Long slender fingers with perfect purple polish, every nail intact and unbroken.

My eyes flash open, and I catch my breath. Every spring, the park erupts in colour. A kaleidoscope of wildflowers covers the ground, native birds wheel above, and wild brumbies roam across the open valleys. Hikers come from all over to follow the trails and lose themselves in the wilderness. Not all are experienced, and many don't realise an underground fault line runs the length of the park. Once upon a time, back before Wildling and some of the nearby towns existed, there were a series of mini earthquakes that caused the land to shift and bow. Like the rumbling of a hungry stomach, the events opened a series of gaping mouths that now sit ready and waiting to swallow up unsuspecting hikers.

Over the past two years, Koda and I have rescued dozens of people who misstepped and fell into one of the ravines, but no matter who they were or where they were from, they all had one thing in common – every one of them came out looking the worse for wear. Filthy clothes, ripped pants, and dirty, torn fingernails from where they tried over and over to climb out.

I close my eyes and picture what would have happened if Lilly fell and tried to get out. Knees scraping against rock. Fingers clawing in the dirt, trying to get traction. Twisted roots scratching the delicate skin of her cheek.

I push the scene away, shake it off, then go back to what I actually saw. No torn clothing. No scratches or scrapes. One shoe off, but other than that, there were no signs she had tried to climb out.

To think she might have wandered out there in the dark and fallen is plausible. The idea she didn't try to get out is not. I glance at Koda, my heart racing, and dare to wonder. *Is it possible that Lilly was already dead when she went into the ravine?*

Chapter Eight

'MIA… It's you.'

I flinch at the sound of my mother's voice behind me. 'Where were you on that one?' I whisper to Koda. 'Thanks a lot.'

I put down my coffee and turn, shielding my eyes from the sun. Like two mannequins from the window of the Country Road store in Winton River, my mother and half-sister Sophie stand over me, dressed head to toe in beige and white.

It's no surprise my mother has angled her back to the sun.

You must always wear sunscreen, Mia. You might have your father's complexion, but that doesn't mean you won't end up looking like an old saddlebag if you don't look after your skin.

The truth is, she couldn't care less about sun damage on my face. It's just her way of reminding me that I look like my father. As if in this town I could ever forget what I look like. The tangle of black hair that mirrors Mimi's.

Even though age has brushed hers with silver, every wild, untamable strand ties me to her in a way I can never seem to unravel. Olive skin, darker than everyone else in town, but still too fair to think I might be a part of the First Nations community, and an athletic frame that works well out in the field, but makes me feel like a work boot at a wedding every time I try to wear a dress.

'Mum.' I greet them with a tight smile. 'Sophie.'

'Hello, Mia,' Sophie replies with a nod. 'You bring your dog to breakfast, then? How... nice.'

I glance at Koda and wonder what Sophie's scream would sound like if he sank his teeth into her ankle. 'He was hassling me all morning for some toasted muesli, so... you know.'

Instead of laughing, her face pinches, and she rolls her eyes. 'No Will then, I take it?' She purposely twists her wedding band, and I'm sure it's to remind me that she has one and I don't.

'He's away in Canberra until Monday night.'

'On the anniversary of your engagement?' my mother gasps, before shooting a look of *I knew it* at Sophie. 'And after what happened out in the park with that awful dead girl?'

I have no idea whether she means Lilly was an awful person or discovering her body must have been awful. I quickly decide it's probably better not to ask. Knowing my mother, it's probably the first one.

'Will has an important job, Mum. He's one step away from being the Prime Minister's executive adviser. He can't just drop everything because of an anniversary or my job.' I hear myself mimic Will's words and immediately want to slap myself. *When did I start doing that?*

'Oh, Mum,' Sophie begins, with a flamboyant wave of her arm, 'remember when Jonathan took us all to La Trattoria Bella in Winton River last month on our wedding anniversary? Wasn't it just divine? And that garlic bread, oh... my... God, right?'

Heat prickles along my neck. 'You all went to dinner in Winton River and didn't invite me?'

'It was a couples thing, Mia, and Will was in Canberra that night... as usual,' my mother says, with yet another eye roll I know she wants me to see.

'Right, but like I said—'

'Yes, yes, his job is very important.'

'It is, Mum. You don't understand.'

Sophie cocks her hip and stares at me. 'What's that supposed to mean? Do you think my father's job as the town GP isn't important? Or that Jonathan's law practice is no big deal? He personally represents Jack Stanton, you know.'

'Yes, I'm more than aware of that, Sophie.'

'Well?'

'Well, what?'

'Well, what did you mean by it? Are you saying Will is

better than Jonathan or *my* father?' As always, she emphasises the *my* in *my father*, reminding me that Gerry is not my biological dad.

I sigh and glance at my mother. It comes as no surprise when, instead of defending me, she takes out her phone and stares at the screen, even though it didn't ring. Sophie is the picture-perfect, blonde-haired, blue-eyed daughter she always wanted. She is the warm glow of morning, streaked with gold and full of promise. By comparison, I've always felt like the coming of twilight, that time of day when the sun fades and you can never really be sure of anything.

'I'm not saying that, Sophie,' I deadpan, giving up and looking away from Mum. 'No one is better than Jonathan. You married the best guy in town, no wait... in the world. Is that what you want to hear?'

She glares back at me, her cheeks visibly warming. 'I did.'

'I know. Congratulations.'

Sophie's jaw clenches, and her perfectly crafted nose bunches up in frustration. 'Well, everyone in town thinks Will's having an affair. What do you have to say about that?'

The shock of her words knocks the wind out of me, and I lean even further back in my seat.

'No one wants to tell you, but I will,' she continues. 'Some woman in Canberra, apparently.'

I swallow down the urge to scream and quickly reach for

the tiny nook behind Koda's ear. Sensing my anxiety, he moves in closer, the warmth of his body pressing against my leg.

'That's... ridiculous,' I manage, but even as I say the words, I know it's not. There was that time before. It was just once, but if Will has met someone else, it would explain a lot.

'Is it, Mia?' she asks. 'I mean, in a way, it's true what you said. He talks to the Prime Minister every day. You eat breakfast with a dog.'

'Koda is a qualified canine search and rescue officer,' I tell her, my voice trembling. 'He saves people's lives.'

'It's a dog, Mia.'

I glance back at my mother, as she continues to scroll on her phone as though none of this is happening. 'Mum, are you really not going to say anything?'

Eventually, she slips the phone back into her bag and looks at me. 'It's true, Mia. I heard the rumours as well.'

My throat thickens. 'I meant about the way Sophie's speaking to me.'

Her eyes linger over me, then she stares down at Koda, an unmistakable look of contempt on her face. 'Mia, get rid of the dog and move to Canberra with Will before it's too late.'

'Get rid of...?' I repeat slowly. 'Did you actually just say that to me?'

'Like your sister said, it's a dog,' she tells me with a toss of her creamy blonde hair. 'It will forget all about you the minute someone else feeds it.'

I bite down so hard on my bottom lip that I'm sure it's about to bleed. 'She's my half-sister, and please don't call Koda *it*.'

My mother and Sophie look at each other and roll their eyes. It's more than I can take. 'You know what… screw you both.'

'Mia!' my mother gasps, her hand flying up to her chest. 'We're in public.'

'I don't care. I don't need this.' I quickly tuck my hair back behind my ear and tighten my grip on Koda's lead. 'Will is not having an affair, Sophie, and Mum… I wish I could say I don't know why you're like this, but that would be a lie. I just wish for once you would take responsibility for your own decisions and stop taking them out on me. Dad was your choice, not mine, and I'm sick of it. Just sick of it.'

'Mia—' she begins, but I cut her off.

'I'm a person. I might not have Sophie's blonde hair and perfect husband, but I'm still your daughter.'

Sophie stares down at me, her brow arched in shock.

'You have something more to add?' I snap at her.

She hitches up her designer bag, no doubt a gift from my mother, and shakes her head.

'Good,' I say, pushing out from the chair and standing up. 'Because we're leaving.'

With every step, I feel their eyes boring into my back as we walk away. My cheeks burn, and the back of my knees tremble. When I'm a safe distance, I fold myself into a park bench and begin to sob.

As I sit and cry, Koda rests his head in my lap. My hand automatically falls across the top of his head, and I try to focus on the texture of his fur. It's a coping mechanism I learned a long time ago, to focus on the feel of something in the present to stop my mind from spiralling into the past. I'm not even sure exactly what it is I'm crying about. The idea that Will might be cheating on me? The fact my mother doesn't love me, or worse, that she doesn't even want to know if she could? Probably all of it – or maybe none of it, and it's just that I can't get Lilly Daniels' dead eyes out of my head.

Chapter Nine

Britt

BACK at home, I punch Lilly's name into the search bar on my phone and hit *News*. Every morning, I check, expecting to see a story revealing the truth about how she died, or at least the findings of the autopsy report, but as I scroll down, there's nothing new. Just the same story from last week about her body being found in the national park.

He got to them somehow. He must have. I toss the phone onto the bed and close my eyes. *Arsehole.*

Not for the first time, I think about telling Mum what happened, but then picture the look on her face and change my mind. I can't. She'd never get it. There's always Juniper, but screw her. Why should I give her one more reason to be perfect? Growing up in the shadow of a sister idolised by the whole town was bad enough. Why should I tell her something that would probably win her an award?

She wouldn't have the guts to confront him anyway. Not after she made everyone so proud by moving to Sydney last year to become some fancy journalist. In the eyes of the town, she might as well be Taylor Swift – only without the singing. Just the parts that make people swoon and carry on like she's God's gift. She'd never come back here and blow it all by writing a story like that. Besides, it's not like she'd listen to me anyway. Why would she? No one else does.

Beside me, the phone rings, and I snatch it up, relieved for the distraction.

'Can you do a shift this morning?' my manager Nate asks, not bothering with a greeting. 'One of the bowsers isn't working. I'll be tied up all day fixing it. Can't be out there and on the till.'

'Yeah, okay. Give me ten to get ready.'

I swing my legs over the side of the bed and grab my work shirt off the back of the chair. Since quitting school last year, Mum has refused to do my washing, so there's every chance it stinks. I sniff check the underarms and deciding it's not too bad, I slip it on. As an afterthought, I double-spray myself with perfume and immediately wonder why I bothered. It's not like anyone paying for petrol is close enough to sniff me, and let's be real, no one's going to give a shit what the servo chick looks or smells like. I wrangle my dark hair into a rough ponytail, tighten it with both hands, and glance into the mirror. It'll have to do.

I grab my bag and am almost at the door when Mum calls my name. These days, our conversations are debates at best, and screaming matches at worst. We've never really gotten along, but since Juniper left and I quit school, things at home have gone down the shit-chute fast.

'You weren't supposed to have work today.'

I sigh and close my eyes. I can sense her standing right behind me. 'Nate called me in. Not like I can say no.'

'Can you turn around and look at me, please?'

I puff out my cheeks, then let the air out slowly. *Here we go…*

When I turn and look at her, my first thought is that if shame and disappointment had a baby, it would look like my mother. Slumped shoulders, pursed lips, her head hanging like there's a chain around her neck with my face on it.

'Mum, don't start.'

'Britt,' she says, steadying herself and finally looking up. 'You're seventeen. It's ten in the morning.'

'Your point is?'

'You've got enough makeup on to be a…' She bites her lip before the word slips out. 'And what? Did you bathe in perfume?'

'Well, if you'd wash my shirt with the rest of the load, I wouldn't have to, would I?'

She rubs at the back of her neck. 'Go and take some of the makeup off. You don't need black eyeshadow at this hour.'

'It's eyeliner. Anyway, I don't have time. I have to go.'

'Britt.' Her tone is a warning – *take the makeup off or we've got a problem.*

I meet her glare, and wonder how long she can hold eye contact without blinking. 'My best friend just died, you know.'

She blinks first, and a small tug of satisfaction rises in my chest.

'I know that, and I'm sorry, but...'

'Finish it, Mum. But...'

'...but she shouldn't have taken God-knows-what and wandered off like that.'

I scoff, staring up at the ceiling. Unbelievable. Everyone in this town is un-freaking-believable.

'That's not what happened,' I whisper to the manhole. 'What?'

I know she's staring, but I don't bother explaining. 'Nothing. Can I just go?'

'Britt, if you know something—'

I shrug and hitch my bag higher. 'What would I know, Mum? I'm just the chick with too much makeup who dropped out of school to work at the servo.'

Mum presses her fingers to her temples like she's trying to stop her brain from exploding. 'Fine. You win. I don't have the energy to argue anymore.'

It's tempting to bolt while I can, but something's off. She never gives up this easily. 'Wait, what's going on?'

'Nothing. I just can't keep doing this.'

'No, there's something.' I tilt my head. 'What is it?'

I quickly run through a mental list of reasons she could

be giving in so easily. *Is Dad sick? Are we losing the house? Could Juniper be...*

'Fine,' she sighs, before I can finish the thought. 'Your sister's coming home for a bit. I thought maybe she could talk some sense into you. You need to go back to school, Britt, and finish Year 12.'

'Oh, my God.' I throw up my hands and turn on the spot. Just what I need, freaking Journalism Barbie coming back and telling me what to do. 'Mum, you've got to be kidding?'

'No, she's already on her way. She'll be here for dinner.'

'I'm going.'

'Britt—'

'I'm going.' I push the door with one hand and don't bother stopping the screen from slapping shut behind me.

'Come straight home after your shift, Britt,' she calls. 'I mean it.'

I stomp down the path as visions of Juniper's perfect hair and glowing skin suddenly begin to suffocate me. 'I wish I was the one who was dead!' I shout loud enough for the entire street to hear. 'I fucking hate it here.'

Mum will be mortified, but at least it'll give her something to do for the rest of the day – worry about what the neighbours think.

Chapter Ten

DETERMINED to clear my head, we walk toward the edge of town and turn left onto Wildling Road. Beside me, Koda sniffs the air, breathing in the scent of wattle and sunbaked grass. To the right stretches the untamed sprawl of the national park, and to my left are acres of pristine farming land, the road a dusty seam between two worlds.

Koda glances up at me, and I smile. He searches my face, and while I can't know for certain, I hope he understands what it means – that just having him beside me is enough.

If we follow the road long enough, we'll end up at Silver Bark River, where, if you're lucky and very quiet, you can sometimes glimpse a platypus unearthing rocks and sticks as it hunts for yabbies and worms. As kids, Jason and I would go there whenever we could, pretending to be in some magical world far away from Mum and Wildling.

With every magpie chorus and low from the cattle, my shoulders ease. Koda's breathing falls in time with my steps, and I begin to push Sophie's stupid accusations out of my mind. And my mother. I should be used to her by now. She was different once, back when Jason and I were little. Still miserable and angry, but at least it was aimed at Dad and not us. Since I've been on the receiving end, it's easier to understand why one day he went out and just never came back. She always told us drugs and drinking got the better of him, but maybe he just got sick of her shit. Because who wouldn't?

The sound of car tyres on dirt cuts through the quiet, and I stop and turn. *Shit, what's he doing out here?*

Behind me, Herm's police car crawls along the road. Knowing I don't have a choice, I stop and wait. When he pulls up alongside us, the window slides down, and he looks at me over his aviator sunglasses.

'You headed to see someone?' He nods up the road.

'See someone? No, we're just walking.'

He stares out the windscreen, chewing gum. The wet squelch between his teeth makes me want to vomit.

'Not thinking about heading to Willow's Crossing, are you?'

'Like I said, I'm just walking Koda.'

'Daley told you not to, huh?' He grins like the Cheshire Cat.

'Daley didn't have to tell me anything. I've got no reason to go there. I already told you that.'

'How long have we known each other, Mia?'

Invisible fingers crawl along my arm, making me shudder. 'A long time, Herm.'

'Since you were a little girl.' He stares out along the road, then turns his attention back to me. 'Didn't I always look out for you? Whenever you got in trouble, who picked up the pieces? Not your mamma.'

I swallow and fix my eyes on a lone tree standing out on the horizon. 'Koda'll get restless if we don't keep moving, so...'

'You know it was me,' he says quietly. 'You know I always took real good care of you.'

'Herm...'

The click of the car door latch makes my heart sink. He's getting out. Sensing the shift in my energy, Koda presses closer, eyes locked on Herm.

'It's okay, mate,' I whisper. 'Everything's all right.'

With one foot on the road, Herm pauses and eyes Koda, as if weighing his chances before pushing the door open and climbing out.

'The thing is,' he says, boots crunching in the dirt, 'I think you're lying about what your dog sniffed out at Jack's the other day.'

'Like I said, Koda just barks sometimes. He likes the—'

'—smell of cow shit. So you said.' He looks around, hands on his hips. 'Thing is, Mia, there's plenty of cows out here now. Probably plenty of shit too, but I don't hear him barking. Do you?'

I follow his line of sight across the paddocks, then back along the empty road. He steps closer, smelling of sweat and cheap supermarket cologne. Beside me, Koda growls.

'Better shut that dog up,' Herm says, leaning in so close I can feel his breath on my ear. 'You know what happens if he bites a police officer.'

'Koda, quiet,' I murmur, too scared to move. 'It's okay.'

Herm lingers, then steps back and hitches up his trousers. 'So, you going to tell me what you're really doing out here?'

Before I can answer, the rumble of an engine draws our attention. Up ahead, a battered red pickup rattles toward us. Rust streaks the bonnet, the bumper hangs loose, and there are no number plates. Behind the wheel sits an elderly woman with a shock of wild grey hair piled atop her.

Mimi.

She pulls up just short of Herm's car and climbs out, a shotgun dangling from her hand. The material of her long dress, painted in swirls of green and yellow, hangs bright against the dull dirt road, and her feet are bare.

'For God's sake, Mimi,' Herm mutters. 'You're driving an unregistered, unroadworthy vehicle and carrying what I can only assume is an unregistered firearm.'

Unfazed, Mimi shrugs and scans him from head to toe. 'Don't need no registration if I don't drive where I ain't s'posed to,' she says.

'And what do you call this?' Herm asks, pointing down at the ground.

'I call it Wildling Road. Private property,' she answers

with a click of her tongue. 'Sarah Stanton's parents own from that red mailbox,' she gestures with the rifle, 'all the way back to that fence rail.'

As the barrel swings past his head, Herm ducks. 'Christ, Mimi. Put the gun down.'

'And from that fence rail,' she goes on, ignoring him, 'to the edge of Willow's Crossing, guess whose property that is? You don't need to answer because we both know damned well it's mine.'

Herm exhales, shaking his head.

'Kiddo, you and Koda go get in the truck,' Mimi says, her eyes trained on Herm. 'You've got nothing more to say to my granddaughter, do you, Drinkwater?'

Herm stiffens and glares at her. 'I ever catch you discharging that weapon, I'll confiscate it.'

'Well,' Mimi says with a sigh as she turns and follows us back toward the pickup, 'you ever around when I discharge this weapon, might be you won't be confiscating anything.'

Chapter Eleven
Britt

MOST times at work, I'm grateful for the quiet. In Wildling, people fill up their cars and trucks with petrol once a week, so it's not like working at one of those bigger stations out on the freeway. There's only the odd trickle of townsfolk and farmers. They say hello and have a quick chat, usually about how hot it is, how cold it is, or how it's windy enough to blow a dog off a chain. Normally, I can't wait for them to get back into their cars and go, but this morning I'd do anything for someone to drive in, just to distract me from thinking about my sister coming to stay.

It's not that I don't love Juniper. I do. I just don't *like* her.

Since we were little, she's always been so worried about what everyone thinks. She's a lot like Mum that way – always wanting to be liked. At school, her grades were almost perfect and she was good at everything. Even now, there's still a shelf in her room crowded with trophies for freestyle, backstroke, and butterfly. I can't even swim. And just to top it off, right up until she left for university, she dated Jack Stanton's son, Bryce, who, of course, every girl in Wildling dreams of marrying someday.

It makes me wonder why Mum and Dad even bothered having another kid. They already had a perfect daughter. Why go and mess it up by having me? It's not like I can ever be her. She looks exactly like Mum, with her shiny blonde hair and tall, athletic frame. I, on the other hand, am my dad. I inherited his brown eyes and stocky build. I like to think I also got some of his attitude, although these days it seems like, along with the kitchen, Mum has remodelled him into something a little more up to date. Into something a little more *functional.*

So that just leaves me, the odd one out. I can't say exactly when I stopped trying, but if you're always falling short, at some point you have to stop reaching, right? Otherwise, it's futile. That's why I loved Lilly so much. She got me, and I got her. Even though our families were different, we were practically the same.

She was an only child and didn't have the burden of a perfect sibling overshadowing her every move, we were different in that way, but she understood what it felt like to be invisible in your own house. My mum was always blinded by Juniper, but Lilly's was more interested in chasing men. Definitely her loss because Lilly was smart. She could've been anything. Deep down, I know she only acted out to get her mum's attention. If Herm was always dragging her to the station, and the good women of

Wildling were banging on the door, accusing her of trying to steal their husbands, Lilly figured her mum would have no choice but to notice her. In the end, all it did was put her in situations no teenage girl should ever be in – like what happened right before she died.

Outside, a familiar vehicle pulls in and stops at the bowser. The shiny black truck has *Willow's Crossing* emblazoned along the door in white cursive, leaving no doubt about who owns it. Luke told me that his dad told him the truck cost a quarter of a million dollars. More than most houses in town.

Bryce climbs out of the passenger seat and I automatically glance into my phone camera to check how I look. Not that it matters. Still, how do you not fantasise about a guy like Bryce Stanton? That wide, magnetic smile hits you before anything else. It'd be easy for him to act like he's above everyone in Wildling, but he never does. Despite his bright blue eyes and family fortune, he's got that boy-next-door vibe. Disarming. Charming. Drawing you in before you even realise it. He was wrecked when Juniper left for Sydney. Maybe because he actually loved her, or maybe he just couldn't believe anyone would leave him – the only son of Jack Stanton and heir to the Willow's Crossing empire.

'Hey, Britt,' he says, pushing open the door. 'Got the morning shift, then?'

'Yep. How else would you want to start the day but right

here?'

He chuckles and heads for the fridges at the back of the shop. His tan jeans and navy collared shirt tell me it's not a workday at Willow's Crossing. He and Jack must be off to the saleyards.

'Cattle or horse?' I ask as he comes back to the counter.

'Dad's on the hunt for a new thoroughbred. Thinks he might have a go at breeding racehorses.'

I roll my eyes. ''Course he does.'

Bryce grins and sets a can of soft drink on the counter. 'I heard Juniper's coming back.'

So that's why he bothered to come inside. News of Juniper's triumphant return has spread.

'Yeah,' I say, mindlessly rearranging things on the counter. 'Apparently. Did she call you?'

'Nah. Mum told me last night.'

I nod and glance out at the truck. 'Did your dad really pay two hundred and fifty thousand dollars for that?'

He follows my gaze, watching his father wipe down the windscreen. 'Yeah. Thereabouts.'

'You know there are kids in Wildling whose parents can't afford groceries, right?'

He looks back at me and smiles. Heat floods my cheeks before I can stop it.

'Dad does a lot for this town, Britt. You know that.'

I purse my lips, trying to seem unimpressed. 'Like I said, can't afford groceries.'

His eyes linger on me, and for a split second, I let myself imagine what it would be like if he looked at me the way he once looked at my sister. If he leaned in and—

The bell above the door rings, and Jack Stanton makes his way toward the counter. Bryce immediately straightens, his tall frame dwarfed by his father's towering presence.

'Morning, Britt. Put the fuel and whatever Bryce has on the account, will you?'

'Sure, Mr Stanton.'

'My son's not giving you a hard time, is he?'

I grin at Bryce, then shake my head. 'Not this time.'

'I hear your sister's coming back. We'd love to have her over for dinner. Be sure to let her know, will you?'

'Will do.' Bryce studies me, and I quickly look away. 'Anything else today, Mr Stanton?'

'No, that's all. Oh—' he snaps his fingers. 'Sarah had an invitation she wanted me to drop off for your mother. I'll leave it with you. Must be in the truck. Run and grab it, son, would you? It's in the console.'

My eyes follow Bryce as he heads back outside.

'Sorry about what happened to Lilly,' Jack says once he's gone. 'Awful thing.'

I nod, swallowing hard against the lump in my throat.

'I know the two of you were close.'

'We were.'

He leans forward, elbows resting on the counter. 'You

know, Britt, girls like Lilly have a habit of getting them-selves into strife. Wildling's no place for that kind of be-haviour.'

His eyes pin me. 'Mr Stanton, I—'

'She made a lot of bad decisions,' he cuts in. 'One of them got her killed.'

His eyes are the same blue as Bryce's, but so much cold-er. A trickle of sweat finds its way along the small of my back. 'Mr Stanton, Lilly was—'

'Trash,' he says flatly. 'She was trash. And you're better than that, Britt. Your family means a lot to my wife and to my son. I'd hate to see them hurt.'

'Hurt... how?'

He steps back and loosens the collar of his shirt. 'Best you just put Lilly's drama behind you. Is that clear?'

'Mr Stanton, I don't—'

The bell rings again, and Bryce comes back, his face flushed. 'I turned the car upside down, Dad. I can't find any invitation.'

'Then I must've left it at home.' Jack taps the counter twice but doesn't take his eyes off mine. 'Nice to see you, Britt. I'll make sure Sarah gets that invitation to your mother.'

I nod, but my throat is too dry to speak.

'Nice to see you, Britt,' Bryce calls over his shoulder.

'You take care,' Jack adds. 'And again, condolences for your loss. Let's hope nothing like that ever happens in

Wildling again.'

I stand rooted to the spot as they leave. Only when the truck pulls out onto the road, do I let out my breath and slump against the counter.

Was Jack threatening me? *Your family means a lot... I'd hate to see them hurt.* Did he mean that if I don't keep quiet, I could end up like Lilly?

Whoever did the autopsy over at Winton River Hospital is already covering up the truth. Now it feels like Jack's threatening me not to say anything about what I know. If I was smart, I'd do just that. Shut the hell up. But how can I when Lilly deserves more than that – and so does the baby she was carrying when she died.

Chapter Twelve

'THANKS, Mimi,' I say, as she fights with the old truck's gears. 'I just needed to get out and walk. Clear my head. I wasn't expecting... him.'

'S' okay, kiddo. No need to explain. Wasn't like I was counting on a visit from you anytime soon.'

I always have mixed feelings when it comes to Mimi. Guilt, frustration, resentment. You name it, and Mimi has the ability to make me feel it. All the bad things anyway. It's not her fault. She didn't choose my parents any more than I did, but it's because of her and Dad that living in Wildling has always been a nightmare.

The fact he just up and left us one night. No explanation. No goodbye. Her self-proclaimed role as a custodian of the land and refusal to sell the farm. Together, they personify everything the farming community of Wildling despises.

It's not that I think Mimi's a bad person, but she's a stark reminder of all the reasons I don't fit in. When I look at her, I remember feeling isolated and unwelcome.

Worst of all, when I look at her, I see my father and feel his rejection all over again.

Is Will going to leave me too? I wonder as we bounce along the bumpy road. Sophie's words echo in my mind, and I try my best to push them aside. Listening to her will do me no good. She's never had my best interests at heart.

'Truth always comes out in the end, kiddo,' Mimi says suddenly. 'You'll see.'

Koda sits perched between us on the bench seat, blocking my view of her face. 'The truth about what?' I ask, leaning forward to look past him.

'About all things.'

That's the other thing about Mimi. She speaks in riddles. She only ever gives you half the story and leaves you to figure out the rest.

'Are you talking about Will?' I press, wondering if the rumour has travelled all the way to the outskirts of town.

She doesn't answer, and I don't bother asking again. She'll only give me something infuriating, like *listen to the spirits of the mountains* or *the answers you seek will come on the wind*. Jason might buy into that hoo-ha, but not me. All I know is that Mimi never gives a straight answer, and it's frustrating as hell.

'Anyway, thanks for coming to my rescue,' I say. 'Herm can be...'

'I know what Herm is.'

I wrap an arm around Koda, grateful he's between us.

There are things I want to ask Mimi, and things I don't. How much she knows about Herm is one of the things I don't.

When we reach the bitumen road leading back into town, Mimi stops the car. 'This is where our journey ends, kiddo,' she says. 'Don't need to give him any more reason to come bothering me.'

'Well, like I said... thanks.'

'You be careful now, Mia.'

She doesn't often call me by name. It's always kiddo. Hearing her say *Mia* makes me pause. 'Careful of what?'

Mimi stares out the window. It'd be easy to think she didn't hear me, that age has dulled her hearing, but I know better. Nothing gets past her. If she doesn't answer, it's because she chooses not to.

'Right, okay. Well, you be careful too, Mimi. And thanks.'

'Don't need to be careful when I've got this.' She pats the shotgun wedged down beside her seat.

I glance at it, and wonder if she's ever actually fired that thing. 'All right... I'll see you.'

'Sooner rather than later, I hope.'

I climb out and wave as she attempts an awkward three-point turn that nearly tears the bumper off. As she drives away, dust billows up, coating us from head to toe. I cough, brushing grit from my face, and glance down at Koda. The white in his fur has turned a mottled brown, and dirt flecks cling to his tongue.

'Look at you,' I sigh. 'We'll stop at the servo and get you some water. It's just up the road.'

After a short walk, I turn on a tap attached to the side of the building and Koda laps the water with his usual deafening slurp. Once he's done, I gather up his lead and head inside to get a drink for myself.

'Hello?' I call out when no one's at the counter. 'Anyone here?'

'Oh, hey, Mia. Sorry.' Britt Davis pulls herself up off the floor behind the counter, and it's immediately obvious she's been crying. Her dark hair is pulled back into a messy ponytail, and what had once been thick black eyeliner is smeared down the side of her face, making her look like a sad and not-so-funny clown.

'You might want to...' I gesture at my own face.

'Shit, has my makeup run?' She disappears again, and I hear her rustling around under the counter. 'Oh my God,' she shrieks. More rustling, then the sound of her blowing her nose, and she reappears. 'Sorry... again.'

I nod and give her a moment, pretending to browse the chocolate bars by the counter.

'They're two for one if you're interested,' she manages.

'No, just the water, but thanks.' I push the bottle forward, and she scans it with a beep. 'It must be a lot, losing Lilly. I know you two were close. How are you coping?'

That's all it takes for her to drop the scanner and burst

into tears. She folds herself over on the counter, her body racked with sobs.

'Hey, you know what?' I try. 'Why don't you come out here for a sec?'

At first, she doesn't move, but then slowly lifts her head and eyes me cautiously before making her way around the counter.

'Koda, go see Britt.'

Immediately, Koda walks over and pushes his nose up against Britt's hand. She looks down at him, and a smile tugs at the corner of her lip. 'Thanks, Mia. I don't usually cry. It's just...'

'Losing someone's a big deal. It's normal.'

'It's not just that,' she murmurs, her eyes still on Koda.

'No?'

Her eyelids flutter as if she just woke up from a dream, and she snaps back. 'It's nothing. Like you said, it's just hard losing Lilly.'

I study her closely. The tremble of her hands. The way she's shifting her weight from one foot to the other. The puffiness around her eyes. 'Britt, is there something else bothering you?'

'No, I'm fine. Just... you know... what you said before.'

Everyone in Wildling knows Britt is a tough-talking, sarcastic girl, quick to cut you down if you give her half a chance. The only stance I've ever seen her take is to be square-shouldered, feet planted, her sharp eyes daring you to have a go. But today she seems rattled, almost vulnerable.

Images of Lilly's perfect nails flash in my mind, and I wonder if Britt knows more than she's admitting. 'You know, it was Koda and me who found Lilly.'

She nods, eyes dropping. 'I know. Thanks.'

I glance outside to make sure there's no one else around. 'Britt, I want to tell you something. Would that be all right?'

'Something about Lilly?'

'Before everyone else got there, I noticed something strange. Her nails were perfect, even the polish. If she'd fallen into that ravine, she would've tried to climb out. I've seen it before. People don't just lie down and wait to die.'

Britt swallows hard. 'Like… if she was already dead when he put her in there?'

'Exactly. Do you think that's possible?'

Her eyes flick nervously. 'This is Wildling, Mia. Anything's *possible*.'

I step closer. 'Well, I think it's more than possible.'

'Nobody else thinks so.'

'But you do.'

She steps away and moves back behind the counter. 'I never said that.'

'But you thought it. You said *when he put her in there*. Who did you mean?'

'No one. Look, I barely know you. I can't talk about

this.'

She busies herself moving things around the counter and won't look at me.

'Can't talk about what?' I lean in across the rows of lollies and chewing gum. 'Britt, let me help. I know Lilly didn't just lie there waiting to die. You're her best friend. Someone has to be held accountable for what happened to her.'

'Why do you care so much?' she snaps. 'No one cared about her before.'

'Because I found her, and I can't get it out of my head.' My voice rises, and I grip Koda's ear to steady myself. 'Shit, Britt. I didn't mean to yell at you. I'm sorry. It's just... it was a lot for me, too.'

She studies me. 'You actually give a shit,' she says finally.

'I do. And I don't think she ended up in that ravine by accident.'

Britt bites the inside of her cheek, her eyes flicking between mine and the floor. I can almost hear the gears turning in her mind as she processes her options. *Should she trust me? Should she let me in?* Her eyes linger on mine just a little longer, then she lets out a long breath and says, 'Herm Drinkwater got Lilly pregnant.'

My breath catches, and I step back, fingers wrapped around the edge of the counter to balance myself. Even though I know what Herm is capable of, the words still shock me. I close my eyes as images of his vile face fill my mind.

'Mia?' I hear her asking. 'Are you all right?'

I nod and quickly re-centre myself. 'Yeah, I just... are you certain?'

Britt nods, and then suddenly pounds her fist against the counter. 'He's such an arsehole. I should have said something, you know? About what he was doing to her. I keep asking myself over and over, why didn't I say something? Why didn't I call the real cops?' Her gaze goes far away for a moment, as if she's still trying to figure it out. 'It was stupid. If I had, maybe none of this would have happened.'

'This isn't your fault, Britt. You can't blame yourself.'

'But I do, Mia,' she whispers. 'I was supposed to be her best friend. I should have done something.'

For a moment, we both stand in silence and I search for the right thing to say. Failing, instead I go with, 'And she'd told him... about the baby?'

'I guess so,' Britt says with a shrug. 'I mean, why else would he kill her? She's, was, seventeen and still a minor. He's a cop. I can't imagine him being too happy about it.'

'You're certain? About Herm being the father, I mean.'

Britt lets her eyes drop. She takes a deep breath and then looks at me. 'People say things about you, Mia. You know that, right?'

My stomach twists, and I nod quietly, bracing for whatever might come next.

'They say that when you were my age, you were always in trouble. Kinda like me and Lilly.'

'That's probably a fair statement.'

'They say you got arrested a lot, then had a mental breakdown. That you got locked away in a hospital for it.' She pauses and watches for my reaction.

'That's all true, Britt, but I'm better now.'

'Do you think there's any chance Herm took you into the station more often than you deserved?'

I eye her cautiously. 'My father left, and my mother kicked us out. I grew up with Mimi, and unless you're my brother, people around here assume who and what you are by your family.'

She nods but doesn't seem convinced. 'Or maybe Herm had other reasons to take you in,' she suggests. 'He took Lilly into the station a lot. Sometimes for things we both did, but he'd put her in the car and then make me go home. You spent a lot of time there as a teenager, Mia. Do you really need convincing that he's the father?'

Chapter Thirteen

I BARELY slept. The encounter with Britt played out over and over in my head as I tossed and turned and stared up at the ceiling. For most people, being awake all night would leave them feeling tired and lethargic, but as I busy myself in the kitchen getting Koda's breakfast and making a coffee, my body is buzzing. I've never felt so wired. Since the moment we found Lilly, it's been nagging at me. Her fingernails. Herm's persistent warnings not to go anywhere near Willow's Crossing, and now finding out she was pregnant.

My mind flashes back to the times I spent at the police station with Herm. Britt was right. I don't need convincing that he could be the father. He's a vile excuse for a man – a predator. To think he could have set his sights on a young woman like Lilly, who had no one to look out for her, doesn't surprise me at all. It's what he does. Now she's dead.

I stir my coffee and watch Koda as he finishes off the last of his kibble. Britt isn't the only one struggling with her conscience. Maybe if I had spoken up about what Herm did to me back then, Lilly would still be alive. Maybe I'm just as much to blame as anyone. I should have. I could have. But I always felt like it was my own fault somehow, like I must have done something to encourage him. Like I must have acted a certain way or dressed too provocatively. Maybe it was the tone of my voice. The way I walked. I thought if I said something, everyone would call me a liar or a slut. Either way, it would be my fault, but knowing what he went on to do to Lilly, I feel even more ashamed.

And what if...

I cast my mind back to Koda's behaviour as we made our way across Willow's Crossing. Someone else was out there. It was a definite alert.

As if on cue, Koda comes over and sits in front of me, staring as though he knows what I'm thinking.

'You were facing north,' I tell him quietly. 'The land is flat in that direction, so if I couldn't see anyone, does that mean...'

Could there be another body out there? I wonder.

For Koda to pick up on the scent, whoever they are, they can't have been out there for more than a week. After that long, human scent deteriorates, overpowered by decomposition and the smell of other functions that take place as a body begins to break down. Only a cadaver dog could detect that kind of scent.

My mind is spinning. If Britt is right and Herm killed

Lilly because she was pregnant, then who else is out there? And why?

I look back at Koda. 'I'm not sure how to tell you this, mate, but I have a very bad idea.'

THE moon hangs low, a lantern illuminating the frost-bitten paddocks of Willow's Crossing. Fences run in perfect white rows, the boards shining faintly as if they've stored the day's light. The air smells of damp earth, and a faint breeze stirs the leaves in the trees just beyond the boundary.

Despite my thermals, beanie, and gloves, the bitter cold seeps into my bones. I pull my parka tighter, hoping to block out at least some of the chill. Being out here in the freezing cold, I'm more certain than ever that there's no way Lilly would have been in that ravine all night without trying to climb out. Absolutely no way.

Koda and I come to a stop at the edge of the park. Our breath hangs in the air as I gaze out over Willow's Crossing. There's no fence on this side. The cattle are all confined to northern paddocks, and Jack's prize horses are tucked away safe in the barn.

'This is it, Koda,' I whisper, turning off my headlamp. 'If we take one more step, we're on Jack's land.'

Lights from the house glitter in the distance. It's almost 10 pm. We're too far away for anyone to hear us, but my heart races at the idea of trespassing in the middle of the night. I've worked so hard to gain the respect of people in Wildling. If we do this and I'm wrong, it will all have been for nothing. Then again, if I do this and I'm right, that's a whole other problem. Either way, I'm setting myself up for a fall, but Koda doesn't make mistakes. Someone is out here.

Beside me, he whines and pulls against his harness.

'I know you don't understand English, Koda, but we need to do this quietly. No barking.'

He licks his lips and prances on the spot.

'Shit, you're going to bark, I just know it,' I say with a sigh. 'What was I thinking?'

But deep down, I know exactly what I was thinking – that Herm Drinkwater is a sexual predator. He did not want me to come back out here. I've never told anyone what he did to me all those years ago, but if he killed Lilly, and maybe someone else, something has to be done.

'Koda,' I whisper. 'Quiet as you can, search!'

He pulls forward, nose to the air, ears alert. I'm not letting him off-lead in the dark. Not that I think he wouldn't come back, but I have no idea who or what could be out here, and I'm not putting him in danger. Instead, I keep a steady pace beside him as he begins to bracket, searching for the scent.

Together, we move silently across the field. From somewhere in the darkness, I hear the sound of hooves rustling against the earth. Koda's ears prick up, and he glances off toward the mountains. I can't see them, but I know they're there. The Sovereign Plains brumby mob.

'It's all right, mate,' I tell Koda. 'They're not going to bother us. Keep going.'

We push ahead, and I keep him close, searching across each section of the field in a sweeping formation.

The breeze picks up around us, clutching my hair and tossing it into my eyes. I direct Koda to move crosswind to give him the best chance of identifying which direction the scent is strongest.

After two hours and no alert, I begin to wonder if perhaps I was wrong. Koda has never given a false alert before, but maybe that day, there was someone out working in the paddocks. Maybe they were just too far away for me to see. Maybe they are very much alive and at home in bed, where we should be. I glance down at my watch. Almost midnight. It's going to be a long, cold walk home.

'I think we're done,' I tell Koda. 'It's for the best. At least there's no—'

Before I can finish the sentence, Koda stops and points his nose to the sky. He sniffs the air and barks in rapid succession. Once, twice, three times, then pulls forward, almost knocking me off my feet.

'In scent,' I whisper, my pulse pounding in my ears. 'Shit, this is actually happening.'

I run as fast as I can alongside Koda as he bounds across the field. Tall grass whips against my legs in the dark, the cold night air sharp on my face. It won't be long now. Once Koda's in scent, nothing will stop him.

After a five-minute sprint across the field, he slows at a spot where the land dips slightly, forming a natural hollow. He sniffs the ground, then begins to dig, his paws furiously working the soil. In my heart, I knew there was another body out here, but now that it's happening, I'm sick inside. As Koda digs, his paws unearth the damp smell of freshly turned soil. Around us, the crickets have stopped chirping, and all I can hear are the laboured sounds of Koda's breath as he digs, desperate to show me the scent source.

I can't let him contaminate the scene, so I pull him back and take his tug rope out of my pack. I haven't seen the body yet, but I know it's there.

'Good job, Koda,' I whisper in the most excited tone I can muster. 'Good boy. Oh, you're such a good boy.'

Koda pulls at the rope, his front feet lifting off the ground with joy. He has no idea that what he's found is likely the remains of a young girl, her life cut short by a monster.

When he's satisfied with his reward, reluctantly, I kneel and take a small set of tools from my pack. A flashlight, small brush, latex gloves, and a trowel. After glancing over my shoulder to make sure we're still alone, I snap on the gloves and get to work.

As I begin to dig, I notice immediately how the earth

feels soft and pliable. In a paddock this big, and so far from the house, the ground should be firmer, compacted. Someone else has been out here digging.

It's hard to control the tremble of my hands as I remove the top layer of soil. Despite the cold air, sweat beads across my forehead, and I wipe at it as best I can with the back of my arm.

Ten slow minutes drag by, each scrape of earth feeling louder in the quiet. Every so often, I glance back toward the house to make sure no one is coming.

When the beam of my flashlight reveals the edge of something pale, I catch my breath and sit back. A piece of cloth, dirt-streaked and torn. Beside me, Koda watches intently, and I whisper a silent thank you to the night sky that I'm not out here alone.

I shift my knees in the soil, take a breath, and will myself to keep going. I've come this far. I can't stop now.

I gag as the first waft of decay reaches my nostrils. A few seconds later, the trowel pushes against something solid, and more than anything, I just want to be home. To be anywhere but here. I put down the tool and carefully brush away the soil. When I see it, my eyes immediately fill with tears, and the skin on my face prickles. The female hand looks unnaturally pale in the moonlight, almost translucent against the dark earth.

For a heartbeat, I can't breathe. The night presses closer, the cold air turning to glass in my throat.

'I don't know if I can do this,' I whisper to Koda. 'I'm not... I can't...'

I sit back on my haunches and let my head loll toward the sky. Above us, the night stretches out, stars unblinking, waiting to see what I'll do next. Beside me, Koda nudges his nose up under my chin. His way of telling me I can do this.

'Why are you always so sure, huh?' I ask, tilting my head to rest against his. 'What if I can't?'

I draw back and meet Koda's eyes. He edges a little closer, a thin whine escaping his throat. Whoever this is, she's been calling out to me, wanting to be found. Not the earth, the dark, or even the privileged hush of Willow's Crossing could silence her.

'All right, mate,' I tell Koda, with a deep breath. 'You're right, I can do this.'

Seconds pass, maybe minutes. Time feels like a blur as I gently remove more soil, careful not to let the trowel touch any part of her. My throat closes, and I stumble back as the outline of her face peers up through the earth. In places, the skin has turned a dark, mottled green. Peeling and blistering make it difficult to tell what she might have looked like when she was alive, but despite her condition, I can guess she would have been no more than seventeen or eighteen. The elements have altered the tone of her skin, but there's no doubt in my mind this was an Indigenous girl. I shine my torch closer and notice an unusual shadow on the side of her head. Reluctantly, I lean in and carefully move her hair. Just behind her right ear, a gaping hole stares back at me, the shattered edges of her skull protruding like jagged teeth around a screaming mouth.

A wave of nausea hits me, and I pull myself up and stumble away. As I throw up, vomit and bile burn the back of my throat. I cough and gag. Someone did this to her. Someone decided she didn't matter. That she was dispensable. The thought forms an ache in my chest that I can't shake, no matter how many deep breaths I try to take.

I wrap my arms around myself in a desperate bid to hold the breaking pieces together. I squeeze my eyes closed as despair and anger take over. Koda whimpers and pushes his nose against my leg. Unable to hold myself up, my knees buckle, and I wrap my arms around him. He stays close as I continue to cry, his fur soaking up my tears. There was a time when I could have stopped this, but I was too afraid. All I had to do was speak up. All I had to do was say his name.

Chapter Fourteen

WITH trembling hands, I fumble with the buttons on my shirt, trying again to pop them out through the holes. I need to get these clothes off. The reek of damp soil clings to me, rot threaded through every fibre of the fabric. I inch my shoulders out of my shirt, and step out of my pants, throwing them both into a heap on the bathroom floor.

I close my eyes as hot water pours over my head, and try to convince myself that I'm not a monster. Whoever she is, she's already dead and has been out there for days. A better person would have called it in immediately. Stayed there by her side until emergency services arrived and took care of her. They wouldn't have gathered their things, removed all traces of themselves, and left the scene.

But that's what I did. I left her there. Alone.

I can feel Koda staring up at me from his usual spot over by the vanity. I haven't taken a shower in private since the day I brought him home. Usually, his presence comforts me, but tonight I feel like I owe him an explanation. I open my eyes and look over at him.

'I just need to think about how to do this,' I tell him. 'It's not like I'm going to let her lie out there forever. I'll call it in, I swear.'

His head drops down between his paws, and he looks up at me, the whites of his eyes showing.

'I know what you're thinking – that I'm horrible, but we need to do this right. If I'd stayed, they would have taken my credentials. It was an illegal search. Then I'd never be able to figure out what really happened. You know that, right?'

It's not as though I expect a response from Koda. I just need to hear myself say out loud that I'm going to do the right thing – that I'm going to make sure she is laid to rest properly.

I need to think. I can't call Herm, and I can't tell Daley. If they alert Jack, he'll raise holy hell that I went onto his property uninvited, but I can't just leave her out there.

I rest my head again against the wall of the shower. More than anything, I just want the water to keep falling long enough to carry the visions of her away. To wash her from my memory.

I reach behind me and turn the tap until the water is scorching. It needles my skin, and I press my palms against the tiles, gritting my teeth just to tolerate it. The burn doesn't drive the images of her away, but I stand there until my skin is red-raw.

When I'm done in the shower, I dress and throw my

clothes into the bin outside. More than anything, I ache to call Will, to beg him to come home, but how would I explain what I've done?

Instead, I pick up the phone and find Jason's number. He's the only one I trust and the smartest person I know. Together, we can figure this out.

When my brother arrives, his hair is mussed, and he smells like sleep. Under the harsh porch light, he looks older. Tired. 'It's four in the morning, Mia,' he mumbles. 'This better be good.'

Over his shoulder, I scan the street outside and notice the first snow of the season drifting down onto the grass. I shiver as I think of her lying out in the cold, and wonder again, what kind of person am I to have just left her there?

'Mia? Hello? It's freezing out here.'

I snap back and grab my brother's arm, quickly pulling him inside. As he trips forward, he pulls away and looks at me as though I've gone mad. 'Okay, now you're starting to scare me. What's going on?'

'Jason, something happened tonight out on Jack's property.'

He looks at me for a moment, then sniffs and scrunches up his nose. 'What's that smell? Is that Koda?'

'Listen to me,' I say urgently. 'We found a body.'

His head snaps back, and he stares at me. 'You what?'

'Out on Jack's property. We found her. She can't have been out there more than a week, or Koda wouldn't have found her. The decomp would have—'

'Whoa,' he says, palms up, signalling for me to stop. 'Just slow down. You and Koda went out to Jack's property in the middle of the night? And without Daley, or an invitation from police?'

'Koda alerted on the way back from finding Lilly.'

'Does Herm know?'

'He knows Koda alerted. He's been threatening me not to go back there.'

'So, you thought the best thing to do would be to go back out there?'

I shrug and pull at the corner of my fingernail. 'He alerted. I had to know.'

'Christ, Mia,' he barks. 'You know damn well I need Jack's support to make the geothermal drilling project work. If you go pissing him off and he pulls his support, I'm dead in the water. You know how much influence he has. Why would you go snooping around on his property?'

'Jason...' I manage, taken aback by his response. 'A girl is dead. She's lying out there right now. That's someone's daughter... or sister.'

He shakes his head, and rubs at his forehead. 'I have everything invested in this, Mia. Everything. Once Will gets the sign-off from Jess, we can start.'

'Jess?'

'The woman he's been liaising with in the Minister's office down in Canberra,' he says with a wave of his hand.

'It's nothing. But, Mia, we need the community on board, and that means Jack.'

'I can't believe this,' I say, getting to my feet. 'You're not even going to ask who she is?'

'Fine, Mia. Who is she?'

'I think she was from the First Nations mob.'

'Right.' He thinks a moment and then says, 'Was it obvious what happened to her?'

'She had a hole in her skull.'

'You're saying someone killed her?'

I take a moment and choose my words. 'Don't you think it's a little odd that two girls around the same age have both been found dead in the past week? And both on or near Willow's Crossing?'

Jason raises his brow. 'You think Jack had something to do with this? Are you serious?'

'Maybe. Or Herm could have done it, and Jack is covering for him.'

Jason stares at me and then paces the length of my living room, which for him is about three strides.

'No way,' he says, shaking his head. 'Why would he do that, Mia? It's ridiculous – on both counts.'

'Then how are two girls dead?'

He stops and folds himself into the couch, head back and eyes closed. I sit next to him and watch him think, praying he will come up with a solution.

Eventually he opens his eyes and turns his head to look

at me. 'I love you. You're my sister.'

I nod. 'I know.'

'Your safety is the most important thing to me. Your credentials too. I know how much working with Koda means to you. What you did tonight could be the end of your career.'

I glance at Koda, and he meets my gaze.

'I know how this is going to sound, but you can't let Jack know you were out there. Or Herm.' He inches forward to the edge of the couch. He has a plan. My shoulders unclench just a little. He thinks a moment longer, then nods to himself, a sign he's made up his mind. 'You have to pretend this never happened. I know it's awful, but you just have to.'

'Wait, what?'

He gets to his feet and looks at me. 'You shouldn't have even gone out there in the first place.'

I stand up and search his face. 'You can't be serious? You want me to just leave her out there?'

'I want you to leave the whole thing alone.'

'I can't. Jason, that's barbaric.'

He shakes his head, and rubs at the back of his neck. 'What's done is done. Having Jack or Herm come after your career won't change that, Mia.'

I want to believe he's saying all this out of love and concern, but I can't let go of the fact that his first response was to worry about Jack pulling support for his project.

'Come after me or your project?'

He steps in and rests both hands on my shoulders. 'Just promise me you won't do anything stupid. Whatever happened to those girls, I'm sure it had nothing to do with Jack or Herm. Jack's farmhands will find the body. Just let it be. Promise me, Mia.'

Reluctantly, I nod and agree. 'Okay, you're right. I just don't know how I'll ever get the visions of her out of my head.'

'Sleep, for a start,' he tells me, as we walk toward the door. 'And wash Koda. He stinks.'

Chapter Fifteen

MUTED light seeps over the mountain range, turning the sky from slate to silver as snow drifts silently across my windscreen. The clock on the dashboard of my Toyota LandCruiser reads 5.33 am.

If Jason thinks I'm going to leave that girl lying out in a paddock, he's lost his mind. Whether he's motivated by concerns for my welfare, his project, or a little of both makes no difference. There's no way I can wake up each morning and go about my day knowing her body is out there. I wouldn't be able to live with myself.

Despite everyone having a mobile in their pocket these days, there's still an old payphone outside the Winton River Hospital. I can use it to call Triple Zero and hopefully get them to connect me directly to the state police instead of Herm. I'll tell them where she is, no extra details. Just the bare minimum, then get off the phone. Hopefully, by the time they arrive on scene, the snow will have erased any sign of Koda and me having ever been there.

The drive feels longer than it should, wrapped in the

kind of quiet that settles before bad weather rolls through. When I eventually reach the hospital, I push open the car door and keep my head down. If this weather keeps up, skiers and snowboarders will start making their way toward the national park, and Koda and I will be on call around the clock. With every step, I try to focus on prepping our winter packs and mentally listing what equipment we'll need. Anything to distract myself from the fact I'm about to go against everything my brother told me to do.

The phone box is just a few metres away. Soon, my part in this will be over, and the authorities can take it from here. What happens to Jack or Herm will be up to the real police. All that matters is the girl's family will have closure, knowing they've said goodbye, and that she is at peace.

'Mia?'

I freeze and look up. Now in his late fifties, Gerry is the kind of man who, when you look at him, you imagine must have been good-looking when he was young. His hair is receding, probably once thick and wavy, and his shoulders, which might have been broad in his twenties, now stoop just a little — probably from the weight of my mother's constant nagging.

'Gerry, it's not even six in the morning. What are you doing here?'

'The hospital was short on triage staff, so they called me in last night. I'm just heading home, but never mind that,' he says. 'Why are you here? Are you sick?'

'Oh... I...' My mind is blank. I have no idea what I can say to explain being here at this hour. 'I was having those heart flutters again. No doubt just my anxiety playing up,' I mutter. 'I thought it was best to come to *Emergency* and get checked out.'

He immediately steps in and takes my wrist between his finger and thumb to check my pulse. 'Did you call your mother?'

I give him a look that says all it needs to.

'Right, well, your pulse is a little elevated. I'll come in with you, so you won't have to wait.'

'That's not necessary,' I tell him, pulling my arm back. 'This isn't anything new, you know that. You're tired. Go on home. I'll be fine.'

He studies me from head to toe. 'Your mother told me what happened yesterday.'

I cast my mind back to the argument we had at the Sweetie. So much has happened since then that, for me, it feels like a week ago.

'I'm sorry, Mia,' Gerry continues. 'For what it's worth, I think Will is a good man. Don't listen to gossip. Your mother and sister are...'

'Awful people?'

He immediately purses his lips as if to stop the wrong words accidentally slipping out.

'It's fine, Gerry. You don't have to say anything. You go

home. I'm okay.'

He looks me over one last time. 'Please call if you need anything. I'll leave my phone on. And Mia, your mother loves you. She's just...'

I nod and smile as best I can. 'I know. Thanks, Gerry.'

When he's out of sight, I make my way toward the phone booth and step inside. After dialling, I wait a moment, and the emergency services operator comes onto the line.

'Triple Zero. Police, Fire, or Ambulance?'

'Police.'

'Just a moment.'

I nervously tap my foot and try to swallow, but my throat is dry.

'Police, what's your emergency?'

'I need to report a body.'

'Hold please.'

Hold? Really?

A couple of moments later, a man's voice comes onto the line. 'New South Wales Police. Can I start with your full name?'

'A girl's body is located in the north-east field of Willow's Crossing in Wildling. The property owner is Jack Stanton. Looks like she's been there a few days.'

Before he can respond, I quickly hang up the phone. Even though I have winter gloves on, I glance over my shoulder to make sure no one is watching, then take a small packet of wet wipes out of my pocket. I wipe down the receiver and keypad, then tuck the packet away.

Seeing Gerry was unfortunate, but he's always had my back, even with Mum. Hopefully, if worse comes to worst, I can trust him to understand.

I climb back into the car and pull the door shut with a thud. I glance in the rear-vision mirror at the space where Koda usually sits and regret my decision not to bring him. It's too quiet without him, and even though he can't give me any advice, sometimes just talking to him calms my nerves.

I start the car, eager to get home and put this entire situation behind me. Even Jack can't control the state police. I did the right thing. Now all I have to do is figure out how to get the faces of two dead girls out of my mind.

Chapter Sixteen

HER name is Hazel Smith. She was sixteen.

News of her name broke yesterday, and by late afternoon, the entire town was buzzing with reporters from Canberra and Sydney, all of them trying to find different angles and opportunities to talk with members of Wildling's First Nations community.

I scroll the news sites, looking for anything new about the case. It must be driving reporters crazy that no one will speak. Having grown up here, I know that when a member of their mob dies, the community enters an official mourning period and refuses to say the name of the person or display images of them for a year. They believe that if they do, it will disrupt the spirit's journey, preventing it from reaching the ancestral realm where passed loved ones will be waiting.

Without access to family members or information from police, all the journalists have to report on is Hazel's name, age, and that she was missing for four days before being found in a shallow grave on Willow's Crossing. Thankfully, there's been no mention of who called the report in, only that *an anonymous source reported the gruesome discovery.*

At home, though, it's another story.

'Are you coming back tonight?' I ask Will, as I cradle the phone against my shoulder and try not to trip over Koda.

'I should be home by eight.'

'Eight?' I pour hot water into the mug and stir my coffee. 'Why so late?'

'Because, Mia, Mondays are hectic, and I have a late meeting with Jess to get the final tick of approval for your brother's project.'

'You can't do that during work hours?' I hear Sophie's voice in my mind. *Well, everyone in town thinks Will's having an affair.*

'There are no ordinary hours here. Everyone works when they need to.'

'Do you spend a lot of time with her?'

I glance around our kitchen and see him standing by the sink, hanging the yellow-and-white check curtains we bought together on Main Street. Over by the stovetop, holding out the ladle to let me taste his Bolognese sauce. In the hallway, helping me clean up the tattered remnants of an old paperback Koda chewed to pieces when he was a puppy.

'What?' He sighs, and I imagine him shaking his head at how stupid I sound. 'Look, just let me get through this meeting, okay? And, Mia, when I get home, we need to talk.'

The spoon clicks against the side of the mug as I stop stirring. 'What about?'

'You know what about.'

'Us?'

'No, about what happened on the weekend.'

Jason must have told him. It doesn't surprise me. Will would hate that I went out there, putting myself and Koda in a dangerous situation. He would also hate knowing what might happen if Jack and Herm found out it was me who called it in.

'Right. It's been a circus in town ever since,' I tell him. 'Journalists from all over the place are here trying to get a story about it.'

'Have you seen Jason?'

'Not since I told him—'

'Stop talking,' he snaps. 'We're on the phone.'

I hold my breath and wait for him to speak again. When he does, he says, 'I'm really disappointed in you, Mia. What you did was stupid. I just... I don't even know what you think sometimes. Anyway, I'll speak to you about it tonight, all right?'

My first reaction is to tell him I'm sorry. The second is to explain myself. But before I can do either, the phone goes dead, and just like that, Will is gone.

Chapter Seventeen
Juniper

I NEVER thought I'd be heading back to Wildling. Especially not this soon and certainly not with my career hanging by a frayed byline. My entire life, all I ever dreamed of was getting out of there. I hated being stuck in a small town. Even as a kid, I knew what I wanted – to be a journalist. To travel and meet people. To tell their stories and see the world. And I could. My parents told me as much as soon as I was old enough to understand.

Junie Bug, you can be anything and anyone you want. You're so special. There's nothing you can't do.

Sydney was supposed to be my way out. I'd traded cow-town quiet for newsroom chaos, swapped snow boots for stilettos and thought I'd make it. As it turned out, my grand arrival barely caused the city to blink.

I pull into a sprawling petrol station on the side of the freeway that looks more like a mini-city than a place to put petrol in the car. As I crack the door open, the air outside feels heavy and damp. I tug my jacket tighter and whisper a quiet thank-you to myself for choosing jeans instead of the skirt I had out this morning. At the bowser, I watch the numbers flick by and try to ignore the delicious smell of greasy hot chips wafting over from the roadhouse. One car over, a middle-aged man with an oversized forehead and a woman in the passenger seat glance at me and smirk. I turn away and sigh. I know what they're thinking, but they're wrong. In the past year, I've lost count of how many times strangers have stopped me on the street in Sydney, believing I'm Margot Robbie or Delta Goodrem. I'm never quite sure how to react to their disappointment when I tell them I'm just me - Juniper Davis. No one special or important. I guess I could take it as a compliment, but it's also kind of depressing to watch someone's shoulders slump because of all the people you're not.

I finish filling up my car and shiver from the cold. The Wildling exit is still an hour away, and already I can feel a bite in the air – the one that tells me there's snow on the mountain. I've only driven a few hours, but there's no denying how far I am from my life in Sydney.

When I asked my boss, *Sydney Daily* editor Lisa Knight, for time off to come home and deal with my teenage sister, initially, she refused. In her opinion, I should be spending every waking moment at my desk trying to make amends for single-handedly almost destroying the paper's reputation.

It happened six months ago when, after writing fluff piece after fluff piece about celebrities and fundraisers, I stumbled across a wiry rodent of a man called Stefano Kutsinoff in a bar just a few blocks from work. He had a missing front tooth and beady eyes that never stopped darting around the room. At first, he'd tried to hit on me, but when he realised I was a journalist, his entire demeanour changed. He leaned in close but wouldn't look at me. He shifted in his seat, this way and that, like something was trying to crawl out from underneath him.

It hadn't taken much prompting, and with just a little encouragement, he spent the next two hours telling me about a former underworld bikie who he *knew for a fact* was behind the murder of a high-ranking Kings Cross police officer who was dirty and on the take. After one more drink, he confided in me that he feared he was next in line because he knew too much.

I'd thought it was my lucky break. I told him that maybe we could help. If I wrote a story, they couldn't kill him. It would look too obvious. I asked if I could attribute quotes to him, and I guess after too many beers and the misguided hope it might save his arse, he said I could. The next day, it was our front-page story. It was the best morning of my life. By the afternoon, he had reneged, and the cashed-up bikie group sent their lawyers after the paper.

Buzz around the office was that my head was on the chopping block, but then Lilly Daniels was found dead, and the remains of Hazel Smith were discovered on Willow's Crossing. Lisa knows Wildling is my hometown. She also knows that under no circumstances do I want to go digging around investigating the people I grew up with. But last night, she made it painfully clear that if I want any sort of career, I've got one chance. Go to Wildling. Get the real story. Or don't come back. She called it *paying my dues*. I call it punishment disguised as opportunity. Either way, here I am, driving straight back into the one story I thought I'd escaped.

A few kilometres from Wildling, the divider markers turn from white to yellow – an indication that snow and ice can sometimes cover sections of road. A warning there could be danger ahead.

Not much further now.

I stiffen at the thought of seeing my sister, Britt. She's always been so rebellious, seeking out attention for all the wrong reasons. I've never been able to understand her. It's like she wants to make her life as difficult as possible. Getting herself into trouble with the police, dropping out of school, and hanging out with Lilly Daniels, who everyone knew was bad news. Mum thinks if I come home and show her that playing by the rules pays off, it will eventually get her out of Wildling and into a different life. One that doesn't get cut short like Lilly's. That's how it started anyway. I left out telling her the part about coming back to try and save my job.

In spring, the cherry blossoms that grow along my parents' street bloom with beautiful pink and white flowers.

It's impossible not to smile when you see them, but today the trees are skeletal and bare. The delicate flowers are long gone, leaving only a network of twisted limbs reaching up against a pale grey sky. I sigh as I drive past, their barren branches making me even more miserable.

'Come on, Junie,' I whisper to myself. 'Get it together. The flowers will make a comeback, and so will you. Just give it time.'

I pull into the driveway and turn off the car. My parents' home is like a lot of the houses in Wildling – a charming cottage painted in soft cream with dark green shutters and a cobblestone path. I open the car door and am immediately enveloped by the scent of eucalyptus and wood smoke drifting over from the neighbours' fireplaces. Behind the houses, the towering mountain range leans in like a room full of relatives gathered to welcome me home.

When I push open the front door and step inside, the first thing I hear is the fire crackling and popping in the hearth. The second is the familiar creak of the loose floorboard Dad always says he's going to fix but never does.

'Mum?' I call out. 'I'm home.'

When there's no reply, I set my bag down and pad into the kitchen. Through the window, I gaze out at the backyard where Britt and I used to play, running around and building snowmen. That was so long ago now, before she decided to tear it all down and hate me.

The old treehouse is still nestled high in the sprawling

tree. The wooden planks are weathered and grey, the paint long faded and peeling. I stare at it and remember all the times I would stand below, shouting up at Britt. She would fortify herself inside, refusing to come down and say sorry for whatever she'd done to me. How good she always was at pressing my buttons.

'Junie, I didn't hear you come in.' I turn to see Mum coming toward me, arms open, her face a mix of love and relief. She pulls me into an embrace, her hand resting on the back of my head.

'Hey, Mum,' I manage as best I can, my face pressed into her neck. Her hair smells like a mix of shampoo and dust. 'I called out, but you didn't hear me.'

'Oh,' she begins, finally letting go. 'I was up the back of the walk-in cupboard trying to find your grandmother's old recipe book. You remember that shepherd's pie you and Britt used to love? I was going to make it for dinner.'

'Mum, I was twelve years old the last time we had that. I think Britt was five.'

'I know, but I thought it might be a nice icebreaker.' She clenches her jaw and looks away. A sign that things are not going well with my sister.

'Is it really that bad with Britt?' I ask. 'Like, shepherd's pie bad?'

'She's just... so angry, Junie. She wears this makeup that makes her look like Dracula.'

Without meaning to, I laugh out loud, and it makes

Mum smile.

'It's so good to see you,' she says, rubbing my arms with both hands. 'Sit down and I'll make us a coffee.'

I pull out a chair at the same worn wooden table where we ate dinner every night. I have so many memories of meals at this table. Britt throwing mashed potato. Our old labrador, Sam, crouched at our feet, licking his lips and hoping for scraps. Debates with Dad as I got older about politics and who should be Prime Minister. Mum beaming at me for no reason other than I ate my vegetables. Britt throwing even more mashed potato.

While Mum busies herself in the kitchen, she fills me in on all the drama that's been going on around town since I left. Lilly's death, Jason Thomas' plan to build some kind of geothermal drilling rig in the mountains, and how Sarah Stanton says even though Bryce is dating the very respectable Charlotte Higgins, he never really got over the fact I moved away.

'You and he could work things out if you decided to stay,' Mum continues, 'which, of course, your dad and I would love. But we know you have your glamorous life in Sydney. We read every one of your stories in the paper, Junie. We have a special order at the newsagent to make sure they save us a copy every day.'

'Mum, you don't have to do that. You can read it on-line.'

'No, I cut them all out and save them in a scrapbook.'

I imagine her down on the floor, scissors in hand, her tongue twisting from corner of her mouth as she concentrates, careful to only cut along the edges. 'Mum, please tell me you're joking.'

'No, I do,' she says, placing the mug down in front of me. 'You want to see?'

The *Sydney Daily* is one of the city's most respected newspapers. It covers politics, crime, finance – actual news. I write filler stories that the real journos laugh about. Dog dress-up contests and who wore what to the ARIA awards.

'No, that's okay,' I tell her. 'I'll take your word for it.'

'We're so proud of you, Junie,' she gushes. 'If only Britt were more like you.'

'Britt's her own person, Mum,' I tell her, sipping my coffee. 'She doesn't want to be like me.'

But Mum waves her hand at me as though I'm crazy. 'Of course she does. That's part of the problem. She always wanted to be like you, Junie. And who wouldn't? You're perfect.'

I bite my bottom lip, wondering for the first time if maybe Britt isn't just rebellious and headstrong. Maybe she acts out because it's the only way to make Mum notice her.

'You don't tell her that, do you?'

'What?'

'That she should be like me.'

'Of course. If she were more like you, she wouldn't have dropped out of school and be spending her days working at the petrol station.'

'You can't say that to her, Mum.'

'I'm just telling the truth.'

I nod, knowing there's no point arguing. 'You're just trying to help her. I get that.'

'Of course you do,' she says with a smile. 'That's why everyone here loves you, Junie. You never make things difficult.'

Chapter Eighteen

I'M in the far west corner of the national park when Mimi's name lights up my phone screen. My full-time job is as a park ranger. Koda and I can only carry out search and rescue operations when we're needed by the police, so in between, we spend our time out here taking care of the land.

I press answer on my phone, then gaze out across the park, counting my blessings that I don't have to work at a job in town.

'Mimi, what's up?'

'Kiddo, I need your help,' she begins. 'Well, Koda's really. Can you come over?'

I can't remember a time Mimi has ever needed help from anyone, and the real reason she's calling probably has nothing at all to do with Koda.

'What do you need him to do?'

'It's easier if I just show you. I'll see you later at my place.'

Before I can respond, the phone goes silent, and I realise she's already hung up.

'Sure, okay, Mimi,' I mutter into the silent phone. 'No problem.'

JUST after 3 pm, I pull up at Mimi's and let Koda jump out wearing just his collar. I have no idea what she wants him to do, but I can't imagine there's any scenario where he'll be tracking or need his work gear.

'You came,' Mimi says, stepping onto the veranda. She's wearing another brightly coloured dress, her hair wild and feet still bare.

'Aren't your toes cold?' I ask, peering up at her. 'There's snow on the mountain.'

She glances down at her feet and shakes her head. 'The original custodians of this land walked barefoot in the snow.'

'Doesn't make it any less cold now.'

'What's that?' she asks, cocking her head.

'Nothing, Mimi,' I tell her, knowing full well she heard every word. 'Well, we're here. How can we help?'

'Come on inside.'

I hesitate and kick at a loose rock on the gravel driveway.

'Oh, come on now, kiddo,' she says. 'You ain't a child no more. What you so scared of?'

The truth is, I have no idea what I'm so scared of. When I was little, Mimi's house was strange and completely different from Mum's place. She had weird rugs on the floor, and unusual smells drifted out of pots bubbling away on the cooktop. Dried herbs dangled from the rafters like sleeping bats, and her shelves were cluttered with feathers, rocks, and jars of things I never wanted to touch. The town whispered that she was a witch. That she cast spells and was to blame every time the crops succumbed to drought, flood, or vermin.

'Got a kangaroo joey inside,' she says with a smile. 'Lost its mamma on the road. You too grown up to like those?'

'No,' I manage, 'I still like them.'

'Wanna come in and see?'

'Why does this feel like Hansel and Gretel?'

'You think I'm gonna try and put you and Koda in the oven?' she asks with a throaty laugh.

I shake my head and look away, embarrassed. 'No, I just...'

'Come on inside. I ain't gonna bite you. Promise.'

I glance at Koda, and he looks back at me, head tilted as if to ask, *what are you waiting for*?

'Fine, but we can't stay long,' I say, as we start up the stairs. 'We have to get home.'

'Can't be late with Will's dinner.'

I don't miss the sarcasm in her voice. 'It's not like that, Mimi.'

"Course not, kiddo. You want tea?'

Inside, I perch myself on a stool at the breakfast bar and let my gaze wander. The kitchen feels smaller than it did when I was a child, yet somehow more alive. The stained-glass window above the sink filters light into soft pools of amber and green that drift across the counter. Wooden shelves bow beneath the weight of mismatched crockery, chipped mugs, and jars of spices with labels written in Latin. A kettle hums softly on the stovetop, steam curling into the air, carrying the scent of chamomile and something I can't place. From where I'm sitting, I can see the old timber dresser in the adjoining room, its surface cluttered with framed photographs, trinkets, and candles that have melted into crooked rivers of wax. Everywhere I look, there are signs of a life stitched together, as though the house carries her memories in its bones.

My gaze comes to rest on a canvas hanging on the far wall. It's at least a metre high and painted with a mix of earthy tones, and brightly coloured green and yellow strokes that together form the shape of a frog.

'One of yours?' I ask, as memories of Mimi painting, her fingers covered in lashings of red and brown, flash through my mind.

'You like it?'

'It's beautiful,' I answer honestly.

'Inspired by Tiddalik,' she tells me, placing the mug down. 'You know about Tiddalik?'

I shake my head and sip the tea. It's so bitter that I shudder, and Mimi laughs.

'Some First Nations people tell a story about Tiddalik the greedy frog who drank up all the water in the land. It wasn't until the other animals found a way to make him laugh that all the water came rushing back out forming waterways and billabongs. That sound like anyone you know?

'The frog?'

Mimi nods and sits down on the stool beside me.

'A greedy frog that gets too big for its boots. Well, yeah, someone comes to mind.'

Without warning, she grabs my hand and holds it between both of hers. 'You and him gonna have a problem soon, kiddo,' she tells me, her tone changing. 'Trust me, he's not someone you want as an enemy.'

'Jack?'

She nods again and pulls me in. 'He's too big for you to take down on your own.'

'Jason came to see you, didn't he?'

'Didn't need to.' She closes her eyes and breathes in and out, slow and deep. 'The spirits are warning me. Telling me you're in trouble.'

'I'm not in trouble, Mimi.'

'Not yet.' She opens her eyes and stares at me, a piercing gaze that makes me squirm in my seat. 'But it's coming, Mia. Looming, larger and larger, just like Tiddalik.'

I pull my hand away and get up from the seat, suddenly remembering why I never liked it here.

'The animals made Tiddalik laugh because they worked together,' she says. 'You need to do the same.'

'You're saying I need to make Jack laugh?' I shake my head and motion to Koda to fall in beside me. 'That makes no sense.'

'No, kiddo. I'm saying you and the other two need to work together. It's the only way.'

I freeze where I am and look back at her. 'Mimi, what are you talking about? What other two?'

'He'll say you walked where you weren't invited, but it's not his land, Mia. You had every right to follow your instincts.'

She must have spoken to Jason. How else could she know I was on Jack's property? 'Well, unfortunately, the law might say otherwise. Willow's Crossing is private property.'

'It's stolen property.'

'That was a long time ago, Mimi. It's Jack's land now.'

'When the third arrow is drawn, it will begin.'

I search her face. Her mouth has pulled into a grim line, and there's genuine concern in her eyes. 'Mimi, what are you talking about?'

'Remember,' she says, getting to her feet. 'Work together.'

I rub my forehead, my fingers moving in small, circular motions over my temples. There's a throbbing pain just above my eyebrows that, by the time I get home, will have become a headache. 'There was never any joey in here, was there?' I ask Mimi. 'Or any job for Koda.'

'You need my help, kiddo, and I know you're too proud to ask for it. Figured best thing was to get you over here and give it to you anyway.'

I nod and head toward the front door, Koda in step beside me. 'All right, Mimi. Well, good to see you,' I manage in a tone that I hope conveys my frustration.

'That's a good dog you got there,' she calls after me. 'He'll show you what you need to do.'

Chapter Nineteen
Juniper

AT around lunchtime, Mum found the shepherd's pie recipe and now she's over at the kitchen bench, doing her best to prepare dinner. Cooking has never been her strong point, but even so, she's launched a full-scale kitchen offensive. Saucepans, spatulas, herbs flying, like dinner is a siege she's determined to win. I'm sure she thinks that feeding the troops will inevitably result in a ceasefire and we'll all just surrender and agree to get along, but I have my doubts.

She refused any offer of help, so instead I'm sitting at the dining table, scrolling and reading story after story about Hazel Smith and keeping an eye on her progress as best I can.

As she scoops the meat out of the pan, I hear the front door and brace myself. Britt is home from work. I have no idea what kind of reception to expect from her. After my conversation with Mum, I can't imagine she'll be happy to see me, especially in the emotional state she's in. She was acting out even before Lilly died.

Mum stops what she's doing, the ladle frozen mid-air, meat sauce on her cheek. I sit up a little straighter, and we exchange a glance. Any minute now.

'Mum, I need to—' When Britt sees me, she stops short and stares.

The first thing I notice is how much she's grown up. How much she looks like Dad, with her thick dark hair and tall athletic frame. The second is the ghoulish eye makeup Mum warned me about. Never mind Dracula, she looks like the Bride of Frankenstein.

'Hey, Britt,' I begin. 'How are you?' As soon as I say the words, I realise how stupid it sounds. Her best friend just died.

She studies my face, taking in every nervous twitch, every tell. It's like she's cataloguing every weak point I have and creating a mental checklist in case she needs it later.

'How do you think?' she says eventually, without a hint of warmth in her voice.

'Right. Sorry.' *Are you all right? Can I do anything? Do you need something?* I search my mind for the right thing to say but come up empty. 'I'm sorry about Lilly,' I try. 'I know she meant a lot to you.'

She holds my gaze for a moment and then nods. I can see the sadness in her eyes, but there's also something else. Something I can't quite put my finger on.

'Don't even think about writing some story about her while you're here,' she warns. 'There's enough vultures circling the town already.'

'That's not why I came back, Britt. I came because I wanted to make sure you're all right.'

'I don't need a babysitter.'

I exchange a glance with Mum, and she gives me a nod of encouragement. 'I know that. I just wanted to see how you are.'

To my surprise, she laughs. The sound is sharp and hollow and hangs between us. I can't figure out whether she thinks what I said is funny or if she just doesn't believe I'd want to help her.

'You're joking, right?'

Clearly, the latter. 'You're my sister, Britt. I want to try and make this better somehow.'

But she shakes her head and stares at the ground.

'What? I do.'

'Bullshit,' she hisses, glaring back at me. 'You want to write a story. You want to come here and play on the fact that everyone in Wildling loves Juniper Davis. You think that will get you info the other vultures don't have access to. Do you think I'm stupid?'

The accusation stings, mostly because she's right. She always was smarter than me. 'Britt...'

'How long are you staying?'

'I'm not sure.'

'You're not staying, staying, though, right?'

'No.'

'Good.'

Her words are acid, but I swallow them down, determined not to let her corrode my good intentions. She's right about the story, but I also want to help her.

Before I can respond, Mum interjects. A bid to defuse the tension. 'Everything will work itself out,' she says with a smile. 'It's just so nice to see you both together here at home.'

Britt holds my gaze a moment longer, and then we both look over at Mum. I nod and give her the best smile I can manage before Britt shakes her head and says, 'Christ, Mum, that meat sauce looks like someone took a shit on your face.'

Chapter Twenty

I PULL up at home and am surprised to see Will's silver Lexus parked in the driveway. He said he wouldn't be back until 8 pm. I glance at my watch. It's not even 5 pm.

'He's home early,' I say to Koda as he jumps out of the back and onto the driveway.

I remind myself to stay calm as we make our way toward the house. Koda trots beside me, his nails ticking on the pavers. Just because Will said we need to talk, doesn't mean something bad is about to happen. This will be okay.

Knee-high rows of lavender line the path. At this time of year, their summer brilliance has faded. The silver-green leaves are beaded with frost, and only a few papery purple heads still cling to the stalks. I breathe in deep, and get the faintest whisper of scent, enough to stir the memory of warmer days even as the cold air needles my skin.

As we step onto the porch, Koda begins to bark. It's playful. The one he usually does when…

I glance over and see my brother's boots just outside the door, one lying on its side where he's recklessly kicked them off the way he always does. Even though he and Will have been working together on Jason's project, the twist in my gut says that's not why he's here.

Inside, the living room feels smaller than it did this morning. In the corner, the wood heater crackles and pops throwing a dull orange glow across my scuffed floorboards. Jason leans against the wooden mantel, arms folded, eyes flicking to the window. Will is over by the couch, hands jammed into his pockets, shoulders stiff. Together, they take up all the space, leaving me pressed against the doorway.

'Mia,' Will begins. 'We need to talk.'

'Can I at least make a coffee? It's been a long day and—'

'This isn't a family catch-up, Mia,' Jason snaps. 'You won't be needing a coffee.'

From the minute I sit down, it's clear what this is – an intervention.

'Mia, I specifically told you not to call the police.' The tremble in my brother's voice makes it clear how angry he is. 'We went over this. I explained to you what was at stake. You've put everything we've worked for at risk.'

'We?'

'Yes, we,' Will chimes in. 'I've worked my arse off in Canberra getting this project signed off. Do you think it's easy getting a bunch of bureaucrats to green-light a geothermal drilling project in a national park? You have no idea what I've had to do, and we're almost there. We're one step away.'

Images of Will charming some government woman over bottles of wine and fancy dinners push their way into my mind. Is that what he *had to do*? I bite my lip to stop from saying it out loud.

'This entire thing hinges on Jack being supportive, Mia,' Jason says, taking over. 'He's not just a big fish in a small pond. He has connections that go all the way to the Premier's office. If he arks up and turns the town against it, we're ruined.'

'I didn't give my name,' I tell them. 'And I drove all the way over to Winton River to call from a phone box. No one knows it was me.'

Jason scoffs and shakes his head. 'Are you really this stupid?'

It's the first time I've ever seen my mother's venom in him. Since we were kids, Jason has been my rock. My ride or die. She resented us both, but bad as it was, I always had Jason, and he was enough. To hear her bitter tone in his voice is like a knife in my chest.

'I couldn't just leave her out there,' I whisper. 'It wasn't right.'

'It's not about that, Mia,' Will says, his voice softening a little. 'What were you thinking, going out there in the middle of the night like that? It's dangerous. Anything could have happened.'

'It was because of Herm,' I manage, inching the sleeve of

my shirt into my palm and clutching it in my fingers. 'He was so adamant that I shouldn't. Koda alerted on the way back from finding Lilly, and Herm was so determined to warn me off going back. I thought…'

'You thought what?'

They both lean in, the intensity of their gaze causing my legs to tremble. 'I thought he knew there was another body out there. Maybe because he did it. Or because Jack did, and he was trying to cover it up.'

They both stare at me. Silence hangs between us, the tension in the room a taut wire about to snap. I immediately drop my head and pull at the corner of my fingernail.

Will shakes his head and steps back. 'Are you being serious? You think Herm is, what? A serial killer? Or Jack?'

'I wasn't wrong about Koda's alert.'

'Anything could have happened to her, Mia,' he says, frustration creeping back into his voice. 'She probably wandered off, just like Lilly did.'

'Oh, come on, Will. You can't really think that, in the space of a week, two different girls who had nothing in common both just wandered off and died either on or near Jack's property.'

'There was nothing to suggest Lilly was murdered. Or Hazel, for that matter.'

'Bullshit,' I snap, finally finding my voice. 'People don't just fall into a ravine and not try to get out. I've seen it a hundred times around the park. No one just lies down and dies of exposure. And Hazel was buried. I saw her head wound. It wasn't an accident.'

'What are you talking about?'

'Lilly's nails were perfect,' I say, glancing down at my own ravaged fingers. 'It was obvious she didn't even try to climb out, and Hazel's head was bashed in. I saw it. I can't get it out of my mind.'

'Maybe Hazel fell and hit her head, and Lilly was probably drugged out and incoherent. There's a million ways to explain how they died, Mia. Why would you jump straight to Herm or Jack being murderers? It makes no sense.'

Jason steeples his palms, then knots his fingers. 'Gerry said you've been struggling again.'

Struggling. Suddenly, my throat is so thick the words get tangled. 'Don't... No... Don't do this.'

'Look, Mia, maybe—'

'No,' I snap, pacing back and forth across the room. 'Gerry saw me when I was going to use the pay phone, that's all. He was coming out of the hospital, so I made up an excuse about my anxiety for being there. I'm not struggling. I'm fine.'

'He saw you?' Will shouts, throwing up his hands. 'Oh, that's just great.'

'He wouldn't say anything.'

'He would, Mia, and he did, to Mum,' Jason tells me. 'She also said you attacked her and Sophie at the Sweetie the other day. Amelia told me the same thing.'

'Oh, that's ridiculous. I did not attack them. I just…'

'What's going on with you?' Will asks. 'You're not yourself.'

'I'm not myself?' I turn to him, my hands trembling. How can he accuse me of acting differently when I barely recognise who he is anymore? 'What about you? You're a completely different person lately. The reason I argued with Mum and Sophie is because they told me everyone in town thinks you're having an affair, probably with that Jess woman you're working with on Jason's project.'

'What?' Will comes forward glaring at me. 'And you believed that?'

Jason steps between us, arms out, trying to calm the situation. I can't help but notice he makes no effort to dispel the accusation. He doesn't even look surprised by it. 'Mia, this still doesn't explain why you put everything at risk to go off on some wild goose chase, thinking Herm and Jack are murderers.' He looks at Will and motions for him to sit down. 'It makes no sense, and I hate to say this, but I think maybe you need to go back on your medication.'

My insides collapse. I want to shout and protest, but that will only prove him right.

'I think it would be for the best,' he continues. 'You're acting crazy right now.'

Crazy. It's the same word Mum used when I was fourteen. She'd been tugging at my arm as I locked both hands around the metal bedhead, knuckles white, refusing to be taken to the clinic in Sydney. It was the last thing she did before she forced us to go and live with Mimi.

'We all think that maybe it would help.'

'We all?' I repeat. 'Who's we all?'

'Mum, Gerry, Sophie, myself,' Jason tells me. 'And Will.'

I stare at Will in disbelief. 'You agree with this?'

'Like I said, Mia, you're not yourself.'

'But there's nothing wrong with me,' I argue. 'I'm not crazy. You're just not listening to me.'

'We are listening, Mia,' Jason says. 'But what you're saying makes no sense.'

I shake my head and turn away to stop them seeing the tears in my eyes. 'You have no idea why I was on medication when we were young, Jason. Or why Mum took me to that place. I wasn't crazy.'

'Mia, I was there, remember? I know what it was like with Mum. It was harder for you because you needed her more. I get that, but—'

'That's not why,' I whisper, unable to turn and face them.

'Then what?'

Koda appears at my side, and I reach down and hold onto his ear. 'Herm,' I begin, the words catching in my throat, 'when I was a kid, he...'

'He what, Mia?'

A hot flush creeps up my neck. A mix of shame and fear. 'When he used to pick me up for the stupid shit I'd do, once we were at the station, he'd take me out the back and…'

'Just… stop,' Will snaps. 'I can't… I don't want to hear this.'

'No, I have to say it,' I say, finally turning to face them both. 'I need to.'

All my life, I've kept what he did to me bottled up inside. An insidious voice that constantly whispered that maybe it was my fault. Making me question why I hadn't spoken up. Asking why I hadn't told someone the first time, the second time, or any of the times that followed. Had his attention, disgusting as it was, been better than feeling like I didn't exist at all? If that's true, then I don't deserve Will's love or Jason's respect. If that's true, there's a part of me that must have been born broken.

'I was thirteen the first time. Sixteen, when it finally stopped.'

Will's head snaps up, and he glares at me. 'Sixteen?'

I nod and roughly wipe at my tears with the back of my arm.

'For three years you let him…?'

'Let him?' I step back. Time stands still and a strange buzzing fills my ears. I squeeze my eyes closed to try and stop myself from falling. *Will thinks it was my fault.*

Jason rubs a thumb along his jaw, staring at the floor-boards as though the right thing to say might be written in the pattern of the wood. 'Is that why you think he killed

Lilly and Hazel?' he asks eventually. 'Because of what he did to you?'

'Huh?' I ask, eventually shifting my eyes away from Will.

'Is that what this is about? What happened to you back then.'

'No, it's because Lilly was pregnant,' I tell him. 'I don't know about Hazel, but Lilly was.'

Jason stares at me a moment, taking it all in. 'There was nothing in the news about Lilly being pregnant.'

'They must have covered it up.'

'Covered it up?' The look of disbelief on my brother's face is enough to make me want to take the words back. 'Okay, let me get this straight. You think Herm is going around town getting teenagers pregnant and then killing them? Wait... is that what happened to you? Were you pregnant?'

Will glares at me. His eyes are hard and unsympathetic as he waits for me to answer. 'No, I wasn't, but it makes sense that he wouldn't want anyone to know about Lilly. He's a cop. She was a teenager.'

'Mia,' Jason comes over and pulls me into an embrace. 'What happened to you is horrible, and I'm so sorry. You should have told me back then. What he did wasn't your fault. I need you to know that.'

I nod and push my head into his shoulder, sobs of relief causing my entire body to shake. I hold on to him as the weight of shame pulls at me, dragging me down toward the hole I'm so tired of trying to dig my way out of.

'That's why Mum made us live with Mimi,' I manage. 'Because of what I tried to do that day. It was my fault.'

When he eventually steps back, I steal a glance at Will. His arms are folded across his chest. He's a fortress, and I am clearly locked out.

'Listen to me,' Jason begins, hands resting on my shoulders, his head dipped to meet my eye. 'I love you. You know that, right? Mum made us live with Mimi because she couldn't cope with being a mum. It wasn't because of you, Mi.'

I nod quickly and wipe at the tears still slipping down my cheeks.

'I'm sorry for what happened to you. I really am.'

'Thanks,' I whisper.

He casts a glance back at Will, thinks a moment, and then says, 'That said, I still think with everything going on, it would be a good idea to have Gerry write you a script.'

I step back and search his eyes. 'What?'

'I just think maybe finding Lilly and Hazel has brought back some trauma for you, and you're not handling it in the best way.'

'Brought back trauma? Jason, Koda alerted, and we found Hazel out there,' I tell him, gobsmacked that he's still not getting it. 'That's not acting crazy, that's a fact. And there's nothing to say it won't happen again. Do you really want that on your conscience?'

'What Herm did to you, and maybe to Lilly, is awful,' he continues. 'It makes him a predator, and at some point, we'll address that, but Mia, it doesn't mean he or Jack are serial killers.'

'Oh... my... God,' I say on a long breath. 'You don't even care.'

He pushes his hair back off his forehead and shakes his head. 'That's not what I'm saying.'

'All you care about is your stupid drilling project.'

'Stupid?' His look of disbelief matches mine. 'Mia, this project could change how the entire world is powered. Do you understand the gravity of what I'm trying to achieve here?'

I search his face for the boy he used to be, for the brother who once loved me unconditionally. With painful clarity, it occurs to me that he's the one person I'll never be able to find, no matter how hard I look. 'Jason, I need you to leave.'

'Mia—'

'Just get out of my house,' I hiss, my voice about to break. 'I don't even know who you are anymore.'

Finally, Will gets to his feet and finds his voice. 'Just go, mate. I'll take care of this.'

This. Like suddenly, I'm nothing more than another problem on his list of things to solve.

'This isn't how I wanted things to go, Mia,' Jason says

as he takes out his keys. 'And for the record, you need to be on medication. The things you're suggesting are just... not possible.'

They exchange one last glance, a silent communication I can't decipher. There was a time when the three of us were inseparable, but clearly, that's no longer the case. It's Jason and Will. I'm nothing more than a thorn in their side – a threat to their well-laid plans.

Chapter Twenty-One
Juniper

WALKING through town, I can't help but marvel at how, despite the world evolving around it, Wildling hasn't changed at all. It's been three years since I was here, and the town is exactly the same as the day I left. It's like coming home to find your old bedroom frozen in time, the pretty ballerina music box still sitting propped open on the dresser.

The community hall stands in the centre of town, flanked by an old sandstone church and the library. As a teenager, I spent countless hours there reading and breathing in the musty scent of the books, letting them take me away to places more exciting than this. At the end of Main Street, the park with its pretty lace rotunda spreads out, the towering Moreton Bay fig still standing over in the corner. My cheeks warm as I remember the sensation of my back pressed against its trunk, Bryce's lips on mine the first time we kissed.

I stroll by Sweet Sips Café, and the aroma of freshly baked bread wafts through the air. To the left, Old Jimmy is wrangling with the specials blackboard, trying to make it balance on the footpath outside the pub.

I stop at the corner of Clyde Avenue and let the sounds of the town envelop me. The church bells, the deafening chatter of white cockatoos up in the trees, and farm dogs barking as they pass by in the backs of utes. I expected to feel claustrophobic coming home, like everything would seem smaller than I remembered, but as I look around, it actually feels good to be here. Like I can breathe again.

It would be so easy, I think to myself as I stroll along, to just stay here. To forget about the pressures of Sydney and instead just slip back into my old life. Once upon a time, I was the sweetheart of Wildling. People trusted me, confided in me, and asked about my plans for the future as though anything was possible. I was going to make them proud. I was going to show them that Wildling could produce more than just farmers and local business owners. I was going to be a name. A journalist in the big city. But unless I can find out what really happened to Hazel Smith and whether she was connected to Lilly Daniels in some way, the reality is, I'm just a girl with a career that's quickly slipping through her fingers.

The sound of laughter catches my attention, and I glance over to the Sweetie where two female reporters are coming out holding cups of takeaway coffee. Edwina Harris, the senior crime reporter from the *Daily Examiner*, and Marcia Hamilton from Channel Nine News. Real journos. Women who have careers to be proud of. Compared to them, I haven't accomplished a damned thing.

The thought distracts me, and not watching where I'm going, I crash into someone. She falls to the ground, her dog's lead quickly tangling our legs together.

'Oh, my gosh! I'm so sorry!' I gush, reaching out to try and unravel the lead. 'I'm such a klutz.'

The brown and white dog licks the woman's cheek, and she quickly reaches out to reassure it. 'Everything's all right, Koda,' she says. 'I'm okay.'

'I was off in a dream world,' I tell her. 'I'm so sorry.'

'It's fine,' she murmurs, her fingers working the knot. 'It was my fault. I wasn't paying attention either. I shouldn't even be here. I took the day off work and… anyway… sorry.'

For a moment we both fuss with the lead, our hands brushing. When she finally looks at me, I notice her eyes are red-rimmed and her skin is blotchy.

'Are you okay?' I ask, not wanting to overstep.

She gives the leash one last tug, pulling it free from my leg. 'You're Juniper,' she says, ignoring my question. 'Britt's sister.'

I search her face for a moment, and then it hits me. Mia Thomas. The girl who grew up with her grandmother on the outskirts of town. Jason Thomas' sister. She was a couple of years above me at school, but I remember how all the other girls tormented her because her grandmother called herself a guardian or a custodian or something like that of the land. They lived out at the end of Wildling Road in a house everyone said looked haunted. All the kids made fun of her. It was awful.

'And you're Mia Thomas,' I reply. 'Long time.' An awkward silence hangs between us and, as always, I can't resist the need to fill it. 'I just got back to town yesterday.'

Across the road, Edwina Harris' laugh rings out again as she sits at one of the outdoor tables in the Sweetie's courtyard.

'You here to write a story about the girls?' Mia asks as we turn to watch the women chatting.

Their bright jackets and flawless hair suddenly make me feel like a drab little field mouse. I glance down at my beige knit sweater and worn jeans, embarrassed at my lame attempt to run off and become someone I'm not.

'Not exactly. Mum thought Britt could use some support. Not sure I'm the right person for it though.'

Mia nods. 'Losing Lilly is a lot for her to deal with.'

Her remark surprises me. 'Do you know my sister well?'

'No, we've only spoken once or twice. Koda and I were the ones who found Lilly. He's a search and rescue dog. We were assigned to the case when she went missing.'

'Oh, that would be a difficult thing to get out of your mind.' I glance back over at the reporters drinking their coffee. 'I guess the media has been on your case then, asking questions about it?'

'Our policy says I'm not allowed to speak to the media,

so no. Besides, finding Lilly's body was enough to rattle me. I don't think I have it in me to deal with reporters as well... no offence.'

'Oh, no, none taken,' I say with a casual swipe of my hand. 'I'm not here for that.'

Despite my sudden bout of imposter syndrome, it quickly occurs to me that Mia is an untapped resource. She found Lilly's body. If I could get her to talk, I'd be way ahead of everyone else. Edwina and Marcia might be real journos, but they're not third-generation Wildlings. It's the one thing I have in my favour.

'Mia, I don't want to be nosy, but you look like you've been crying,' I begin. 'Since my sister still won't talk to me, maybe I could offer you a shoulder instead?'

She looks away, clearly embarrassed.

'I'm fine,' she replies, refocusing her attention on gathering up her dog's lead. 'Just... you know, life stuff.'

'I imagine it must have been hard on you, finding Lilly like that. Small town like this, we all know each other, even when we don't.'

She nods and glances at her dog. It looks back at her, and the connection between them is clear to see.

'I... ah, yeah... it's a tricky one,' she says eventually. 'And now, Hazel.'

'You found Hazel as well?'

'No, it wasn't me,' she says, maybe a little too quickly. 'I don't know who found her. Have they said anything more about it on the news?'

I shake my head and continue to study her. The way she's shifting her weight and pulling at her fingernails. If she was the one who found Hazel, why lie about it? A tingle of excitement runs through me. So far, the media hasn't reported a cause of death for Hazel. All I've heard on the grapevine is that it looked like she fell and hit her head. But if Mia found her body, she would have seen her injuries. She'd know if something more sinister had taken place. Maybe that's why they're taking so long to confirm what happened. Maybe it wasn't an accident after all.

'There hasn't been any new information reported that I know of,' I tell her. 'It must be hard for her family, still not knowing for certain how she died.'

'It would be,' Mia replies. 'The whole thing is terrible.'

I agree and think about my next words carefully. I have to do this just right. 'Well, it was nice seeing you, and thanks for chatting with my sister,' I tell her. 'For what it's worth, I appreciate that at least she's had you to talk to. All we can do now is hope they find whoever is responsible.'

I turn as though I'm about to leave, like I care little about her response, all the while praying she responds from her heart instead of her head. *Come on, Mia, give me something to work with.*

'I hope so, too,' she says.

And there it is.

Despite a pathologist's report showing Lilly died of exposure, and radio silence on Hazel Smith's cause of death, Mia has just confirmed what she doesn't want to say – that she thinks someone is responsible for at least one of the deaths. In my book, that means there's every possibility the sleepy town of Wildling has become home to a murderer.

Chapter Twenty-Two
Britt

'HERE,' Luke says, handing me a blister pack of Valium. 'That's it for a while. If I take any more, Dad's going to notice.'

I nod and stuff the pills into the pocket of my denim jacket. We're sitting on the aluminium grandstand down at the footy oval, and all I want to do is get this over with. It was a long shift at the servo, the afternoon wind is arctic, and I just want to go home.

'What's up with you lately?' he asks. 'It's not like you to be on it this hard. You all good?'

'Am I all good?' I repeat, turning to face him. 'Are you kidding me?'

'Well, are you? Least I care enough to ask.'

I stare at him and wonder what the hell I was thinking ever letting this numbnuts touch me. *Am I all good?* My best friend is dead, and he's asking something that stupid.

'No, Luke, I'm not all good,' I say with a shake of my head. 'What a stupid question.' *Why can't he be a grown-up?* I think to myself. *Why can't he be more like*

Bryce?

'Well, geez,' he shouts, throwing up his hands. 'Sorry for even asking. Sorry for even giving a shit!'

'Settle down. What's your problem?'

He doesn't answer, and instead turns away and links his fingers behind his head. There's skin off his knuckles, and the outline of a bruise forming.

'What happened to your hand?'

He quickly unlinks his fingers and shoves his hands back into the pockets of his worn-out cargo pants. 'Nothing, just... frustrated, I guess.'

'How's the other guy?' I say it with a smirk, but he doesn't return my attempt to make peace.

'Nah, it was just the wall at home. Dad says I gotta pay for the stuff to fix it now. Arsehole.'

I nod and stare out over the field. 'You've been weird since Lilly died.'

From the corner of my eye, I see him turn to look at me. 'Am I supposed to just act like I don't give a shit? I thought out of everyone, you'd get it, Britt. We were all friends.'

Anger crawls up the back of my throat, and it takes every ounce of willpower not to scream at him. Lilly and I were soulmates. He was nothing to her. How dare he measure his loss against mine? Against the sadness that has seeped into every part of me. But as I try to find the words, something about the slump of his shoulders forms a question mark in my mind.

'Is that all you were?'

'Is what all we were?'

'Friends. Were you and Lilly just friends?'

'What's that supposed to mean?'

I shift my body to face him. 'Like I said, ever since it happened, you've been acting different.'

'Different how? Because I'm sad she's dead?'

'No… I don't know,' I say with a shrug. 'Just different.'

He scuffs the toe of his sneaker against the step and sniffs, digging his hands deeper into his pockets.

'Are you going to answer me?'

'What do you want me to say?'

'Just tell me. Did anything ever happen between the two of you?'

Without answering, he pulls himself up and begins climbing down off the grandstand.

'Luke?'

'What do you want to hear, Britt? Shit.'

I don't care if Luke slept with someone else. It's not like I love him, but would Lilly do that? Sleep with him behind my back? I get up and follow him down, the gaps forcing me to take each step one at a time.

'Say it,' I demand when I eventually reach the ground.

'No.'

I push him in the chest with both hands, and he stumbles back. 'What the hell, Britt?'

'Say it!'

'Say what? That I screwed Lilly? So what? It was once. Now she's dead, and it's weird.'

'When?' My hands curl into fists at my sides.

'I don't know. Whenever.'

I stare at him, and suddenly every part of him annoys me. His messy hair and pointy nose. His tall, lanky frame and the way his shoulders are always stooped like the branch of a weeping willow. 'Tell me when, Luke, or I swear to Christ... Was it while we've been seeing each other?'

'Like you care,' he quips. 'You want to screw someone else.'

'What?'

'Oh,' he shouts, turning in a circle, his arms out. 'You really think I don't know you're gagging to root Stanton?'

'Well, I haven't.'

'Only 'cause he doesn't want you.' He shoves his hands back into his pockets and kicks at the grass.

'Prick,' I swear. 'Tell me when and stop trying to turn it around.'

'I don't know. Like two or three months ago, maybe?'

His answer sends prickles of disbelief across my cheeks. Two or three months ago.

'Was it you?'

'Was what me?'

Freezing wind whips my hair into my eyes as I study every twitch of his face, every flinch of his body. 'Was it you who got her pregnant?'

'What?' He takes two steps back as his mouth falls open. Until this moment, I've never seen someone's face change colour before my eyes. 'Lilly was pregnant?'

Luke is a lot of things, but he's never going to grace the silver screen for his acting abilities. He didn't know about the baby.

'Yeah,' I tell him. 'Three months.'

He swallows and looks away. 'Are you saying...'

'I don't know.'

'Shit.'

'On the day she died, she said she was going to see the father,' I tell him. 'Did you see her?'

When he doesn't answer, my heart skips a beat. A tear slips over his cheek, and suddenly it hits me. 'Jesus, Luke – you loved her.'

He shakes his head but won't look at me. 'It wasn't me, Britt. She never came to see me that night.'

I sigh and let my head fall back. 'What are you even doing with me if you were in love with my best friend?'

He slowly backs up and folds himself down onto the first step of the grandstand. Without warning, he drops his head into his hands and begins to sob.

All I can do is stand and watch as I simultaneously split into parts. The part of me that's furious he did it and wonders why her and not me, even though I don't love him either. The part that feels betrayed by my best friend. The part that's angry because now I can never ask her why she did it, and the part that feels sorry for him because despite what she did to me, I love her, too.

'I'm sorry,' he manages between breaths. 'It was a shit thing to do. I just never thought I had a chance with her until that day.'

'Right,' I reply. 'Thanks a lot.'

'She wanted nothing to do with me after that one time. I knew she liked someone else. She wouldn't say who though.'

I try to find a place in my head and heart where I can pack this moment away and never think of it again. I stare out over the field unable to look at him any longer. 'So, who do you think it was?'

'Who do I think what was?'

'The person she liked.'

'You don't know?'

I shake my head and push my hair back, embarrassed to realise that maybe I didn't know as much as I thought about the girl who was supposed to be my best friend.

For a moment, Luke goes somewhere in his head as he stares up at the sky like he's trying to remember something.

'Luke? What is it?'

He snaps back and nods his head. 'Now I get it.'

'Get what?'

'I saw her that afternoon. I was...' He holds my gaze a moment, then shrugs like he can't be bothered trying anymore. 'Screw it. I was following her, all right? She was being distant. Wouldn't answer my texts, call me back, nothing. I thought maybe it was just one of her head games to try and keep me on my toes. You know what she was like, always needing to try and control everything and everyone. So, I followed her to see what was going on.'

'And?'

'And she went to the cop shop. I thought she was going in, but then she pulled out her phone and it looked like she was texting someone. About fifteen minutes later, she got picked up.'

'Got picked up?' I step in closer. 'Picked up by who?'

He hesitates and my heart races so hard I can hear it thumping in my ears.

After a long, deep breath, Luke steadies himself and says, 'Jack Stanton.'

Chapter Twenty-Three

WILDLING Police Station is a squat, drab building, more like a tired old house than a place of authority. The blue sign above the door is worn and faded. Some of the bricks are chipped, and the windows are dusty. It's been twelve years since I stepped inside, but as I push open the front door, bile rises in the back of my throat and instantly I'm a teenager again.

Inside, it still smells the same. The musty scent of old files and mildew hits me first, followed by a faint whiff of burnt toast curling in from the kitchenette out the back.

Koda nudges my leg with his nose, and I look down at him. His brown eyes are soft and quiet, an anchor when my world feels like it's tilting. I run my fingers through his fur, grounding myself in the rise and fall of his breath. I can get through this. I have to.

'Hello? Is anyone here?'

I'm not the same person I was back then, I tell myself. *I can do this. I can prove to Jason and Will that I'm not crazy.*

'Well, well,' Herm mutters as he comes around the corner, his fingers wrapped around a coffee mug with the words *World's Okayest Cop* written across the front. I look at it and bite my tongue to stop from saying what comes to mind. 'Can't say I ever expected to see you in here again, Mia.' He puts the mug down and loops his thumbs through his belt. His hips tilt forward as he rocks back on his heels. 'What can I do for you?'

I count to three in my head, willing myself not to fall apart. 'I know what you did to Lilly.'

Herm raises an eyebrow, pretending not to understand, but I catch a flicker of recognition in his eyes. He shifts his weight and strokes what looks like the beginnings of a moustache. 'Do you just?'

I nod and step in closer to Koda. A single bead of sweat trickles along my lower back. My insides are trembling, and I swear that if I were to glance down at my feet, I'd see the battered-up trainers I wore as a teenager instead of my grown-up boots. 'You're not going to get away with this,' I manage. 'What you did to me... and to Lilly, is not okay.'

He nods to himself and then stares past me out toward the street. 'As I recall, Mia, it was more than okay at the time. In fact...' He sets his gaze back onto me and moves in closer, the scent of stale coffee and sweat drifting across my face. '... if I'm not mistaken, you used to enjoy coming here. Quite a lot, as I remember it.'

'That's not true.' I step back, the old floorboards creaking beneath my feet. 'I was just a kid.'

He grins at me, but his eyes are flat and dull. 'Tell you what. I'm going to let you in on a little secret. You and Lilly both got exactly what you wanted. Now, you can tell yourself as many little fairy stories as you like, but at the end of the day, you never said no, did you? You never told anyone. You never fought me. You enjoyed yourself, and that's okay. It's nothing to be ashamed of.'

I swallow the lump in my throat and reach down, desperately feeling for Koda's ear. When my fingers find his fur, I quickly hold on, trying to steady myself. 'I hated it. You know that.'

'Did you though?' He steps in even closer, and although my mind screams at me to run, I'm frozen to the spot.

This whole place reeks of things left to fester and rot. His breath touches my cheek, and I feel the first tremble of my jaw.

'See,' he whispers into my ear, 'even now, you don't run, Mia. Even now, you still want it.'

'You killed Lilly because she was pregnant,' I whisper, pushing through my fear. 'And Hazel. I know what you did.'

Herm immediately pulls back and glares at me, his face darkening. His eyes flick to Koda, realising for the first time that I'm not completely alone.

For a long moment, we just stare at each other, the air between us thick and still.

'Why would I do that?' he asks eventually. 'If Lilly was

pregnant, that's news to me, and extremely unlikely since I had a vasectomy a long time ago.' He pauses to let his words sink in. 'She was in love with me. She came here willingly, maybe not at first, but in the end, I had to tell her to stop or people would start to notice. She was upset about it, sure, but there were no hard feelings, and I certainly didn't kill her.'

'That's a lie.'

But he smiles and shakes his head. 'Nope, that's a fact. And as for Hazel, can't say I ever met her.'

I gather the courage to search his eyes, desperate to see some hint that he's lying, but he just stares back, daring me to question him.

'Then you're covering for Jack,' I say. 'One of you killed those girls.'

He laughs out loud and once again rocks back on his heels. 'You think Jack's a murderer? Do you really think he'd risk everything he's built over trash like Lilly and some Aboriginal girl?'

'I...'

'You know what I think? I think you went out onto Jack's property, even after I told you not to, and found that girl's body. You carried out an illegal search. I could have your credentials, Mia, but I won't,' he says, finally turning away and walking back to his desk. 'Do you know why? Because you're clearly unstable. You need help, and haven't I always been there for you?'

'I don't want your help,' I tell him, blood pounding in my ears. 'There's nothing wrong with me.'

He nods slowly and reaches for the phone. 'Everything is going to be fine, all right, Mia?'

'What are you doing?'

'I'm calling Will. He needs to come and get you.'

'No!' I shout, stepping forward. 'Don't!'

Herm freezes, the phone hanging in mid-air. 'You're spiralling, just like the last time.'

'That was because of you,' I whisper. 'I didn't want to hurt myself. I just wanted it to stop.'

His gaze lingers over me, and his eyes go soft. He nods and tilts his head, then lets out a breath. 'Well, be that as it may, I can't take that risk.'

He tucks the phone into the cradle of his shoulder and begins to dial.

'Stop. Just don't. Please...'

He clicks the receiver button with his finger and shrugs the phone out from under his ear. 'Just like always, I can't say no to you. I guess that was always the problem, wasn't it?' he says. 'I'm too soft when it comes to you. I let you keep coming here as a teenager. I never stopped you from graduating search and rescue, even though I knew deep down you were unstable. I even let your dog there ride in the backseat of my cruiser. And now you've come here accusing me, a police officer, of killing two girls, and I'm just going to let it slide.' He shakes his head in mock disbelief.

'I'll tell you, I'm starting to wonder if I might be the crazy one in all of this.'

My head spins. I didn't keep coming back here, did I? There were a few times when Jason went hiking and wasn't back before sunset. I came and asked Herm to have someone try and find him. Every time, he was always waiting, leaning over the counter, eyes bargaining before I even got a word out. I close my eyes and see the red and blue lights of his cruiser cutting through the dark, catching me for spray painting or smoking or some other stupid thing. Had I known he would? Is that why I did it?

I can feel him watching me. His eyes exploring every expression, clocking the twitch of my lip and the pulse of anxiety across my temple.

'Poor Mia,' he whispers. 'You never could get out of your own way, could you? How about we just pretend none of this ever happened? There'll be no more wild accusations, no more threats, and I won't tell Will about this. It will be our little secret.'

Our little secret.

The words echo through my mind, pulling me back to the first time he said them. I was thirteen. His hands were cold on my thigh. I was crying. The memory sparks something, and I suddenly stand taller, braver. I never wanted to come here. Not ever, and I can't let him do this to me again.

I step forward and see the first flicker of fear in Herm's

eyes. 'You and I don't have any little secrets anymore,' I tell him. 'I told Jason and Will what you did to me. They know what you are.'

For a moment, he stares at me, his eyes clouding with confusion. 'You wouldn't.'

'I would,' I say, feeling stronger with every word. 'You want to call Will? Fine, call him. Call my brother. Call anyone you want. It doesn't change what you did, or the fact that I'm going to find out who killed those girls.'

'You're sick, Mia,' he tries again. 'You need...'

'...help,' I answer. 'Yeah, so I've heard, but I'm still going to find out the truth.'

Without another word, I turn and walk out. My heart is racing, but I keep moving, Koda by my side, his steps matching mine.

Outside, the sun feels too bright, too harsh. I pause, sucking in the cool, fresh air, and crouch beside Koda. He immediately presses his head into my hands, and I bury my face in his fur.

Together, we sit like that for a long time. Just the two of us.

Chapter Twenty-Four
Juniper

NOW that I know for certain there's more to this story than the police are letting on, I'm determined to find out what really happened. I can't let my insecurities get in the way. I messed up in Sydney, but now I have a chance to fix it – a real chance.

Hazel was found on Willow's Crossing, and Lilly just outside the boundary. If Mum's right, there's one person in Wildling who will be more than happy to tell me anything I want to know. Better still, he's perfectly placed to know every detail.

Bryce Stanton.

'Thanks for coming to meet me,' I tell him with a smile, as we wander through the park down by Main Street. 'It's good to see you.'

He grins and lets his eyes linger over my face. First on my eyes, then travelling down to my lips. 'I can't believe you're actually back, Junie. Never thought I'd see the day.'

I slowly steer him toward the sprawling fig tree, knowing it will spark memories of the two of us. 'I know, it's weird, right? After three years away, I thought things would be different here, but everything feels exactly the same.'

'Not everything.'

I search his face, trying to decide what to say. The day I left was the first time I'd ever seen Bryce cry. 'For what it's worth, I'm sorry about what happened with us,' I begin. 'It was never about not loving you, Bryce. I just had to try and make something of myself. Away from here.'

He nods and tucks his hands into his jeans pockets. I almost forgot how good-looking he is, with his Zac Efron smile and those bright blue eyes. I quickly remind myself I'm here for the story, not to get caught back up in a relationship. But he's just so damned handsome...

'I get it, Junie,' he tells me. 'Sometimes I imagine what it would be like to just get on a plane and never come back. Forget all about Willow's Crossing and my parents.'

The admission surprises me. I remember seeing our third-class teacher, Ms Spannagle, down at the pool once sunbaking in a red two-piece bathing suit. Out of her modest brown skirts and collared shirts, she was almost unrecognisable, and something about it just felt strange to me. In my mind, she lived in the classroom. She didn't wear swimmers or lie in the sun, and it's the same with Bryce. He is Willow's Crossing, and Willow's Crossing is him. Seeing him in another life would just feel wrong.

'But you love the farm. And what would your mum do if you left?' I laugh out loud at the thought. 'She'd have a meltdown.'

He laughs, and the sound makes my heart skip a beat. *Shit.*

'Yeah, she's... a lot. Always loved you though, Junie. Dad too.'

For a couple of minutes, we walk in silence, and it feels easy. Familiar. It's tempting to just enjoy the moment instead of worrying about the story, but I want more than this. More than being Bryce Stanton's girl.

'How's your mum coping with everything that's happened?' I ask, hoping he'll speak freely.

'Those girls, you mean?'

'Yeah. It's not quite business as usual in Wildling.'

'Nope, it's sure not.'

He doesn't elaborate, and I search for the right thing to say next. 'Have the police said anything more about Hazel?'

'Anything more like what?'

It could just be the distance that's grown between us, but something about Bryce suddenly feels different. Almost like he's on guard.

'Like, why she was found on your property?'

He stops walking and turns to face me. 'Not yet. Why do you ask?'

I shrug and try to brush it off. 'Just curious, I suppose. It's not every day a dead girl turns up in your back paddock. Did you know either of them?'

I take a few steps forward but stop when I realise he's not walking next to me. When I turn back, he's glaring at me in a way I've never seen before. 'Bryce?'

'Did you want to see me so you could write a story?'

My throat thickens, and I glance away. He'll know if I lie. He knows me too well.

'Answer me, Juniper,' he snaps. 'Is this for a story?'

I naively thought Bryce would be so keen to please me that our conversation would be open and honest, that he would consider my questions, and we'd talk it through. But from the way he's staring at me, I can see I've overestimated my effect on him. His face hardens, and his eyes narrow. His lips press into a thin, tight line as he waits for an answer I have no clue how to give.

'I'm not sure yet,' I say, trying to sound genuine. 'There's talk of there being a murderer in Wildling. I mean, a murderer. In Wildling. It's unbelievable.'

To my surprise, Bryce laughs out loud, but it sounds different this time. 'A murderer? You have to be joking, Juniper?'

'Two girls are dead for no apparent reason.'

'Lilly Daniels was a drug user. We all knew that. What happened is no surprise to me or probably anyone.'

'So, you knew her?'

'Not really. I'm just saying there's no murderer, so don't go writing shit that makes people think there's some lunatic murdering girls and using our property as a dumping ground. That's the last thing we need.'

'I wasn't going to write that, Bryce. I'm just trying to figure out what happened to them.'

'Well, like I said, Lilly was a junkie. And the other one... well, Christ, Juniper, how the hell would I know what those people do or how she ended up on our property?'

I've never known Bryce to talk like this. He was always so softly spoken, almost humble. He used to hold my hand so gently. His touch was loving, reassuring. I felt safe with him. But now, as I look at his face, sneering and flushed with anger, he looks like a stranger to me. 'You know what? Let's just leave it. You're probably right.'

'Are you going to write the story?'

'I don't know. I'll see what I can find out, I guess, and—'

Before I can finish, Bryce grabs my arm and drags me toward the tree. The base is so wide that it will be impossible for anyone to see us behind it. As teenagers, that was the allure. Complete privacy to explore each other without anyone ever seeing a thing. But now it feels dangerous.

'Bryce, stop it,' I tell him, trying to pull out of his grasp. 'Let me go.'

His fingers are wrapped around the top of my arm, and he drags me across the park so quickly I almost lose my balance. When we reach the tree, he shoves my back against the trunk and leans in, leaving only centimetres between his face and mine. Memories of him causing my legs to tremble come rushing back. I used to want to pull him in so close that not even air could come between us. I ached for his touch, his breath against my skin. But now all I feel is fear.

'If you write anything like that, or say that I said anything, we're going to have a problem. Do you hear me?'

'Bryce, let go of me,' I tell him. 'You're scaring me.'

'The last thing my family needs is more bloody reporters swarming around the front gate. Just leave us alone. Mum is getting triggered by the whole thing. Dad says it's just like back when she was a kid and Aunt Missy died, so just leave it, all right?'

'All right, I'm sorry. I'll leave it. You have my word.'

Instantly, his face softens, and he steps back, letting me go. 'Thanks, Junie. I knew I could count on you.'

I nod quickly and rub the aching spot on my arm where his fingers pressed into me. He studies my face for a moment and then gives me a beaming, radiant smile. 'Good girl. I knew you'd listen. I always loved that about you the most. Come on, I'll walk you back to your car.'

As we walk, I cast my mind back. Was Bryce always this way, and I just didn't see it? I sneak a sideways glance at him. He catches it and smiles.

'You look just as beautiful as ever, you know.'

I force a smile. 'Thanks, Bryce.'

'You know, when you left, I just...'

'What?'

'I don't know,' he says with a shrug. 'It was like you took

all the sunlight with you, Junie, and all I could see were dark clouds.'

'I'm sorry,' I tell him, quietly scanning the park for anyone who might come running if I were to scream. 'But you have Charlotte now, right? She's nice.'

He nods and shrugs. 'She's not you.'

'Well, that might be a good thing,' I say with a laugh, to try and ease the tension.

'I wanted to hurt you so much when you left, Junie,' he says, his jaw tightening. 'So much.'

'Bryce... what?'

'The idea that you could do something like that. Just leave the way you did.' He looks me over and shakes his head. 'I wanted to hurt you like you hurt me.'

The hair along the back of my neck prickles. My car is only a few metres away. If I ran, I could almost make it before he caught up.

'That's the only reason I started dating Charlotte. I hoped someone would tell you. I know you always hated her.' He laughs, an embarrassed look on his face. 'Did you even care?'

I feign a sigh of relief and shrug. 'Charlotte the harlot? All she ever did through high school was flirt with you in front of me. What do you think?'

He laughs, and it's the one I recognise. 'It was always you, Junie.' He pauses. 'Still is, if I'm being honest.'

We reach my car, and I pull the keys out of my bag. 'It

was nice to see you, Bryce,' I lie. 'For what it's worth, I'm sorry for what I did. Leaving town like that. Like I said, it was never to hurt you.'

He shrugs and glances away. 'You're here now. That's something.' When he looks back at me, it's with an intensity I can't remember ever seeing before.

'We'll talk soon,' I say, making my way around to the driver's side door. 'I'll message you.'

'You better,' he says, slapping the roof of my car twice with his palm. 'I'll be waiting.'

Chapter Twenty-Five
Britt

THE discovery of two dead teenage girls in less than a week has the entire town on edge. You can feel it when you walk down the street. There's an energy in the air, cracking and buzzing like something's about to explode. It's all anyone can talk about. They whisper at the checkout in the IGA and speculate over coffee at the Sweetie. The rumour mill is running wild. Every detail of Lilly's life dug up and spread out in the sun for all to see.

Then there's the vultures.

Yesterday, three different reporters with camera crews came barging into work, hurling questions and trying to get me to go on camera. Eventually, I locked myself in the bathroom and called Nate to come and cover for me.

All the locals still think Lilly wandered off and died from exposure, but the blow-ins from the city are trying to link her death to Hazel Smith, the First Nations girl found out on Willow's Crossing.

Did Lilly and Hazel know each other? Were they friends? Did they hang out in the same circles?

Their stupid questions are all the same. They have no clue how Wildling works. First, there's the farming community. They live on sprawling acreages on the outskirts of town, running beef cattle and Merino sheep. How well they do usually depends on the weather. The drought we had a couple of years ago threatened a few of them with bankruptcy, same as that time it wouldn't stop raining for months on end. Of everyone, they have the most say about what happens in Wildling, and they're rich compared to the rest of us. There's a few average folk scattered in pretty houses here and there along the river and at the base of the mountains, but most of Wildling is divided into two sections. Hazel lived on the local mission, a tiny settlement on the river about three kilometres south of town. I'd seen her at school, but she never mixed with any of the white kids. Lilly lived to the north, about the same distance away, in an area the farming kids call the slums. The houses there aren't government-owned, but most of the people who live there are either single parents renting, old people who still live in run-down places they bought back in the '70s, or graziers who went broke and have no place else to go.

One to the north. One to the south. And never the twain shall meet.

I learned that in high school and say it a lot about this town. The place is so divided. It's like Wildling is a huge rock in the middle of a river, splitting the current in two, each side rushing away from the other. Beats me why.

Water is water, and people are people. All comes from the same place, but there's no way Lilly and Hazel would have ever been friends.

When someone knocks on the front door, I get up off my bed and pad over to the doorway to listen. It's probably another vulture. Mum knows to turn them away. For now, Juniper hasn't asked me anything, but I know it's only a matter of time. She won't be able to help herself.

'Britt, there's someone here to see you,' Mum calls out. 'It's not a reporter.'

'Who is it?'

'Can you just come out here, please?'

I let out a long sigh. The last thing I feel like doing is talking to someone, but reluctantly, I tighten my ponytail and shuffle off down the hall. When I get to the living room, Mia Thomas is sitting on the couch.

'Mia,' I say, slightly taken aback that she would just turn up at my house. 'What's up?'

'And don't go anywhere,' Mum interrupts before she can answer. 'Your sister will be back from town in an hour. I want the two of you to spend some time together, please.'

I roll my eyes. 'Can't. I have work this arvo.'

After a way-too-dramatic eye roll, my mum finally leaves the room, and Mia looks at me. 'Can we talk? I have a couple of questions I'd like to ask you.'

I nod, and she follows me out the back. The yard is freshly mown, and Dad has swept all the autumn leaves off the veranda – more signs that Juniper's back.

We sit down at the picnic table where my family always had Sunday night barbecues, and I wait for her to speak. It doesn't take long.

'Herm wasn't the father,' she says, not bothering to make small talk. 'He couldn't be. Physically, I mean.'

'You don't beat around the bush, do you?'

She shrugs and looks at me unapologetically. Any time I've ever seen Mia, she's had her dog with her. It's strange to see her sitting across from me alone, almost like one of her limbs is missing.

'Where's your dog?'

'He's at home,' she says, gazing down at the space beside her. 'I wasn't sure if I could bring him here, so...'

'You could have. We like dogs. We used to have one. A Labrador named Sam. He—'

'Britt... can we stay on track?'

I stop mid-sentence and stare at her. There's something different today. The way her hair is bunched messily on top of her head instead of wrangled back into a neat ponytail. Her brow seems tight, but her shoulders are sagging. I want to ask if she's all right but instead hear myself say, 'How do you know he wasn't the father?'

'He told me.'

I pull back, not bothering to hide my surprise. 'You went to him?'

'I didn't mention you. There's a situation with Will

and my brother. I had to. It's a long story, but your name didn't come up, you have my word. He did say he'd had a vasectomy, though, so he can't have been the father.'

I have no idea what Mia's boyfriend or brother has to do with this, but my mind is reeling that she confronted Herm. Either she's a whole lot gutsier than I thought, or a lot stupider.

'Britt, I'm sorry to ask this, but are you sure Lilly was pregnant?'

'A hundred per cent,' I tell her. 'I saw the test.'

'Then someone else was the father.'

'And you believe that creep?'

She shrugs and nods. 'I do. I have no idea why, given what he is, but I do.'

She looks away, and it's clear that what he did all those years ago has stayed with her. 'I know you found Lilly, but I don't get why you're doing this,' I tell her. 'Why would you confront Herm? It's not like you knew her or anything. If you keep pushing, you know what's going to happen. Jack and Herm run this town.'

Mia chews the inside of her cheek. Her eyes narrow a fraction, and then she says, 'I grew up in the slums. When I was a kid, before Jason and I were sent to live at Mimi's, we lived one street over from Lilly's place. You know what Herm did to me. Lilly wasn't so different than I was at her age. Maybe if I'd had the courage to say something earlier I...'

'… could have stopped it,' I finish.

She nods, and I finally understand her. The sadness that lingers behind her eyes. The reason she's so attached to that dog. All her life, the people she's trusted have let her down. That, I get.

'Screw him,' I say. 'He's such a prick.'

'He is,' she agrees. 'But do you really think he killed two girls?'

I think back to what Luke told me in the park yesterday. Trusting people is not something I'm very good at, but the last thing I want is for people to keep thinking Lilly was a headcase or an addict who just wandered off, delusional and on drugs. Maybe Mia is the right person to tell. I'm just not sure.

'I'd kill for a smoke,' I say instead.

'You really shouldn't smoke, Britt. It's bad for your health.'

'Like living in Wildling isn't?'

'Fair point,' she replies, a grin touching the corner of her lip.

It's the first time I've seen any hint of a smile from her, and something about it feels real. Like she's an actual person. Like maybe I could trust her. 'You know what? Screw it,' I begin, deciding to take a chance. 'I found out yesterday that on the day she died, Lilly was outside the police station.'

'Okay, but that still doesn't—'

I hold my hand up for her to let me finish. 'But instead of going in, she climbed into Jack's truck, and they drove away.'

'Jack Stanton?'

'The very same.'

'You're sure?'

'Hundred per cent.'

I watch as Mia sits back and takes it in. 'The night she went missing, did Lilly say anything to you about what her plans were?'

'She said she was going to talk to the father about the baby.'

'She said that? The father. Not Herm specifically?'

'Yeah.'

Mia thinks for a moment and then glances down at the empty space where her dog would usually be. 'You don't think...'

'What?'

She leans in close enough to whisper. 'You don't think Jack could be the father?'

'All I know is that Herm was abusing her. That's a fact. And she was pregnant. Also, a fact. Why Jack picked her up that day is anyone's guess. I mean, if what Herm said is true about having a vasectomy, then maybe? I mean... it's pretty out there, though, Mia.'

We stare out over the backyard, both lost in our own thoughts. There's a part of me that wants to climb up into the old treehouse and never come out. I think back to all the times I hid in there just to make the world go away. Surrounded by pillows, pens and notebooks. Juniper never would leave well enough alone, though. She was always down on the ground, shouting up at me to come out and apologise for something. Always interfering. *All these years later*, I think, *and still nothing has changed.*

'Okay,' Mia says, interrupting my thoughts. 'I appreciate your honesty. I know this must be difficult to talk about.'

I shrug because I don't really know what to say.

'I really am sorry for your loss, Britt,' she continues. 'I hope in time things get a little easier for you.'

She gets to her feet, and I automatically stand as well. 'I better get back. Thanks for talking with me.'

Even though she didn't tell me, I know it was she and her dog who went out to Willow's Crossing and found Hazel Smith. For now, her secret is safe. I'm not going to tell anyone. But the thing about Wildling is, nothing stays secret forever.

Chapter Twenty-Six
Britt

AFTER my shift, I'm supposed to be meeting Luke down by the river. He wants to talk more, but I just don't have it in me. All I can think about is that someone else was the father of Lilly's baby. If it wasn't Herm and it wasn't Luke, that means there was another secret she was keeping from me. *Could it have really been Jack?*

A block away from work, I stop and take out my phone. I'm going to text Luke and say that I can't make it tonight. Screw him. Why should I bother after what he did? I punch out the text, not bothering with niceties, and slip the phone back into my satchel. When I look back up, my heart skips a beat. Bryce and his mother are walking toward me.

'Hey, Britt.' Bryce beams at me with a grin wide enough to light up the entire town. He's wearing jeans and a black polo shirt with *Willow's Crossing* embroidered over the right breast pocket.

'Bryce.' I return his greeting with an awkward nod and instantly hate myself for being so weird.

'You heading to work?'

'Yep.'

'How are things with your sister being back?' Sarah asks, looking me over like she can't possibly understand how Juniper and I could be related. 'Will she be staying long?'

'I really couldn't say, Mrs Stanton.' She looks so perfectly put together in a long floral skirt and pink blouse. The pearls around her neck sit flat against her throat, clasped by a tiny diamond that glints in the sun.

'Jack said he invited her to dinner. You're welcome too, of course.'

'Mum, they don't want to come to dinner,' Bryce says, shooting her a look. 'Sorry, Britt. Just ignore that.'

I'm about to nod and let it go when the conversation with Luke plays over again in my head. *About fifteen minutes later, she got picked up. Picked up by who? Jack Stanton.*

'You know what, maybe we will come to dinner,' I reply, knowing Juniper will do anything if it means getting inside goss for the story she wants to write. 'In fact, my evening just opened up. Would tonight work?'

'You really don't have to,' Bryce says.

'No, I want to. Juniper will too. I finish at five. We could be there by six o'clock?'

Sarah gives Bryce a warm look as if to say, *Look what a wonderful mother I am*, and then says, 'That's perfect, Britt. We'll see you both tonight.'

'DINNER and then we're out,' Juniper whispers as we walk toward the towering front door of Willow's Crossing. 'I had a weird run-in with Bryce yesterday. I don't want to be hanging around here too long.'

'Weird like what?'

'Just weird,' she says. 'Mum made me come because you wanted to, but we're not sticking around.'

'Oh, bullshit, Juniper. You came because you're trying to write a story and want the inside scoop,' I say with a shake of my head. 'Do you think I'm stupid?'

My sister stares at me, clearly deciding whether it's worth trying to deny it. 'Why did you want to come anyway?' she asks instead. 'I don't recall you ever wanting to visit Willow's Crossing with me in the past.'

We're almost at the door. The last thing I want to do is help Juniper's career, but knowing her, she's going to write the story anyway, and we're here now. 'Because the day Lilly died, she was last seen getting into Jack Stanton's truck.'

'Britt, what?' Juniper gasps as the door opens.

'Girls, welcome,' Sarah says with a smile. 'Come on in. I hope you like roast lamb.'

Huddled at the end of a polished mahogany table long enough to host a wedding party, I begin to wonder if this might be the most awkward dinner anyone has ever had since the invention of dinners. On the wall behind us, generations of long-dead Stantons gaze down, their painted eyes following our every move. Jack has barely said a word. Sarah keeps giving us tight, polite smiles. Meanwhile, Bryce won't stop staring at Juniper, who is desperately trying to keep her eyes trained on the plate in front of her.

They don't know it yet, but all that's about to change. If Jack thinks veiled threats at the service station are enough to scare me into silence, he's dead wrong. Screw this family. I'm about to blow the whole thing up.

I put my knife and fork down and clear my throat. 'Mr Stanton, it occurred to me that I never thanked you for picking Lilly up from the police station the afternoon she died,' I begin. 'Herm Drinkwater is not a nice man. He was always hassling her and hauling her in for things that never hurt anyone. At least she was shown some kindness on the last day of her life.'

He stops slicing his lamb, the knife hovering over his plate. 'You must be mistaken there, Britt,' he says eventually. 'I didn't pick Lilly Daniels up from anywhere.'

'Oh, it must have slipped your mind. She was outside the police station, and you picked her up in your truck.' I look over at Sarah. 'My friend was across the road. He saw it.'

Bryce stops chewing and looks over at his father. Beside me, Juniper stiffens. I don't dare look at her, but I can feel it.

Jack slowly places his utensils down and wipes his

mouth with the corner of a linen napkin. 'You accusing me of something there, Britt? Because I'd like to remind you, you're a guest in this house.'

'Accusing you? No, I was thanking you,' I tell him, feigning surprise. 'Lilly didn't have many people in her corner. I thought it was nice that someone of your standing would take the time to give her a ride.'

He holds my gaze, and I reach under the table to try and stop my legs from shaking.

'Oh, wait. I remember now,' he begins, reaching out to give his wife's hand a reassuring squeeze. 'Herm got a call, said he had to go over to Winton River and didn't want the girl wandering the streets. You know, after getting picked up for whatever it was that day. Asked me to drop her home since I was heading through town.'

'Well,' I manage, battling to hide my disappointment. Trust him to come up with something and weasel out of it. 'Like I said, I appreciate it.'

He nods and bites the lamb off his fork. Around the table, everyone's shoulders drop with relief. They smile and look back at their plates, clearly relieved that everything is right with the world again.

What they don't notice is that Jack doesn't blink, and his eyes remain fixed on mine.

'WHAT on earth is wrong with you?' Juniper hisses the moment we get back into her car. 'Are you insane?'

I yank at the seatbelt, over and over until I feel like I'm going to scream.

'Britt, I'm talking to you.'

I give up on the seatbelt and stare out the window, even though it's so fogged up I can't see a thing.

'Britt, answer me,' Juniper tries as she leans across and gently pulls the seatbelt over my chest until it clicks into place. 'What was that about?'

'You wouldn't understand,' I huff. 'Besides, it makes no difference. You saw what happened. Whatever he says, everyone just believes it. He might as well have killed her in the middle of Main Street. Nothing would happen.'

Juniper lets out a sigh and rests back against her seat. 'Who told you Lilly got into Jack's truck that night?'

'Just forget it. Whatever. Doesn't matter.'

For a moment, the car falls silent. Somewhere in the darkness a cow lows and I almost jump out of my skin.

'Britt, I'm on your side,' she says eventually. 'Just talk to me.'

'Why? So you can put it in a story? I know that's why you came back here.'

She turns the set of car keys over in her palm. Lights along the driveway cast long shadows as we sit in the car, the air between us thick with all the things we've never said.

'Are you going to drive or what?' I ask, just wanting the night to be over. 'They're going to come out if we keep sitting here.'

'Fine, Britt. Have it your way,' she says, putting the key into the ignition. 'But at some point you're going to tell me what that was about, and how you know who picked Lilly up that day.'

Suddenly the whole situation feels hopeless. Compared to Jack and Herm I'm a bug. Worse than that. I'm a bug under their shoe. Like he was ever going to care what I said. I was fooling myself to think I could make any difference or find justice for Lilly.

'Luke Mittigan was in love with Lilly,' I say as she starts the car. 'That's how I know.'

'Your boyfriend, Luke?'

She looks over at me, aghast, and it's humiliating to say the least. I shrug out of my jacket, then toss it into the back. 'He's not my boyfriend. Then or now. Anyway, he followed her and saw her get into Jack's truck.'

'And no one saw her again after that?'

'Am I on the record?' I ask with a roll of my eyes.

'Britt...'

'It's fine, Juniper,' I say with a sigh. 'Not to be on the record, that's not okay, but I know why you came home. I never thought it was for me.'

'But it was for you, Britt. Partly, at least. I mean... things in Sydney are not like Mum and Dad think. The truth is, if I don't get this story I'm going to lose my job.'

I stare over at her, unable to believe that maybe perfect Juniper's life isn't so perfect after all.

'I don't want you near the Stantons on your own,' she adds. 'Do you hear me? Not any of them, especially Bryce.'

'Why Bryce?'

A shadow flickers over her eyes when she says, 'Because he's not the same person he was when I left.'

Chapter Twenty-Seven
Juniper

BRITT'S words play over and over in my mind.

...he followed her and saw her get into Jack's truck.

In Britt's eyes, last night's attempt to call Jack out was a failure, but I don't agree. When put on the spot, he feigned remembering picking Lilly up as a favour to Herm, but I'm not buying it. In fact, I've never been more certain that the Stantons are somehow involved in whatever happened to those girls. But what doesn't sit right is the idea of Jack and Lilly being involved. Jack's not the type to risk everything for some fling with a teenager. But there's nothing he wouldn't do to protect his family – including lying. So, what if it hadn't been him who picked up Lilly Daniels in the Willow's Crossing truck, but Bryce?

I pull into the petrol station and start filling up my car. I need to clear my head and heading out to one of the trails that leads through the national park, with its towering gum trees and patches of melting snow, feels like the perfect place to think things through.

I have so many memories of growing up with Bryce,

Jack, and Sarah. Laughing until my sides ached as Jack tried teaching me to drive a tractor out in the paddocks of Willow's Crossing. Sarah and I, our hands ghostly white and covered in flour, when she taught me how to make homemade bread in her kitchen. And Bryce. He was my first real love. To write a story that casts suspicion over the family would destroy the lives of each and every one of them.

As the weight of my memories presses in, I can't help but wonder if I have it in me to do it – if I can betray the people I once called my family, even when every instinct tells me I should.

I glance up as a journalist I recognise, Stewart Hartigan from Channel Ten News, and his cameraman walk past me toward the shop. From behind the counter, Britt looks out and her face pales. I know Stew. He's like a dog with a bone when it comes to getting the inside scoop. There's not a chance he won't harass my sister until she's in tears. As they step inside, I shove the petrol nozzle back into the bowser and march toward the door.

Inside, Britt is holding her hand up to the camera, trying to block her face. 'I don't want to,' she's telling them. 'Just leave me alone.'

'Hey!' I shout out, causing them both to turn. 'How about you get out of my sister's face?'

They turn toward me, and I don't miss the look of shock and unexpected pride in Britt's eyes.

'That you, Davis?' Stewart asks. 'Would have thought you'd be collecting unemployment benefits by now after that stuff-up with Kutsinoff.'

'Just leave my sister alone, okay? It's enough already. She doesn't know anything.'

'Yeah, yeah,' he says, motioning to his cameraman to park the rig. He looks me over, and I shudder. 'You end up getting the chop from the Daily, there's a spot for you on my crew. Damn, those titties would look hot on camera.'

'Like I said, just leave her be. And don't speak to women like that. It's disgusting.'

He walks by, slow enough to make sure I feel his eyes run over every part of me. 'Sure thing, Davis. Whatever you say.'

When they're gone, I approach the counter where Britt is looking at me in a way I've never seen before.

'Wow, you actually had my back,' she says. 'Thanks.'

Her makeup isn't quite as heavy, and her hair is pulled back into a neat ponytail.

'Of course,' I tell her. 'I always would. I hope you know that.'

She shrugs and looks away. I don't push it any further. 'Anyway, I'm going to take a walk and try to clear my head.'

'In the park?'

'Yep.'

'Cool, you got water? Snacks?'

'What?'

'Water and snacks. Do you have enough?'

I nod and stare absently around the shop. 'I think so.'

She comes out from behind the counter, and I stay silent as she brushes past me, collecting packets of chips, energy bars, and bottles of water from the fridge. 'Here, take these.'

'Britt...'

'Just take them.'

'Well, here,' I dig around in my pocket for money.

'I don't want your money.'

'But you'll get into trouble.' I glance up at the security camera above the counter. 'Your boss will know.'

She follows my line of sight up to the camera. 'That thing hasn't worked in years,' she tells me. 'Anyway, like I give a shit.'

I hold her gaze and smile. 'Well, thank you.'

'Enjoy,' she says, turning her back and walking back to the counter. 'See you tonight.'

OUT in the park, I take in the cool, crisp air and feel myself start to relax. The smell of eucalyptus mixed with damp earth is a scent so undeniably Wildling that even with everything going on, it feels like I can breathe out here. Especially now that Britt is coming around. Maybe there's hope for us yet.

The track twists and turns. Before long, my feet crunch against shallow patches of snow, stirring up the rich smell of decaying leaves. There are so many layers to Britt, and she's so smart. It's always been hard to decipher her moods and Machiavellian tactics to get attention. Last night was a perfect example of her ability to be manipulative, but I think she's on the right track about Lilly being picked up in the Willow's Crossing truck.

A loud wolf whistle pierces the air, and I clutch at my chest in fright. Up on a branch, a currawong tilts its head and stares down at me, its bright yellow eyes stark against black plumage.

'You scared me,' I tell it, with a shake of my head. 'Quiet.'

I've missed the sounds of the national park. Birds like the currawong with its unique whistling, the raucous call of kookaburras, and the delicate choral of magpies. When we were young, Dad would bring Britt and me out on walking safaris in search of elusive yellow-tailed black cockatoos. They would often fly in groups of three, their haunting high-pitched cry reaching our ears before they came into view. An Australian history teacher, Dad would explain how some First Nations mobs told Dreamtime stories about a white cockatoo that flew too low over a bushfire causing its plumage to turn black. He'd say that for him, the story felt like a reminder of how the experiences we have in life can change us completely. That if an event is significant enough, sometimes we can come out the other side looking almost unrecognisable.

Is that what will happen to Wildling? I wonder. When the truth finally comes out, will the town ever be the same again?

As I walk deeper into the bush, the snow gums move closer together. I hop from rock to rock across a small stream, the steady flow of clear, cold water providing a temporary distraction from the thoughts colliding in my head.

Eventually, I reach for my phone to check the time and see the *no signal* icon in the top right corner. I automatically glance back the way I've come and wonder how far I am from the entrance to the park. A flicker of worry sparks in my chest when I realise I'm not completely sure, but I push it aside. I've walked through this park a thousand times. I know it well. When we came with Dad, we used to get intentionally lost as a way to add to the magic of the day. We pretended to be the first people who ever set foot on each rock, to touch each tree, to walk each trail. And we always found our way home.

I calm myself and turn, preparing to retrace my steps, only to find that a few metres back, the trail splinters off into three paths. Each seems to wind its way into the depths of the bush. I quickly try to recall which I took, but all three trails look maddeningly similar.

I spin slowly in place, trying to suppress the panic rising in my chest. I scan the trails for any sign, any clue, that might jog my memory. I see a twisted tree that seems familiar, but they all look so similar.

As I head back along the path, I convince myself that I'm on the right track. I glance at my watch. It's 3.43 pm. Around me, the shadows are growing quickly, the air turning from light and crisp to dense and cold. It can't be more than an hour back. That means the bush should spit me out just before 5 pm. It will be almost dark by then. I pick up the pace, my feet skipping between a walk and a run every few steps. This has to be the way. It has to be.

At 4:30 pm, I stop and try to catch my breath. In the distance, I hear the sound of the river I crossed, but it's a long way off. I pull my jacket tighter around me. In less than half an hour, it's going to be dark, and I don't seem to be any closer to the trailhead.

After a few hesitant steps forward, I stop, knowing there's every chance I'm walking deeper and deeper into the park. Behind me, the path is almost indistinguishable from the rest of the bush. My chest heaves, and I try to swallow down the lump in my throat. I need to stay calm. But as I glance up and see the sun sinking lower, the first tear slips over my cheek. The temperature will be below zero overnight. I can't stay out here. I quickly take out my phone to call Triple Zero, but my stomach falls when I see only a black screen. The battery has died.

'No, no, no,' I cry. 'Shit.'

I think back to the safety of my car, the musky aroma of Mum and Dad's wood heater, and the comfort of pulling a blanket up over my chest. Around me, the bush is growing dark. It smells wet and cold, a mix of moss, earth, and dank sadness. 'Oh my God,' I sob. 'What do I do?'

If I can just find my way back to where the trails split, I can try one of the others. If that doesn't take me home, the other one will. The process of elimination. It's all I can do. I crouch and pick up a stick, breaking it in half and planting it upright in the ground. If I get disorientated and find myself back here, at least I'll know not to keep going this way.

'You can do this,' I whisper to myself. 'You'll be all right.'

I straighten up and turn back, hopefully heading for home.

Chapter Twenty-Eight

THE call from Daley is almost a relief – anything to break the tension between Will and me. Since the argument I had with him and my brother the other day, things at home have been unpleasant, to say the least. Tonight, I made his favourite dinner – eggplant and zucchini lasagna, but all he's done is sit across from me, pushing it around the plate with his fork.

'Hey, boss, what's up?' I answer as I get up and leave him sitting out in the kitchen.

'I need you and Koda to come in.'

His tone causes my stomach to tighten. I glance out the window. It's been dark for more than an hour, and it can't be more than one or two degrees outside. 'What's happened?'

He pauses, and I feel the first skip of my heart. 'It's Juniper Davis,' he says. 'She's missing.'

'Juniper's missing?' My mind immediately flashes back to my collision with her on the street a few days ago.

'According to Dave and Sue, she went for a walk in the

park this afternoon. Had a few things on her mind. She must have lost her way. It's been a while since she was here.'

'No ping from her mobile?'

'Last one was three hours ago, just north of Kincumber Creek. Phone must have died.'

And they've called in the police?'

'They have. Herm specifically asked that you do the search. He told Dave and Sue you know that side of the park better than anyone. Promised them you'd be best placed to find her.'

'He did?'

'Your last search must have impressed him.'

Or he's hoping I'll accidentally fall off a cliff in the dark.
'Let me get our things. We'll be there in fifteen.'

As we pull into the gravel car park of the ranger station, I turn off the engine and glance at Koda in the rear-vision mirror. He immediately meets my eye and lets out a frustrated whine. He knows why we're here. It's time to work.

Inside the ranger station, the atmosphere is tense. Daley is hunched over a map spread out on the table. His eyes flicker over me as we enter, nodding in acknowledgement.

'Thanks for coming in, Thomas. It's cold out. Time is a factor.'

I nod, my heart tightening. I know the trails up around Kincumber Creek well. They're dense and winding. Treacherous at night.

In the small visitors' room, Juniper's parents are huddled together, their faces pale and drawn. Daley follows my gaze. 'Don't go in there making promises you can't keep.'

I hold his eye for a moment and then signal for Koda to follow me. 'Dave, Sue, this is Koda,' I tell them. 'He's the best chance we have of locating Juniper.'

Sue looks us over. She has a tissue clutched tight in her fist, and her eyes are red from crying. 'Thank you for coming to help.'

I nod quietly and run my hand along Koda's head. 'My dog will find her. It's what he does.'

Dave is holding his wife tightly. He manages a weak smile. 'Promise me you'll find our Junie,' he whispers, his voice cracking. 'Please, Mia.'

Before I can respond, Herm marches in, shoulders back and barking orders. 'Mia, SES volunteers are already covering the lower trails. We need you to go higher. You and the dog can navigate the kind of terrain they can't. You good to go?'

I glance around the room. A volunteer named Melissa Metcalfe is packing a first-aid kit with methodical precision, while Tom Stilling, one of the other rangers, checks and rechecks his GPS device.

'Daley, can you brief me on the search grids?' I ask, moving closer to the map. 'Koda's nose can do the work of twenty people, but we need to be smart about it. Show me exactly where the phone last pinged.'

Daley points to the spot on the map where Juniper's

phone signal was last detected. 'We've divided the search into four quadrants. You and Koda take the upper eastern trails. It's the most challenging terrain, but if anyone can navigate the area, it's you two.'

I nod quickly, my mind already racing through the familiar paths. When I've decided where we should start, I kneel beside Koda and give him a scratch behind the ear. Daley hands me a radio, and I clip it onto the strap of my pack.

'The ground is still damp, and there's patches of snow, so watch your step in the dark. It might get slippery,' he tells me. 'We'll be monitoring all channels. Stay in contact, Thomas. We don't want any surprises, you hear me?'

I close my eyes and carry out one last mental check of our gear. When I'm confident that I have everything we'll need, I get to my feet and together Koda and I step outside into the frigid night. If Juniper was just going for a walk, she won't be equipped for this type of cold. We don't have much time.

'Okay, Koda, let's do this,' I tell him. 'Every minute counts.'

OUT on the trail, my headlamp creates a bobbing circle of light as we push ahead, quickly leaving the other searchers behind. I glance back at their strobing flashlights, dancing like fireflies against the night sky. It's protocol to search in designated quadrants, but they're not going to find her back there. The trails up around Kincumber Creek are a labyrinth. If you don't know the area, they can take you around and around in circles, each one up to fifty kilometres of winding, rocky terrain that will inevitably lead you right back to where you came from. The only question is, which one is she on?

Juniper Davis. Somehow, she'd got me to admit I thought Lilly and Hazel were murdered. I hadn't been paying attention. It didn't hit me until I got home that day what had happened. Today, she told her parents she was coming out here to try and clear her head. Was it because of what I said? Is it my fault she's lost out here in the cold and dark?

'Easy, Koda,' I murmur, as we manoeuvre through a patch of scratchy blackberry bush. Thorns scrape against my jacket, and I try quickly to navigate him away, so he doesn't get caught in the prickles.

On a search like this, I would usually let Koda off-lead. He would go ahead, find the scent source, and return to me. But it's dark out. I trust him implicitly, but I won't risk his safety. There are too many potential dangers that I can't see, and so instead I keep him close, which also means I have to try and match his pace.

Cold air burns the back of my throat as we dash through the park. Koda's nose twitches as he moves forward, weaving back and forth in a methodical pattern. His tail wags slightly, a sign that he's focused on the job. Every so often, he looks back at me, and I encourage him to keep going.

When we reach a small clearing, I hear the faint sound of running water. Kincumber Creek is only a few metres away. I pause and scan the surroundings with my torch. My mind drifts back to our last two searches. Their lifeless bodies flash through my mind, but I quickly push the thought away. This time, it has to end differently. We are going to find Juniper alive. We have to.

A sharp bark from Koda snaps me back to the present. 'Good boy. Show me.' He immediately bounds toward the creek, caring little about the freezing water as he dashes across.

With no time to step from rock to rock, I run after him, my water-resistant pants and boots useless against the freezing water.

On the other side, the terrain is treacherous. The wet track is slippery underfoot. Koda stops suddenly, his nose pressed to the ground, sniffing intently at a particular spot. His body is tense, his ears perked up. I crouch beside him, examining the area. There's nothing visible, but I know from Koda's behaviour that Juniper was on this path.

He quickly barks, once, twice, three times, then pulls against his harness. As best I can, I press the button on my radio to contact Daley and the others.

'In scent,' I call as we dash forward. 'Eastern side of Kincumber Creek. Right where the phone pinged. Won't be long now.'

Suddenly, my foot slides out, sending me sprawling forward. I manage to break the fall with my hands, but the jolt leaves me breathless. Koda is instantly at my side, whining softly, his nose nudging my cheek.

'I'm okay, mate,' I assure him, pushing myself up and wincing as I test my ankle. It throbs, but I can still put pressure on it. We can't afford to stop.

The track is steep and uneven. Rocks jut out at odd angles, making it tricky to navigate with only the light of my headlamp. Cold seeps into my bones, and my feet are aching.

Would she have come all the way up here? It seems unlikely, but Koda is sure. As he pulls me forward, a sense of dread settles in my stomach. Lilly's lifeless eyes. The colour of Hazel's skin.

Without warning, Koda halts. His ears prick up, and he tilts his head, listening to something only he can hear. He barks sharply and looks at me, his eyes filled with urgency. I strain to hear something – anything that might tell me Juniper is still alive, but all I hear are the sounds of the bush.

'Juniper?' I shout as loud as I can. 'Juniper, it's Mia. Can you hear me?'

I grab my radio and call Daley. 'We're closing in. I don't have audio or visual confirmation yet, but I'm certain she's here.'

'Great work, Thomas. Find her and get back here.'

'Will do, boss.' I click off and focus all my energy on Koda. 'Find her.'

Together we sprint forward, Koda leading the way. As he closes in on the scent, his body language shifts into high gear. Every move is deliberate, as he quickly weaves back and forth in a zigzag pattern, systematically covering the area to pinpoint the scent source.

'Almost there, Koda,' I encourage him. 'Almost there.'

Occasionally, he pauses, head snapping up as he re-assesses the scent's direction. His sniffing is audible now, a rapid succession of short, sharp inhales and exhales.

'Juniper?' I call again. 'Juniper, can you hear me?'

Koda pivots left, guiding us down a familiar trail that I know will eventually loop back to the creek. A few metres in, he stops, nose to the ground, inspecting a stick placed deliberately in the middle of the path. His quick, urgent barks leave no doubt – Juniper must have put it there to mark her way.

'Juniper? It's Mia. Can you hear me?'

I close my eyes, tilt my head, and listen. She has to be here. Koda doesn't make mistakes.

Chapter Twenty-Nine
Juniper

THE cold is biting. Every breath feels like a shard of ice tearing into my lungs. When the trail led around in circles, I decided to take shelter under a low-hanging tree branch to try and conserve what little warmth I have left.

I gave up bargaining a long time ago, but with nothing left to lose, once again I close my eyes and promise that if someone finds me, I'll make a change. A difference. I'll do something that makes my life count.

I shiver and bite down to keep my teeth from chattering. Around me, the darkness presses in, thick and suffocating. Each rustle, every snap of a twig, sends adrenaline coursing through my body. My mind is a whirlwind of what-ifs, each one darker than the last. *What if no one finds me? What if I don't survive the night? What if, what if, what if?*

Mum and Dad must be frantic by now. Someone will come. They have to.

I shift slightly, trying to find a more comfortable position. The ground is so hard and so cold. I strain my ears, listening for any sign that someone might be nearby. I think I hear a bark, but it's faint and far away. Could it be real, or am I imagining things? Has Mia come looking for me with her dog?

I open my eyes and peer into the darkness. I want to believe it. I need to believe it. I quickly make another promise that if Mia gets me out of here, I'll do whatever it takes to find justice for Lilly and Hazel, and for Britt. She lost her best friend. She deserves closure as well. To hell with everyone in Wildling hating me. The girls deserve to have someone held accountable for what happened to them. Not so I can save my job, but because it's the right thing to do. Even if it was Bryce who killed them.

Suddenly, a bark pierces the silence. Undeniable this time, I sit up straighter, my heart racing.

'I'm here!' I shout as loud as I can. 'Help! I'm here!'

Another bark. Closer. Then another.

'I'm here!' I call again. 'Can you hear me?'

'Juniper?' a woman's voice calls back. 'It's Mia. Stay put. Koda will find you.'

'I'm over here!' I call again, getting to my feet and waving my arms. 'Over here!'

The sound of Koda's frenzied barking cuts through the darkness, and then I see it – a beam of light illuminating the surrounding bush.

'Over here!' I call again. 'I'm here!'

The sound of twigs and leaves crunching under their

feet draws closer, and my heart swells.

'Juniper,' Mia says with a sigh, as their shapes emerge from the darkness. 'Nice night for a walk.'

Relief bursts out of me in a mix of laughter and tears. 'Oh... my... God, Mia,' I gush, throwing my arms around her. 'Thank you. I... I don't know how I got so lost.'

She shrugs and smiles. 'It happens, but we're going to get you out of here.'

Her movements are practised and precise as she slips off her backpack and grabs her radio. 'Daley, we've got her. She looks good. I'll give her some fluids, check her vitals, but I don't think we need a medevac. Tell the ambos to meet us on the main trail. She should get checked out at Winton River just to be safe.'

Mia wraps me in a silver thermal blanket like the ones I've seen on news stories about people rescued from the mountains, then pours a hot drink from a small metallic thermos. She is calm and methodical – the complete opposite of how she seemed when I saw her last.

'Drink this and try to warm up,' she tells me. 'We'll head back in five if you're up to it.'

She gives Koda his reward for saving my life, a chew rope that he grabs with obvious delight, and I watch in awe at her ability to control the situation. We're out here in the middle of a freezing, dark national park, and yet she is completely unfazed.

'You're amazing,' I manage. 'You saved my life.'

'Koda's the amazing one,' she tells me with a warm smile. 'Aren't you, buddy? Hey?'

She ruffles the fur around his neck, and it's clear to see how much the dog means to her.

'Mia, can I ask you something?'

She straightens up and turns her attention back to me. 'Sure, what is it?'

I hesitate, considering my words, then decide there's probably no use in trying to tiptoe around it. 'I know you said otherwise, but were you and Koda the ones who found Hazel Smith's body out on Willow's Crossing?'

She studies me for a moment and then crouches to put Koda's chew rope back into her pack. 'What makes you ask that?'

'Just watching the two of you,' I tell her. 'I think maybe he gave you a sign there was something there, and you trusted him enough to go back and check.'

'Let's just get you back to base,' she says. 'It's been a long afternoon.'

'Those girls were killed, and their bodies discarded out in this cold. Whoever could do something like that isn't human, Mia. He needs to be stopped. You know that.'

She searches my face, clearly contemplating what to say next. 'Juniper...'

'You don't have to say anything, but I know it was you and Koda who found Hazel. You're invested in this too.'

'More than you think,' she says with a long sigh.

'Then let me in. I came here to help Britt. I thought that was going to be by… actually, I don't know what I was going to do, but maybe the best way I can help is by finally doing my job.'

'You'd write about it?'

'Once we're sure what happened, yes.'

Mia stares out into the bush, and I pull the blanket tighter around my shoulders.

'We'd have to be one hundred per cent certain,' she says eventually. 'There's no room for mistakes here.'

I nod quickly. 'Agreed.'

'You'd be willing to take on Jack Stanton?'

I think back to what Britt told me. Whether it was Jack himself or Bryce, it's still taking on the Stantons. 'I am,' I tell her. 'If he's responsible.'

'You think it was someone else?'

'I think we have a lot to talk about,' I tell her. 'When I'm not half frozen to death.'

Chapter Thirty

DOWN by the river, the late afternoon air feels heavy and damp. Fog has laced through the trees, and soggy ground sucks at the soles of my boots.

The thought of Jason and Will finding out what I'm about to do knots my shoulder blades. Will and I are already on tenterhooks, but how can I just pretend none of this is happening? And Jason. He's already threatening to medicate me, but every night when I jolt awake, the stench of Hazel Smith's decomposing body clogging my throat and Lilly's dead eyes staring at me through the dark, I know that I have to make this right – no matter what.

Juniper emerges from the tree line first, a notebook held tight against her chest like it might shield her somehow from what lies ahead. Behind her, Britt trails along, hands shoved deep into her pockets and a dark hoodie pulled up over her head.

As I watch them heading toward me, Mimi's words run through my mind.

When the third arrow is drawn, it will begin.

All three of us have a reason to be here, and all three of us have something to lose – but maybe together, we can find justice for Lilly and Hazel.

'Hey, Koda,' Juniper says, leaning down to scratch behind his ear when he trots over to meet her. 'How are you, hey? How are you?'

'Have you recovered from yesterday's walk in the woods?' I ask her.

'It was a walk in the woods all right,' she replies, rolling her eyes. 'I don't know how to thank you and Koda for coming to save my arse.'

'You're alive. That's enough.'

She nods and glances back at Britt, still making her way over. 'She doesn't trust me, not completely, but she's here.'

I nod and look past Juniper at Britt stalking toward us. I was so much like her at the same age. Rebellious, righteous, and completely raw.

'So,' I begin when Britt catches up, 'we all have our theories on what happened to Lilly and Hazel. The best thing might be to put everything we know on the table and see where we end up.'

Juniper nods. Britt kicks a stone and watches it roll almost to the waterline. Neither of them says anything.

'Fine, I'll start. I guess by now it's no secret that Koda and I found Hazel's body out on Willow's Crossing. I also spoke to Herm. He didn't know Lilly was pregnant, and I don't think he was the father.'

Juniper's eyes widen, and she stares at Britt. 'Lilly was pregnant?'

'Yeah, like three months,' Britt replies. 'I knew about Herm, so I just assumed it was him. Now I'm not so sure.'

'Wait,' Juniper says. 'Catch me up here. You knew *what* about Herm?'

Britt glances at me, and I nod that it's okay.

'Herm was abusing Lilly... sexually,' Britt begins. 'It's what he does.'

Juniper's mouth forms a silent O as she stares at her sister in disbelief. 'What do you mean, *it's what he does?*'

'She means he's done it before.' I hesitate and then add, 'To me, and maybe other girls as well.'

'Oh, Mia...' Juniper steps forward, but then stops short, clearly unsure of whether she should hug me or give me space.

'It was a long time ago. I never said anything. I should have.'

'Then, she was last seen getting into the Willow's Crossing truck the day she died,' Britt adds, returning the conversation to Lilly. 'That can't be a coincidence.'

We all take a moment to think, the rush of the river behind us filling the silence.

'I saw Bryce the other day,' Juniper says eventually. 'I thought he'd help me, but he was... weird.'

'Weird how?' I ask.

She stares out toward the river for a moment. I follow

her gaze and notice the water level is rising. Snowmelt from the mountains pushing against already swollen banks.

'I don't know… aggressive,' she says. 'He grabbed me by the arm.'

'He grabbed you?' Britt repeats, instantly standing up straighter.

'It's fine,' she says with a wave of her hand. 'I mean, it was scary, but he didn't hurt me. It did get me thinking though.'

I step in closer. 'Tell us.'

'Well, what if it wasn't Jack driving the truck?'

We stare at each other, no one wanting to be the first to say it out loud.

'Shit,' Britt says eventually, breaking the silence. 'Can someone just say it? It was Bryce.' She kicks at a stone with her foot and stares at us. 'Look at what we've got. He was weird and aggressive to you in the park, Juniper. Luke said something about Lilly liking someone, so with this being Wildling, there's every chance that was Bryce, right? On the day she died, Lilly said she was going to talk to the father and was seen getting into the Willow's Crossing truck. Despite the bullshit Jack came up with, it seemed like he had no idea what I was talking about when I brought it up at dinner the other night. So, it had to be Bryce behind the wheel, not Jack. He must have flipped out about the baby and killed her. Now his dad and Herm are just protecting him. Typical freaking patriarchy.'

We all exchange a glance. 'But what about Hazel?' I ask. 'How does she fit into this?'

'That part, I have no idea,' Britt says. 'Lilly didn't know her. I never saw Bryce with her, or Herm, for that matter.'

'Could there be two killers?' Juniper asks.

'I think you've been listening to too many true crime podcasts,' Britt quips. 'The idea that there's even one murderer in Wildling is hard enough to believe.'

'All right,' I begin, my hands stretched out in front of me. 'We all think it's plausible that Bryce killed Lilly, and Jack and Herm are covering for him. What we don't know is how Hazel fits into this.'

'That, and we have no proof of anything,' Britt adds.

'I can't write anything unless we find proof,' Juniper says. 'Trust me, I learned that lesson the hard way.'

Britt pulls a cigarette out of her pocket and balances it between her lips.

'Don't even think about lighting that thing,' Juniper tells her.

'You're not really supposed to smoke in the park,' I add.

Britt shoves it back into the front pocket of her hoodie and rolls her eyes.

'The first thing we need to figure out is whether there was a connection between Lilly and Hazel that we don't know about,' I say. 'Maybe that will tell us something.'

'Hazel's community won't talk to anyone,' Juniper says. 'Every journalist from here to Timbuktu has tried. No one is willing to speak.'

'I can go talk to Lilly's mum, maybe look through her stuff,' Britt suggests. 'There might be something in her room.'

Britt's voice trails off, but my mind is already somewhere else. If Hazel's parents won't open up to outsiders, we need someone they trust. Mimi has always considered herself a custodian of the land, much like the First Nations community. Her love for the national park and its rivers, mountains, and valleys has made her the only person in Wildling ever able to walk both sides of the line.

My jaw clenches. I hate the idea, but there's no doubt in my mind. If we're going to solve this, we need Mimi.

Chapter Thirty-One

TOWERING mountains loom over us, casting long shadows as Mimi, Koda, and I climb out of my LandCruiser.

Mimi walks ahead, her gait steady as we move through the fringe of the national park. She moves like she belongs here, as though the bush might bend around her.

In a clearing just up ahead, Hazel's parents are waiting. They stand close together, heads bowed, bracing themselves against more than just the chill. Her mother's dark eyes glisten, and her father's shoulders sag as if the weight of their grief has bent him in half.

'Hello,' I manage, as Koda walks up and offers his head for them to pat. 'I appreciate you both coming out here today.'

They nod and look to each other for support. Seeing their pain makes me worry this was a bad idea. If I've brought them out here for nothing, then all I'm doing is making things worse.

Mimi stops and turns to me, her eyes catching mine. 'Still your tongue. Listen before you speak. The land always talks first.'

I nod and press my lips together, the pressure in my chest making it hard to breathe. Hazel's mother briefly rests her hand on Koda's head before I call him back and he sits beside me, ears pricked, watching intently.

'They're here,' Mimi says softly as we step into the clearing. 'The spirits. I feel them.'

Hazel's mother breaks into sobs, her husband's arms pulling her in tight. Tiny flakes of snow drift from the sky, dissolving against her skin like brief, fleeting touches.

We're only metres from Jack's property line. This is as close as I dared bring them to where I found Hazel. Jack would never allow this gathering on his land, but the boundary doesn't change what happened here.

'The mountains know. The air remembers,' Mimi whispers as though she can read my mind.

I look her over. She has dressed with care. Her usually wild hair is woven into two braids, and a shawl the colour of wattle leaf is wrapped around her shoulders. Her bare feet press into the earth, the sight of her naked toes sending goosebumps along the length of my arms. She closes her eyes, then tilts her head as if listening to something only she can hear.

'You want to understand?' she asks quietly. 'You need to listen to what the spirits of the land are saying.'

The wind stirs around us, carrying with it the faint scent of snow gum. Branches creak overhead, and the world narrows until Mimi's voice is all I can hear.

'Two young roos bounded across this earth,' she begins, her tone low and steady, 'joyful and full of life. But a dingo came upon them, envious and angry. Its strike was swift. Fatal.'

The words crawl across my skin. My thoughts spin, threads tying themselves together. Hazel died first, before Lilly. Had Bryce been seeing both of them? Did they find out and turn against him? If Lilly and Hazel had threatened to tell Charlotte, or worse, Jack, could it have been enough to send him into a rage?

...envious and angry. The strike was swift. Fatal.

My pulse hammers. Maybe Lilly's death wasn't about the baby at all.

'You shouldn't be out here.' Jack's voice suddenly booms across the quiet landscape. 'I don't want you doing your voodoo bullshit so close to my boundary line.'

He stands defiantly on his side of the fence, hands planted on his hips, legs spread and anchored to the ground.

'You got no say about what we do out here,' Mimi tells him. 'This ain't your land.'

'Not yours either,' he snaps. 'The national park belongs to the government, and this land belongs to me.'

'Call it what you want,' Mimi tells him. 'That will never be your land.'

Jack laughs, his head tilting back. 'Everything is my land, old woman. Even that shack you call a house. It's only a matter of time.'

Koda pulls forward, a low growl rumbling in his throat.

'And don't think you're fooling anyone, Thomas,' he says, turning his attention to me. 'I know it was you who came sniffing around out here and called the police.'

He has no proof, I remind myself. If he did, the state police would have been knocking on my door by now.

'You stay away from her,' Mimi warns. 'She ain't none of your concern.'

Jack steps up to the fence and glares down at her. 'Everything that happens in Wildling is my concern.'

'While ever you stand on this land, you're bound by the will of the mountain,' she tells him. 'Everything out here has a balance. What's taken must be returned. And you've taken more than your fair share.'

He considers her, then tosses his head back and laughs. 'Say whatever you want. People in this town might call you a witch, but your superstitions are just that – hocus-pocus bullshit.'

'There's debts that need repaying,' she tells him, her voice unwavering.

Around us, a sudden wind blows in off the mountain. Icy and cold, it steals Jack's hat, sending it tumbling off across the field.

'They've whispered the truth into my ear,' Mimi finishes. 'And mark my words. The balance will be restored.'

Chapter Thirty-Two
Britt

I'M heading over to Lilly's place to ask her mum about any connection with Hazel, even though I already know the answer – there wasn't one. Lilly wasn't the type of girl to have a bunch of friends. We had that in common. I was her person, and she was mine.

Or was she?

Before all this, I believed Lilly's flaws made her perfect. The way she refused to be a *good girl*. The way she said whatever was on her mind. Her disregard of rules, expectations, and boundaries. Like her namesake flower, *Lily of the Valley*, she was impossible not to admire and maybe beautiful enough to hide the fact she was poison.

When I get to Lilly's, I knock on the door and step inside. The first thing I see is her mother, Trudi, perched on the edge of the couch. A narrow beam of light seeps in through drawn curtains, catching strands of her hair, the colour of decaying autumn leaves. Her foot jitters a restless rhythm against the floorboards, and the house smells of stale smoke and spilled beer. A stained coffee table slumps under the weight of ashtrays and empty bottles.

She drags deep on a joint pinched between her fingers, then closes her eyes as she exhales. Without a word, she passes it to the man beside her. He has sinewy arms and a shaved head. A tattooed rose sprawls across the left side of his neck like it bloomed there by mistake.

Lilly never had a chance.

'Haven't seen you since it happened,' she says. 'Funeral's next Wednesday.' The guy hands back the joint, and she takes a long drag. 'Burying my own kid. Can you believe it?'

I tense and close my eyes. I want to scream that all she had to do was pay attention, but there's no point. She's probably too stoned to even understand.

'Ms Daniels— '

'Trudi.'

'Right... Trudi, um, do you know if Lilly ever hung out with that girl Hazel?'

'Who?'

'Hazel,' I say again. 'The First Nations girl they found out on Willow's Crossing last week.'

Trudi purses her lips, then shakes her head. 'Nah, never heard about any First Nations girl,' she says eventually, the words shrouded in smoke haze.

'Did any other friends ever come here to see Lilly?'

'Nope.' She takes another long drag, then blows the smoke out in rings. 'You want a hit?'

It's tempting, but that's not why I'm here. 'Nah, I'll pass, but can I take a quick look around her room before I go? I think I left a sweater the last time I was here. Mum's hassling me about it.'

She gestures up the hall with her arm. 'She loved you like a sister,' I hear Trudi say as I head toward Lilly's room. 'She really did.'

I stop and swallow down the lump in my throat. Maybe I shouldn't go snooping through her room. Maybe it would be better to just let her rest in peace. She certainly never found it in life.

'There was one guy who came over,' Trudi calls out. 'Just one time. Good-looking, well-dressed kid. If she was smart, he wasn't just a friend, if you know what I mean.'

My pulse quickens, and I turn back. 'Do you know who he was?'

'Thought it was the Stanton boy, but she swore black and blue I had it wrong.' Trudi flings her arm out in a dramatic gesture. 'Called me a drunk and druggie. Told me what the hell did I know?'

'Right,' I say with a nod. 'When was this?'

She shrugs and drops the butt of the joint into the ashtray. 'Don't know. A few months ago. Four, maybe five.'

'Not less?'

She turns and stares at the man beside her. 'Nah, he weren't on the scene yet. You've been here now, what, three months?'

'Somethin' like that,' he mumbles.

'Was before that.'

'Right. Well, I'll just have a look for the sweater and be on my way then.'

Inside Lilly's room, I close the door and press my back against the wood. I don't want to go through her stuff. It feels intrusive, especially now I know there were things she wanted to keep from me, but if Trudi is right and Bryce was here, there might be something in her room we can use to prove he killed her.

'Sorry, Lilly,' I whisper, as I step toward her dresser, 'but this is Wildling, and you should have known better than to try to keep a secret in this town, especially one that includes the Stantons.'

Chapter Thirty-Three
Britt

I SWEAR I can feel her watching me. If I didn't know better, I'd think she was standing over in the corner, twirling her hair and laughing as I rifle through her things. She'd love thinking she out-smarted me, that she'd hidden the answers somewhere I couldn't find. Not in a bad way. She'd just enjoy the challenge of seeing who was craftier, her or me.

You know what she was like, always needing to try and control everything and everyone.

Luke's words play back in my mind, and I wonder if subconsciously I blocked out the parts of Lilly's personality I didn't like. Maybe I was always so close that I only saw glimpses of her and never the whole. Her infectious laughter and disregard for the opinions of others. The way she made it feel like anything could happen at any moment. Maybe if I'd found the courage to step back a little, I would have seen the entire picture. Maybe I didn't want to.

'What am I even looking for?' The room is empty, but as

I say the words, I catch myself glancing toward the corner, still certain I can feel her there. 'Would Bryce have written you a note? Did you print a photo?'

I sit down on the edge of her bed and look around the room. It still smells of her – that vanilla-scented perfume she always wore. I hated how it always got up my nose, but knowing this might be the last time I ever smell it forms a lump in my throat. Being here in this room makes it hard to believe she's really gone. There are so many pieces of her, and yet none of them can make her whole again.

An eclectic mix of artwork and photos covers the walls. Some she drew, others she collected because they spoke to her in a way the people in Wildling couldn't. There are photos of us drinking, smoking, and hanging out with Luke down on the grandstand at the oval. As I peer at them, it hits me that there are no normal pictures. The obligatory road trip, movie night, or high school graduation. There's no light, only darkness. Why were we always so angry at everything?

Her clothes are strewn haphazardly across the floor, a mix of jeans, singlets and jumpers. There's no rhyme or reason, no seasonality to it, just a mess of garments discarded as she tore through the room in a whirlwind of Lilly-ness. But amidst the mess, there are also glimpses of a different side to her, one not everyone got to see.

On the dresser, between makeup brushes and jewellery, is an old, worn copy of Wuthering Heights. I doubt anyone in Wildling would believe Lilly Daniels read the classics, but it comes as no surprise to me she might like this book filled with passion, revenge and longing – all the things Lilly was made of. I flip through the pages and notice something handwritten on the inside cover. I recognise her loopy scrawl immediately.

He shall never know I love him, and not because he's handsome, but because he's more myself than I am. Whatever our souls are made out of, his and mine are the same.

I stare down at the words she'd written. Was it supposed to be about Bryce? They were nothing alike. He's a doting son, reliable and predictable, as vanilla as that awful perfume she wore. If Lilly was the summit, he was the base, rock-solid while she reached for the sky.

Or so it always seemed.

A thought occurs to me, and I put the book back down on the dresser. Before I dropped out of school, we studied Wuthering Heights in English class. In it, the main character, Catherine, hid her journal in a secret panel of her bed. I walk over to Lilly's bed and stare at it. It's not a gothic oak bed by any means, but if she had a journal, maybe this is where I'll find it. Not under the mattress or pillows – too obvious. I strip the bed back, throwing the sheets and blankets onto the floor. Nothing. Even though I know it won't be there, I haul up the mattress, revealing the skeletal frame and slats, but still nothing.

'I always thought we could tell each other anything,

Lilly,' I whisper. 'I'm trying to find out who did this to you. It sure would help if you could tell me whether you kept a journal.'

I stand still and silent, waiting for a sign. A movement. A ghostly whisper. Anything that might point me in the right direction. When none comes, I push my hands onto my hips and stare at the mess I've made. Somewhere in this labyrinth of clothes and sheets and Lilly could be a journal, but I have no clue where. Without her help, I have no chance of finding it. I reach up and grab the edge of the mattress to pull it back into place, and that's when I feel it. Zipped into the mattress protector, an oblong shape the size of a small book.

A mix of excitement and anxiety thrums through me as I take the small leather journal out and tip the mattress back onto its frame. I quickly remake the bed as best I can, then tuck the journal into my backpack and take one last look around her room. This will be the last time I'm here, surrounded by her things – by her. It will be the last time I smell her vanilla perfume or look at the photos of us up on the wall. It doesn't escape me that it may also be the last time I think of her the way I do now. Lilly was larger than life – something I could never be, someone whose presence allowed me to uncover parts of myself I would never have the courage to find on my own. Once I read her journal, some of that might change. I've already lost her once. The idea of losing her again makes me ache, but I have to know, and maybe she can take me on one last ride as I try to figure out who killed her.

Chapter Thirty-Four

BEING out in the park with Mimi had a profound impact on me. There was something about seeing her connection to the land that flicked a switch. For so long, I shunned her beliefs, but now I'm not so sure.

Will always told me I should make more of an effort to get to know her, to appreciate her the way Jason does. A part of me was always determined not to listen because I wanted him to see the differences between my brother and me as a quality rather than a flaw. But it was always going to be a hard sell. Jason and his magnetic personality, coupled with his support of Will's career goals, makes it almost impossible for me to compete.

At least now, I think as I stir the vegetables, I can tell him I've seen the light – that just like Jason, I'm ready to get to know Mimi and open myself up to what she may have to teach me.

Outside, his car pulls into the driveway as the first drops of rain begin to fall. Koda whines at the back door to go out, and I wonder why he always seems to time his toilet breaks to coincide with bad weather.

'All right, but be quick about it,' I tell him.

I glance around the kitchen, making sure everything is neat and tidy. On the drive home, I decided not to tell Will about Jack's threat – that he suspects it was me who found Hazel and called the police. Telling him will just start another fight, and I want tonight to be about making amends. I want us to get back on track before he heads to Canberra in the morning. By the time he finds out Juniper, Britt, and I have been looking into the case, we'll have figured out who did what, and if Bryce really did kill those girls and Jack covered it up, his influence over the town will cease to matter. Even he won't be able to talk his way out of that.

'Hi, I'm making stir-fry,' I say as he walks in and dumps his pack on the floor by the dining table. I glance at it and feel my throat catch. 'You spent the day out in the park?'

Before he can answer, Koda runs in and shakes, spraying rainwater all over the both of us.

'Goddamn it,' Will swears, wiping himself down and glaring at Koda. 'Christ, Mia, can you at least get a towel?'

My pulse quickens as I put down the tongs and hurry to fetch some towels. I've never known Will to look at Koda with such anger. He's only ever showered him with love and affection.

'Here you go.' I pass him the towel and kneel to dry Koda. 'How was your hike?'

He pats down his pants and shirt and then drops the towel on the floor beside me. 'It gave me some time to think.'

Butterfly wings flutter in my chest. 'About what?'

'Everything,' he replies. 'Mia, we should talk.'

My heart sinks. When you love someone, the last thing you ever want to hear them say is *we should talk.*

I consider whether I should stand or sit at the table, but the ache in my chest tells me it's probably safer to stay on the floor. 'Sure, okay. What's on your mind?'

He pulls out a chair and sits down. 'There's really no easy way to say this. I've decided to move to Canberra.'

I freeze and silently scream at myself to stay calm. It makes sense. The commute must be terrible for him, but we can work this out. I can go down there sometimes. He can come up here.

'We can make that work,' I reply, battling to keep my voice steady. 'How do you want to go about it? Will you come back on weekends, or...'

He takes a deep breath, avoiding my eyes. 'No, I think we should end things,' he says, each word hitting me like a punch to the gut. 'It's Jess. I've been seeing her for a while, and... I'm moving down there to be with her.'

'But you said that wasn't true.' I search his face, desperate to find even the slightest crack, a tiny passage back to where we started. Back to the place where he used to love me.

'I'm sorry,' he continues. 'I don't want to hurt you, but I can't keep doing this. She's where I need to be.'

My fingers grip Koda's fur, and he turns to look at me. If it hurts him, he doesn't let on. Instead, he licks my cheek and moves in closer.

'But we're engaged... I thought... you said...'

Since I was a child, I've gazed at Will with dream-lit eyes, imagining the life we would build together. It can't all come crashing down. My mind scrambles for the right words. Ones that will make him stay. We have a lifetime of history. Year after year, we've watched the seasons change. Snow has given way to sunshine, leaves have turned gold and drifted down around our feet. Koda has grown from a puppy wriggling in our arms into a beautiful, capable search and rescue dog. We've held each other up, reached out in the dark, and woken wrapped in the warmth of what I believed was always. This woman, whoever she is, has known him less than a year. A handful of months can't erase an entire life.

'I'm sorry, Mi, really.'

The fact that he calls me *Mi* gives me a sudden burst of hope. It feels familiar and reassuring. He's still Will and I'm still Mia. I can fix this. I can change his mind.

'Can we just talk about it?' I ask. 'If there's something wrong, if I'm different somehow, I can change back.'

He shakes his head and looks away. 'It's not you, Mia. I'm different. I live in a different world now.'

'Then show it to me,' I reply, inching toward his legs. 'Let me be a part of it with you. We've always been a part of each other's lives, Will. Ever since we were kids. We've always found a way. It's you and me.'

'I need to be in Canberra, and you belong here with Koda. Wildling is your home.'

I force back the tears as my voice breaks. 'You're my home.'

He sighs and moves his leg further away. 'I've made up my mind. I'm sorry.'

Don't beg him, I tell myself. *Whatever happens, don't do that. You're better than that.*

I close my eyes as a barrage of images flash through my mind. I've never been in this house without Will. As soon as I was old enough, he rescued me from Mimi's and we laughed and kissed, folding our clothes away in the same closet, swearing to each other that nothing would ever change. That just like the mountains and rivers, we were forever.

My stomach folds in on itself as the sickly scent of stir-fry curdles in the air. I press my palm hard against my chest, trying to hold myself together.

'Please don't go,' I whisper. 'Just give me another chance. I can change. I can be more like her. Just tell me what to do. Who to be.'

'Mia, stop it,' he snaps, getting to his feet. 'You're better than this.'

I know he's right, but now that I've started, I can't stop. Any boundary I had has already been crossed. 'Please, Will,' I beg, sliding myself forward and wrapping my arms around his legs. 'Please don't leave me.'

'For God's sake,' he says, nudging me away. 'Get up off the ground.'

Instead, I collapse over my knees as the sound of something breaking escapes my chest.

'Jesus Christ,' I hear him say with a sigh. 'I have to go.'

'No...' I grab at his ankle as he passes by, but again he shakes me loose and swears out loud.

'For Christ's sake, Mia, get your shit together. You're embarrassing yourself.'

I hear him walk back down the hall and into our bedroom. I know he's gathering things to take. Things he'll need at her place.

I glance at Koda, and consider following him. Barricading myself across the doorway so he can't leave. Shouting at him. Throwing things at him. Trying to hold him, kiss him, make him remember that he loves me somehow.

At the other end of the house, the front door opens and a cold wind rushes in along the hall. If I don't do something now, he'll be gone. My leg flinches, ready to move, but the rest of my body feels weighted to the floor. I hear the click of the lock closing and the scream of silence that comes after.

My face falls slack, and my eyes burn as Koda lies down

next to me, his head pushing into my lap.

I don't know how long we sit out on the kitchen floor together, but when I finally stop crying, the rest of the house is dark and everything is still. Freezing air bites the skin of my cheek. The kitchen smells like charred smoke. It's quiet aside from sounds of the house creaking in the wind, and Koda and I are the only two left in it.

Chapter Thirty-Five
Britt

ALL I want to do is go home and read the journal, but of all nights, Nate has chosen now to come down with the flu. I've only ever worked a night shift once before. Even though this is Wildling and there's never been a robbery in the town's 140-year history, he still thinks it's dangerous to have a teenage girl behind the register at night. *Even more so when she's investigating a murder.*

At least it's quiet and I'll be able to read between customers. Under the counter, I have the biggest bag of chips I could find on the shelf, two chocolate bars and a box of tissues. I figure that covers all bases, and screw Nate if he thinks I'm paying for them. It's the least he can do for making me come in for a night shift – and in the rain.

I haven't told my sister or Mia that I found the journal. I have no idea what's inside and, loyal to the end, I want to make sure there's nothing incriminating that could make Lilly look bad, especially when she's not here to defend herself.

With a stomach full of hummingbird wings, I open the

journal. 'Okay, Lilly,' I breathe. 'Here we go.'

The first half of her entries are what I expected. It's hard pushing through the detailed recollections of the things Herm did to her, but at least we have evidence against him now. Even if he didn't kill her or Hazel, he'll have to answer for sexually assaulting a minor – so there's that.

I flick through a few more pages of typical Lilly-isms, talking about how much she hates her mother, her dreams of being a model and how much she longs to get out of Wildling.

Then I reach the first mention of Bryce, and that's where things get interesting.

17 January

OMG I can't believe I just had sex with Bryce Stanton! I don't even know how it happened. I was lying on the grass in the park to get away from the sound of Mum screwing some loser in her bedroom, and he just appeared out of nowhere. We talked, and he's actually so funny. And that smile. Damn. He told me all about working on Willow's Crossing with his dad, and how one day it will all be his. Then he looked so sad when he talked about how he can't imagine being there all alone once his mum and dad are gone. He's an only child like me, so I get it, but I can't believe that someone like him would ever be worried about being alone. He's Bryce Stanton. He looked so lonely, and I couldn't stop staring at his lips. Next minute, we were behind that huge tree, kissing. I didn't mean for it to go any further, but it was so intense, and I felt so connected to him. It was hot, and I was only wearing a cotton dress. When he turned me around and pulled my underwear to the side, I closed my eyes and just let him. It was so exciting, being out there where someone might see us. It was nothing like with Herm the Worm. Back when he used to touch me, I wanted to be sick, but that was all a long time ago. That freak only likes girls who are too young to fight back. Like, vomit.

19 January

I can't stop thinking about Bryce. The way he touched me. The sound of his voice. It's probably stupid, but I keep thinking about what my life would be like with him. The two of us living out on Willow's Crossing together. His mum and dad would flip if they knew he liked a girl like me. I know they want him to get back with Britt's sister Juniper, but she's long gone. And he's still dating that prissy bitch Charlotte Higgins, but I know there's something between us. I felt it. I need to tell Britt. She never says anything, but I know she has a crush on him. But it's not like she has a chance with him anyway, and I didn't start it. He made me put my number in his phone before he left. When he texts, I'll tell her, and she'll just have to accept it. If she doesn't, bad luck.

24 January

It's been five days, and he hasn't text. What the hell? I

didn't get his number. I didn't think I had to. He was so into me, like so much. He wasn't faking it. I would have known. He was so worried about ending up with no one and I'm right here, like, I want to be with him. Compared to him, every other guy in Wildling is an idiot. They don't talk the way he does, and they sure don't look like he does. He's all I can think about now. I can't remember ever wanting anything this much. My life could be completely different with him. I could be someone. I wouldn't have to be the girl from the slums whose mum is a screw-up. I could be Lilly Stanton, the girl who has her own horse and lives on Willow's Crossing. Why doesn't he just text?

27 January

Still nothing. I wish he'd never come over that day. Before that, being Bryce's girlfriend had never even crossed my mind. Now it's all I can think about. Wait, OMG, what if I put my number in his phone wrong? He doesn't know where I live, and it's not like he can just go to the servo and ask Britt. Like, he knows we're friends. We talked about that, but it would be weird with her being Juniper's sister and everything. Maybe I should go over there. What if he thinks I gave him a fake number? Screw it. I'm going over there.

6 February

Bryce Stanton can go to hell. I can't believe he told me to leave. 'It was what it was, Lilly. You can't just turn up here. What if my parents see you?' That's what he said. That whole thing in the park was a load of shit. The sad eyes and what if I end up alone speech. Everyone in Wildling thinks he's such a good guy – the perfect son. What a load of shit. I just wanted it so much. How can I go back to my normal life now? There must be something I can do.

Lilly's journal entries taper off over the next few weeks. There's the odd rambling about wanting to live at Willow's Crossing and cursing at Bryce, but nothing new. I read one entry on Valentine's Day where she saw him walking hand in hand with Charlotte on Main Street, so she let his tyres down while they were in the pub having lunch, and another where she sat out on the drive of Willow's Crossing until three in the morning just staring at the light spilling out of his room.

But then an entry dated 16 February catches my attention, because the first line is all written in capitals.

16 February

OH MY GOD I AM BLESSED!!!

I'm pregnant. Like, actually pregnant, and Bryce Stanton is the father. I have no doubt in my mind. I haven't slept with anyone else since that day in the park, and the test came up positive. I had a feeling when my period was late, and my boobs were so sore, that something was going on, but I didn't dare to hope. But I'm having Bryce's baby. I knew it was meant to be. This is going to change everything. I want to tell Britt, but I can't. Not yet. I don't want to jinx it. Once I get to three months, I'll tell her. Once he knows, he'll change his mind about everything, and his parents will be fine. They'll love the idea of having their first grandchild – a grandchild who is entitled to everything on Willow's Crossing. It's actually going to happen. My dream life is going to come true. I can't believe it!!!!!!

I put the journal down and stare out over the shop, trying to figure this out. Lilly wouldn't lie in her journal, but Bryce couldn't have been the father. The only time they had sex was six months ago. By the time she died, she would have been showing.

20 February

I told Bryce about the baby. I waited for him at the end of the road that leads to Willow's Crossing, and when he drove by, I flagged him down. When I got in the car, he started cursing, calling me a stalker, but then I told him about the baby, and instead, he called me a liar. I told him I was happy to prove it, so we drove all the way to Winton River, where I could buy a pregnancy test without anyone seeing me get out of his car. He brought me home and came in while I did it. When he saw I wasn't lying, he looked like he was going to pass out. He started carrying on about how his parents will freak out. He said he'd pay for an abortion, but I told him there's no way I was going to kill our baby. That's when he lost it. Said I had to or else he'd find another way to make sure I didn't have it. Whatever that's supposed to mean.

I turn the page, and the first thing I notice is that the next entry is dated a week later.

28 February

I lost the baby. One minute I was pregnant, the next I was covered in blood and almost screaming from the pain in my stomach. At least I was at home when it happened, and no one saw. It's a strange feeling, like kinda empty and lonely, which is weird because it's not like I even met the baby. It's a shit feeling, though. The idea of being a mum was growing on me. I imagined having someone who would love me more than anyone else in the world. I've never had that. Shit, now I'm crying. I want my baby back. If only I could still be pregnant. If only... I could get pregnant again.

Chapter Thirty-Six

TWO days ago, the rain stopped, and the snow began. Rain carries a rhythm, a pulse against the window that reminds you the world is still alive. Snow is different. Its silence presses against the earth, bringing with it a chill that has settled in my bones.

Daley has been calling relentlessly. By morning, the mountain will be inundated with skiers and snowboarders. He'll want me to be on call, but I can't. I haven't left the house since Will walked out. We're almost out of food. I can't let Koda go hungry, but the idea of going to the shop makes me want to be sick. By now, everyone will know. When they see me, they'll whisper and stare. I'll be the laughingstock of the town, Sophie and my mother undoubtedly writing all the punchlines.

Without him here, the house feels different. The rooms are wider, emptier, like they're holding their breath. The patch of carpet at the end of our bed where he used to leave his clothes mocks me, a reminder of how I would get so angry when he didn't throw them in the washing basket and how now I'd do anything to see them lying there. Visions of him hover in every doorway. The way he'd watch me, how he'd walk in already mid-sentence before I could even look up. What felt like a home has become a cluster of empty rooms and memories. Spaces that once cupped our love in their hands, now calloused palms, weathered from the storm that was Jessica.

When a knock comes at the door, answering it is the last thing I want to do. I can tell from Koda's reaction that it's Jason. He's probably come to check on me. He would have been the first to know. He probably knew long before I did. They speak about the drilling project every day, and he already mentioned Jess, so he knows who she is. The idea that he could have known something like that and kept it from me provides just enough spark to pull me up off the couch.

'You knew,' I hiss before he even steps inside. 'You knew, and you never said a word.'

'Whoa,' he replies, palms out in front. 'Settle down. I didn't know. No one did. Do you really think I'd keep that from you?'

I shrug, and my shoulders drop forward, any energy I had quickly draining away. 'I don't know. I don't know what to think.'

'Can I come in? Last time I was here, you threw me out, so...'

'If you want,' I mumble. 'I don't care.'

He follows me over to the couch, where I slump back into my pile of chocolate wrappers and empty soft drink cans.

'Mia, this is not healthy,' he says, looking around. 'You can't just give up and sit here in squalor.'

I focus my eyes on a small crack in the wall and stare at it for so long my eyes go fuzzy.

'Mia, are you listening to me?'

I nod but don't say anything.

'Are you taking care of Koda? Has he eaten?'

'Of course he's eaten.'

'Mia?'

'He's eaten. I wouldn't neglect him, Jason. He's all I've got.' On cue, Koda crawls into my lap as best he can and nuzzles my hand.

'If it's too much, I can take him for a while.'

I snap back and stare at my brother. 'Take him?'

'Just until you're feeling better.'

'You're not taking Koda anywhere,' I say firmly, my hand coming to rest across his head. 'Not ever.'

'Okay, all right. I'm just offering.'

'Well, don't,' I snap. 'Koda stays with me. End of story.'

For a moment, we sit in awkward silence before Jason eventually asks about work. 'Daley called?'

'Only a million times.'

'You're not going in?'

I shake my head.

'What if someone gets lost?'

'What if I'm lost?' I mumble back and then add, 'Have you talked to him?'

'Mia...'

'Just tell me, Jason. Have you talked to him?'

'I have to. He and... she... they're finalising the permits for the drilling rig.'

'And?'

'And what?'

'Did he say anything?'

'He said he feels like shit about it.' Jason sighs and shakes his head. 'He also said he's where he wants to be.' My brother glances down at the shiny diamond ring still on my finger. 'You have to find a way to accept it, Mi.'

I follow his gaze and stare longingly at the ring. It's so beautiful. So full of sparkling potential. 'I can't make myself take it off.'

'Give yourself time,' he says. 'But not too much. Enough to accept it, but not so much that you're wallowing.'

'I just lost my entire life.'

'It feels like that, sure. But you didn't. Not really.'

I scoff and roll my eyes. 'What would you know about losing anything?'

'What's that supposed to mean?'

'It means you've never had a bad thing happen to you your entire life. You're Jason Thomas, hero of Wildling.'

'Whatever,' he says, sighing and getting to his feet. 'I'm going to head off. You need to go back to work.'

'Well, it's true,' I snap, suddenly filled with venom. 'Everyone loves you, even Mum. I'm sick of it.'

'Call if you need anything.' He glances back at Koda one last time. 'I meant what I said about Koda. I'm more than happy to take him.'

'I bet you are,' I snap. 'You'd love that, wouldn't you? Taking the one thing I have left. Then you'd have everything. Koda, Mum, Will – the entire town.'

'You need to calm down.'

'Don't tell me to calm down,' I shout, moving Koda off my lap. 'You have no idea what it's like to be me, Jason.'

'So, tell me,' he says, planting his feet. 'Tell me how terrible it is to be Mia.'

My emotions have taken over. I can't see what he's doing. If I calmed myself enough to think this through, I'd keep my mouth shut, but I don't.

'I was abused by that disgusting excuse for a man, Herm Drinkwater. I found Lilly dead in the ravine. I saw Hazel's remains up close and personal. Do you have any idea what a body looks like after almost a week out in the elements, Jason? What it smells like? Mum and Sophie hate me, and now Will's left me for some other woman. That's how terrible it is to be me. Not that you'd have any idea what it's like with your perfect life. So once again, please just get the hell out of my house. I can't even look at you.'

He studies me for a moment, then nods. 'You're right, Mia. That's too much for anyone to cope with. I'll speak to Gerry.'

'What?' I step back and stare at him.

'I'll speak to Gerry about getting you some help.'

'I don't need help, Jason. I just need you to leave.' My heart is racing. This is exactly what he wanted. A way to discredit me, or worse, to have me so drugged up on medication I can't cause trouble with Jack.

'Maybe a break would help.'

'Like a holiday?'

He bites the inside of his cheek and shakes his head. 'Not so much a holiday but—'

'You want to have me committed?'

He screws up his face and looks away. 'Don't be so dramatic, Mia. It's voluntary admission, like before. Somewhere nice, maybe up in Sydney. It helped last time, right?'

'Mum took me there when I tried to kill myself. That was because of Herm. This is nothing like that.'

He closes his eyes and rolls his shoulders, stretching out his neck. 'Mia, I have so much on my plate right now. I really can't deal with this. Just let someone help you. I'm not qualified for this level of crazy, and I can't do it right now.'

I stare at my brother open-mouthed, unable to believe what he's saying. 'You'd actually put me in a hospital because I'm upset my fiancée left?'

'Mia, you know how you are. You can be a danger to yourself.'

'I was fourteen.'

'Even still.' He gazes across the room. 'Look at this place. It's a disaster, and I'm willing to bet…' He turns and strides down the hall.

'What are you doing?' I call, hurrying after him. 'Jason, this is my house. You can't just barge around…'

Before I can finish, he tears open the door of the fridge. 'Nothing,' he says, staring at the barren shelves. 'You're not eating. Is there anything for Koda?'

He steps to the left and opens the pantry. Empty shelves yawn back at him, waiting to be restocked.

'I was going to do a shop today,' I snap. 'Not that it's any of your business.'

He closes the door and turns to me. 'You need some support.'

'This is such bullshit. Don't act like you're doing this because you care about me. You just want me out of the way, so I don't keep looking into Jack and interfering with your precious drill.'

'What?' He steps back and stares at me. 'Jack? You don't still think Wildling is full of serial killers?'

'Don't make it sound like I'm crazy.'

'I'm not,' he says, hands up in mock protest. 'I'm actually trying to help you. You're my sister, but, Mia, you're not thinking clearly. Just listen to yourself. You think Wildling has a serial killer. That's insane. You're not eating. You have nothing here for Koda's dinner. Let Gerry help you. You know he's always had your best interests at heart. Even if you think I don't, at least talk to him. Will you do that, please? If he says you're fine, then you're fine.'

'Two girls are dead, Jason. It's not like I'm making it up.'

He leans in and rests his hands on my shoulders. 'I love you,' he says, catching me off guard. 'I get that finding those girls has affected you. I mean, shit, Mia, either of them could have been you back then, right? It's triggering. I get it. That's why you need to talk to someone.'

I sigh and let my head drop forward. I'm so tired. 'Please just go and leave me alone.'

'I'll send Gerry over,' he says from the door. 'Everything's going to be okay, Mia. You'll see.'

Chapter Thirty-Seven
Juniper

WHEN Britt doesn't pick up the landline at the petrol station, I grab my keys and head out to the car. I've sent her a dozen messages and called her mobile phone at least five times. I don't like the idea of her being alone in that petrol station at night, not with everything that's going on. I just wanted to check she was all right. Now I can't get hold of her.

On the way over, I try calling Mum again to ask if she's heard from her. It's Tuesday night. That means everyone, including my parents, is at the pub for trivia night. When I get her voicemail, I leave another message asking her to call me and try the petrol station's landline again. Still no answer.

With panic building in my chest, I turn into the driveway and switch off the engine. There's no other cars here, and at first glance, the shop looks empty.

I climb out and half run toward the door. 'Britt!' I call out as the tiny overhead bell rings my arrival. 'Are you here?'

I scan the shop, and my breath catches when I see the overturned confectionery stand. Packets of chips and bags of lollies are strewn across the ground. To the right, a magazine display has also been tipped over. The faces of TV soap actors stare up at me from the floor, their glossy smiles at odds with the surrounding chaos.

'Oh my God, Britt? Where are you?' I shout, panic pulling at my chest. I dash behind the counter, heart racing, and find her bag half open on the ground. I crouch and pick it up, my fingers brushing against her wallet and phone still inside. Her keys dangle from the zipper, clinking softly as I lift it up.

'Britt!' I scream, louder this time. 'Britt!'

I spin in a circle, my eyes searching every corner of the shop, even though I know she's not here. 'Britt! Shit...'

I fumble, digging around in my bag for my phone. When I find it, I call Triple Zero and wait impatiently for someone to answer. When a woman's voice comes on the line, my words tumble out in uneven bursts as I explain as best I can that my sister is missing.

She asks a few questions. My name, our relationship, when I last saw Britt, then instructs me to wait until the police arrive.

She hangs up, leaving me in a silence that suddenly feels too loud. My pulse hammers in my ears. I pace a few steps, then stop. The air around me feels heavier now that I've admitted out loud that she's gone.

I jump at the sudden vibration in my hand, then glance at the phone as my mother's name flashes across the screen. For a moment I just stare at it, trying to figure out what I'm going to say.

'Mum?'

'Junie, oh my God. Herm just told us,' she cries into my ear. 'We're on our way.'

'Wait, Herm told you?'

'He was here at the pub when the call came in from the State Police. We're all coming, Junie. We'll find her. We have to. I'll see you in a minute.'

I crouch to pick up Britt's bag and phone, and that's when I see it. The corner of a leather-bound journal stashed behind the store's Wi-Fi router. I flip it open and know right away that it doesn't belong to my sister. The writing is too loopy and neat. There's a page marker about halfway through. Britt must have been reading this before she disappeared. I quickly skip to the marked page.

1 March

I have to get pregnant again, like right now. It's the only way Bryce and I have a chance of being together. He already thinks I am, so it's not like he'll question it. When I tell him I couldn't go through with an abortion, it will be too late. I know he'll come around to the whole thing. My baby will be the heir to Willow's Crossing. All I have to do is get pregnant, and I've got two options. That creep Herm, who would almost do it in his pants at the opportunity to sleep with me again, and Britt's boyfriend Luke, who never takes his eyes off my tits. The thought of encouraging either of them makes my skin crawl, and I feel bad about Britt. I wasn't going to tell her about being pregnant, but I'm pretty sure she saw my test on the dresser the other day. She doesn't know I lost the baby, so she can vouch for me that it's true. I have to focus on the end goal. A baby, Bryce, and life at Willow's Crossing.

I stare down at the page in disbelief. This is Lilly's journal. Bryce got her pregnant, and then what happened? She lost her mind? She willingly let Herm have sex with her and seduced my sister's boyfriend all so she could trick Bryce into thinking he was still the father?

I sit back in the chair and try to steady my breathing. After what I saw of Bryce in the park, he would not have reacted well to finding out Lilly was pregnant. But what about Hazel? I glance out toward the empty road. Mum and Dad will be here any minute. I need to find out the rest, but I don't have much time.

4 March

Bryce keeps texting, asking if I've booked a date to go to Winton River, but I've been ignoring him. Last night I let Luke come over, and we did it in my room. Mum wasn't home, and I got rid of him as soon as it was over. I feel really shitty doing that to Britt, but I made him swear never to tell her. It's not like I want to steal him off her or anything. I've been to the police station a few times as well. Thinking about that makes it hard to sleep, so I have to put headphones on to try and block it out. It's like every time I close my eyes I can see and feel him. It's gross. But whoever ends up being the father won't matter. All anyone will ever think is that it's Bryce's baby, and like they say, it's not a lie if you believe it.

20 April

Shit, I got my period. I could have sworn one of those idiots had managed to get me pregnant. I should have known. They're both losers. Even worse, I saw Bryce in the park this morning with one of those Aboriginal girls. He wasn't 'with her, with her', not like he was with me, but I could see him leaning near our tree, and she was walking over to him. Not that I think he's going to start dating her or anything. Officially, he's still with Charlotte. But I need him focused on me. I'm going to tell him I'm keeping the baby and there's nothing he can do about it. That should get his attention.

Something bangs against the outside wall, and I almost leap out of my skin. I stand and peer out into the dark, but can't see anyone. It's probably just the wind. I take one last look around and then glance at my phone. It's been five minutes since Mum called. They must be almost here. I glance back at the journal. I have time to read a little more.

22 April

I went to Willow's Crossing tonight. I was going to wait outside and text Bryce to come out and talk to me. I thought in the dark with no one around, maybe we could get things back on track, but she was there. That Aboriginal girl from the park. I saw them walking back up toward the house from the paddocks, and he was holding her hand. Why would he do that? Does he actually like her?

26 April

I've asked around, and her name is Hazel Smith. Like, I guess she's pretty or whatever, but what's he thinking? He can't date her. His parents would have a fit. Jack hates the Aboriginals.

Outside, blue and red lights flood the petrol station driveway.

Herm's here. My parents' car pulls in right behind him.

There's no way I can give the journal to Herm, so reluctantly, I shove it into my handbag and step out from behind the counter. Outside, I can see my mum bent over. She's sobbing, and my dad is trying to comfort her. Herm glances in, says something to my parents, and then together they turn and walk toward the shop.

Jesus, Britt, where are you?

Chapter Thirty-Eight

WHEN Gerry arrives at my door, he has that look on his face – the same one as when I was a teenager. Part love, part sympathy, part doctor. Back then, he led me out of our family home to the car where Mum was waiting in the front seat. She'd given up trying to forcibly drag me out and instead left Gerry to *talk some sense into me*. Her head was down, her face mostly obscured by a scarf so no one in town would see them carting me off to the *funny farm*.

After a couple of weeks, the doctors at the Delta Clinic in Sydney's Northern Beaches diagnosed me with bipolar disorder. They said it involved a chemical imbalance that triggers depression, that it was why I'd tried to kill myself. At the time, I just stayed quiet and went along with it. It was better than telling them the truth – that I had PTSD as a result of Herm's constant sexual abuse. That most days, I wished for death, just to stop hearing and feeling him on me.

'Hey, Mi,' Gerry says with a sorrowful smile. 'Jason called. I guess you know why I'm here. Can I come in?'

I nod and pull Koda in closer.

'Your brother told me about Herm,' he says, as we sit down on the couch. 'I wish I'd known.'

I shrug and close my fingers tight around Koda's ear. Gerry stares down at his tan leather loafers.

'We could press charges against him,' he offers. 'It's not too late.

I imagine the feast everyone in town would have on that. As if they weren't already swollen, their seams bursting with stories about me and Will and what a failure I am. 'I'm not really up for that right now, Gerry.'

'Well, someone should.' He swallows and lifts his face to look at me. 'Jason said he thinks you need a break. Finding those girls would be a trigger for anyone with your past, Mia, but he says you think Herm and Jack are serial killers. Is that true? Do you think they're responsible for the deaths of Lilly Daniels and Hazel Smith?'

'No, I don't,' I say truthfully with a shake of my head.

Gerry smiles as best he can and breathes out. 'Well, good, because you know that's a little far-fetched, right?'

'I think it was Bryce.'

Gerry's shoulders sag, and his head drops forward. 'Mia, please trust me when I tell you, no one killed those girls. It was misadventure. Lilly died from exposure, and Hazel, well, just between you and me, I heard from the forensic pathologist in Winton River that she fell and hit her head.'

'Hit her head?'

'That's right.'

'But she was buried. And why would she be out there in the first place?'

'Mia, your brother told me it was you and Koda who went out and found her. I know you saw her remains firsthand, but it was dark and must have been a terribly upsetting experience. Are you certain she was intentionally buried? She had been out there almost a week in the wind and weather. Perhaps the elements covered her over, enough for Koda to have to dig just a little.'

I shake my head to try to clear my thoughts. 'That doesn't explain what she was doing out there.'

Gerry shrugs. 'There's been a lot of talk around town lately, mostly from your grandmother, about the Stantons stealing land. Jack's pressuring her to sell, and she's getting the entire First Nations community up in arms about it. Maybe Hazel went out there to try to damage his property in some way as payback or to cause trouble. You know what teens are like. I couldn't say for sure the reason, but she fell, Mia, maybe in the dark? I don't know. But it was an accident. They're going to release the findings later this week.'

My head is spinning. *That's what happened to Hazel? An accident?*

'Mia, I agree with your brother. You need care,' Gerry continues. 'Would you let me help you?'

'That's really what happened?'

'Yes.'

I close my eyes and try to think. 'You know the medical team over at Winton River. When they did Lilly's autopsy, was she pregnant?'

'Pregnant?' Gerry asks, sitting back. 'No, not that I'm aware of.'

'You're certain?'

Gerry nods. 'There was nothing to suggest that in the report.'

Lilly wasn't pregnant. Britt must have been mistaken. That means Bryce had no reason to kill her, and Hazel died because she fell. It was just an accident.

'Mia, have you thought about harming yourself?' Gerry is asking.

I shake my head. 'No, I'd never leave Koda.'

'Is that the only reason?'

'I only need one.'

He nods slowly. 'Koda needs you to be well, Mia. So do a lot of other people.'

'Like?'

'Like all those who'll be heading up the mountain.'

I roll my eyes. The thought of caring about strangers up on the mountain seems impossible when my entire world is crashing down around me.

'I'm not sure I have it in me to rescue people at the moment, Gerry.'

'It mattered to you once.'

'So did a lot of things.'

'You still have a life, Mia, even without Will.'

'But I don't want it,' I say with a sigh. 'I grew up in the dirt, Gerry. I should have known. Girls like me don't get to be with men like him. I should have known this would happen eventually.'

His face pulls tight, and I catch the pulse of his jaw.

'I don't mean I'm going to kill myself. I'm just saying, this, what's left, I don't want it. I can't stop thinking about him there with her. It's too much.'

It's a mistake to cry, but I can't hold it in. I fold myself over and begin to sob. Heaving, wracking, choking tears that steal my breath. Gerry pulls me into an embrace. He smells like Old Spice, the way a father should, and it's better and worse all at once.

'Let me help you, Mia,' he whispers. 'I could write you a script, but I'd rather you not be here alone and medicated. I know you have Koda, but what if there's a minute, just one minute, that it's not enough? What if...'

'I won't, Gerry,' I manage between sobs. 'That was a long time ago.'

'But going away, it helped you back then, didn't it? It provided you with some space to think and breathe.'

'That was different. I did it because of him.'

'You did it was because of the trauma he caused. This isn't so different,' Gerry says, pulling back to look at me. 'Will betrayed you, and finding those girls... There's no shame in feeling things, Mia. I just want someone to be there to guide you through that process. To build a house, first you need a solid foundation. Do you understand? To rebuild your life, first we need to fix what's broken. There are people who can help you do that. You don't need to do it all by yourself.'

'But Koda...'

'I'll take care of Koda,' he says.

'Mum would never—'

'Let me deal with Mum.'

I sniff and glance down at Koda. I would never take my life and leave him alone. Never intentionally. But what if Gerry is right? If none of what I thought is true, then how can I trust my own judgement? When I tried to take my life, it wasn't meticulously planned out the way some people do it, the way they find peace in planning the details of their death. For me, it was impulsive and desperate. I didn't think it through at all. I didn't consider how it would feel, what pain it would cause Jason, or even the finality of it if I'm being honest. I just wanted to be able to close my eyes without feeling his hands on me. I would have done anything to exorcise the ghost of him that hovered over me everywhere I went. It had taken only a few minutes to make the decision. Even less to take the knife out from the kitchen drawer. Gerry's words echo in my mind. *What if...*

'How long would I have to stay there?

'Just a week. Just so I know that you're safe.'

'I'm scared, Gerry. I don't want to be away from Koda.'

'You can't be a good mum to him like this, Mia. He needs you to take care of him, and right now you're not even taking care of yourself.'

I cup Koda's face in my hands and look into his eyes. He's the best friend I've ever had. He depends on me for everything. His entire life is dictated by what I do and what I provide. His food, his walks, where he sleeps, where we go, and what we do. Every part of his day is decided by me. What if I make the wrong choice? What if I'm not paying attention and something happens to him? What if he has to watch me die?

'Just a week and then I'm coming home,' I say with a sigh. 'No longer.'

'Would you like me to take Koda to the house?'

'No,' I say, shaking my head. 'I want him to go with Mimi.'

Not so long ago, I wouldn't have dreamed of leaving Koda with anyone, especially Mimi, but I know in my heart that's where he will be safe.

Instead of questioning it, Gerry nods and tells me he'll make sure Koda gets there safely.

'Get some things packed. I'll go and make all the arrangements. I'll be back to collect you in an hour.'

Chapter Thirty-Nine

Juniper

HERM has assured us he'll do everything in his power to find Britt, but as we wait back at the house for an update, I'm filled with a growing sense of unease. After everything I've learned, how can we trust him to do the right thing? I quickly decide that if she isn't found in the next hour, I'm taking matters into my own hands. To hell with him if he thinks I'll just sit here hoping he'll do his job. Britt is my sister. Even if she can't depend on Herm, she can depend on me.

I take out the journal and open it up to the last page I read. Maybe there's something inside that triggered Britt to react. I can only hope the answer to where she is might be in the pages of Lilly's journal.

28 April

I don't know how it happened. It just did. Now everything has changed. Last night I went back to Willow's Crossing. I just wanted to talk to Bryce, but as I walked up the path, I heard laughing. It was far away, but I knew in my gut it was her, that bitch Hazel. He was with her again. With every step, I got angrier and angrier. Who was she to get in the way of my plans? I kept hearing her voice, like it was guiding me or something, like it was supposed to happen. When I found them, they were out in the paddock. She was trying to pull her dress back on. I shouted that she was a slut, and Bryce immediately took her side. The worst part was when he pulled her in behind him like he was protecting her from me. I hated her so much when he did that, like I could have just ripped the skin right off her bones. I'd had his baby inside me. She was nothing and no one. I shouted that I was keeping the baby, and she started crying. When he turned around to console her, I picked up a rock and held it behind my back. Then, just like it was meant to be, one of the cows bellowed, and he stepped away to see if something was there. I swear it just happened on its own. I don't remember thinking anything or deciding to do it, but next minute, Hazel was on the ground, her head caved in, and my fingers wrapped around the rock. It was all warm and sticky and covered in blood. In the moonlight it looked black instead of red. I was thinking about that when Bryce pushed me so hard that I fell. He crouched over her and kept shouting, 'What did you do? What did you do?' I just sat there like I was numb. I should have freaked out, but I didn't feel anything. When Bryce turned around, even in the dark, I could see his face was pale and tears were pouring down his cheeks. When he yelled that he was calling Herm, I didn't know what to do, so I threatened to tell everyone that he was the one who killed Hazel. I'd say he brought her out here to tell her it was over because we were having a baby. I'd say I made him let me be there, so I knew for sure he'd told her. They got into a fight. She pushed him, and he pushed her back. She fell and hit her head. That's what I'd say. When he realised I was serious, he sank to the ground. It was weird because all of a sudden, I wondered what I ever saw in him anyway. Crying like that over some Aboriginal girl. I realised I didn't even want his stupid baby. Then, just like that, it was clear to me. I didn't need to be pregnant. I already had enough leverage over Bryce Stanton to make him give me anything I wanted.

I gasp and stare down at the page. Lilly killed Hazel. Then she planned to blackmail Bryce. In the days that followed, she must have managed to push him over the edge. Enough to make him kill her. I leaf through the journal. There's only two entries left.

29 April

Now that I have Hazel's death to hold over Bryce, it doesn't matter if he finds out I'm not pregnant. I've told him I want $250,000, or I'm telling the police. Not Herm, the real ones in Winton River. As soon as he pays up, I'm getting the hell out of here and never coming back. Maybe I'll go to Europe or America. I could be a model or an actress. With that much money, I can be anything I want.

1 May

It's been two days. He still hasn't paid. He thinks he can bluff me. He has no idea who he's dealing with. I've just told him I'm going to tell Herm. At the very least, he'll shit himself that his dad will find out. Maybe that will change his mind about paying.

I flip the page, and when there are no more entries, I close the cover over.

Britt must have read this and let her emotions get the better of her. She must have called or texted him. I put the journal down and shake my head in disbelief. Why would Britt do that without telling me?

Then I remember the page marker. It was tucked into the middle of the journal. Britt didn't get up to the part where Lilly threatened Bryce.

None of it makes any sense, and time is ticking. I grab my keys and head toward the front door.

'Where are you going?' Mum calls from the couch where she's tucked up under Dad's arm like a broken baby bird.

'Just for a drive to clear my head,' I tell her. 'I won't be long.'

Everything points to Bryce picking up Lilly and then killing her. Now my sister is missing. Lilly didn't have anyone to look out for her, but Britt has me, and I'm not wasting any more time.

I pull up outside Mia's house and almost leap out of the car. There's a light on inside. She's home.

Racing up the path, I try to un-jumble the words crashing around inside my head. I need to tell her everything I read in the journal. She needs to know that we were right about Bryce, but when she opens the door, I'm suddenly no longer worried about how to explain it. Her hair is tied up in a haphazard ponytail, and her pink T-shirt has at least three stains down the front. From the smell of her, I don't think she's showered in days.

'Mia, what the hell?' I gasp as I stare at her, my mouth open in shock. She doesn't answer right away, and I glance over her shoulder into the living room. What could be a cosy room room is a mess of neglect. Dust motes drift through the air like ghosts. The couch sags beneath a pile of clothes, and a half-empty wine glass sits on the floor beside it. Even the fireplace looks tired, its cold mouth full of days old ash.

'Will left me. He's in love with Jessica. Gerry is taking me to a *clinic*,' she says, using her fingers to create inverted commas in the air. 'It's for the best.'

Her tone is flat, accepting. I have no idea who this person is or what's happened to the Mia I've been getting to know, but this isn't her.

'Mia, listen to me,' I begin. 'Lilly had a journal. There's so much I need to tell you, but Bryce killed her, and Britt is missing. I don't know for sure, but he may have taken her to the national park just like he did with Lilly.'

I expect her to stare at me wide-eyed and worried, but there's almost no reaction at all. 'Mia, did you hear me? Bryce killed Lilly. Britt is missing. We need to find her.'

She continues to just stand there, holding onto the doorframe and staring at me through vacant eyes.

'Gerry will be back any minute,' she manages. 'He's taking me to Sydney.'

Frustration pulls at my chest, and I will myself to stay calm. I step forward and wave my hand in front of her face. 'Mia, did you hear what I said? Britt is missing.'

She shrugs, and I want to slap her, just to see if it shocks her back from whatever dark place she's gone to in her head. 'Can I come in?' I ask instead.

'He'll be back any minute.'

Certain she won't stop me, I step inside and try not to gasp at the state of her house. The curtains are drawn, stopping the outside world from pressing in against the glass. The television screen glows faint blue, soundless, and casting shapes across the floor. Mugs and crumb-speckled plates crowd the coffee table, and on a dish sits a candle that's been lit for so long it's puddled into itself.

'Mia, please listen to me,' I try, drawing my eyes back to her. 'I need your help.'

Koda presses himself against her leg, his eyes never leaving hers.

'Hazel fell and hit her head. And Lilly wasn't pregnant,' she says, her voice no louder than a whisper. 'No one did anything. It was all in my head.'

'What? No, Mi.' I step in close and peer at her. 'I read Lilly's journal. She was pregnant. Bryce was the father, but she lost the baby. She was the one who killed Hazel. She wrote it herself in the journal.'

Mia gazes at me, and I can see a part of her mind ticking over. 'She did?'

'It's not in your head.'

'It's not?'

'Come with me.' I gently guide her to the kitchen and sit her down at the table. 'I'm going to make you a coffee.'

As I boil the kettle, Mia strokes Koda's head and manages to smile at him.

'It's normal to be upset after a breakup,' I begin. 'And you've been through a lot. It would be strange if you weren't upset. That doesn't mean you need to be institutionalised.'

'But I tried to kill myself.'

I spin around and stare at her in shock. 'Tonight?'

'No, when I was a teenager,' she tells me, her voice empty. 'Because of Herm.'

My heart aches for her. I want to say the right thing, something that will make her realise she's stronger than this. 'That was a long time ago,' I tell her. 'You were just a kid. Whose idea was it for you to go into care?'

'My stepfather... and my brother.'

I nod slowly, the pieces falling into place. Potentially upsetting Jack so close to launching his drilling project is the last thing Jason Thomas would want, but I can't believe he's gone so far as to try to have his own sister sent to a mental health in-patient centre.

'Mia, listen to me,' I say, putting the steaming mug of coffee down in front of her. 'You do not need to go to a treatment centre. I saw you the night you came to rescue me. You're a strong and accomplished woman. I've never met anyone who can go out and do the things you do. I was genuinely awe-struck that night. Do not let your brother or anyone ever tell you that you're anything less than perfect, exactly how you are. If Will can't see that or it doesn't suit Jason's agenda, then screw them, Mia. Do you hear me? Screw them. You have Koda, and you have me. That's all you need.'

Mia's eyes linger on mine. She thinks a moment, then slowly pushes up out of her chair. She's unsteady on her feet, but finally taking it in. 'Yeah,' she whispers eventually. 'You're right. Screw them.'

Chapter Forty

I WARM my hands on the mug of coffee and try to brush the cobwebs from my mind. Since I was a child, all I ever wanted was to be like my brother, but as the years passed, and it became clear I never would be, a single question hung over me – how do you forgive yourself for all the things you never become?

Maybe I did put myself in situations for Herm to abuse me. Maybe I did lash out instead of letting people in. Maybe I did push Will away because deep down I thought I didn't deserve him. Maybe I tried everything I could to punish myself just for being me.

But what if Juniper is right? I might not be Jason, but perhaps it's time to ask myself a new question. *What's so wrong with being me?*

There are things I can do that he can't. Things I have that he doesn't. Things I won't stand for that he will – and one of those things is letting the men of this town think they can do whatever they want.

Edgar Stanton stole most of the farming land in

Wildling from the First Nations people. Since then, every generation of Stanton men has taught their sons they're better than everyone else, that they're smarter and more deserving. As a result, Jack grew up to be heartless and shrewd, his son Bryce watching on with feverish intent, destined to inherit his father's privilege and intolerance. Now he thinks he can get away with murder.

If no one acts, this will be the legacy of Wildling – a patriarchy that allows young women to be abused and murdered at the whim of white men carrying a licence of wealth and power around in their pocket.

'Do you think Jack knows what Bryce did and is covering for him?' I ask.

Juniper thinks about it and then nods. 'From how he reacted to Britt at the dinner, I'd say yes.'

'And Herm. He knew that Hazel was out there.' I shake my head in disbelief. 'This has to stop,' I whisper, mostly to Juniper, but also to myself. 'They're monsters.'

'I know,' she agrees, 'but Mia, we have to find Britt. I can't do it without you and Koda.'

'You're certain he would have taken her out to the park?'

'No, but he killed Lilly, and that's where you found her.'

We both turn at once as Koda barks and steps into the hall.

'Sorry, the door was unlocked,' Gerry says, glancing back over his shoulder. 'I was worried that maybe...'

He stops in the doorway and glances at Juniper. Behind

him is Jason.

'I'm fine, Gerry. In fact, I think I'm better than I have been in a while.'

'But you're still going to the centre,' Jason adds. 'You have to, Mia.'

My perfect brother, with the entire world stretched out at his feet. In his way, he loves me. Enough to convince himself that sending me away is as much for my own good as it is his. In his mind, I get a week of care and comfort, he gets his proposal signed off, and Jack gets to feel like he gave the final nod. Everyone wins. It's how things always go, but not today. Not anymore.

'No,' I tell him, the strength of my voice surprising me. 'Bryce killed Lilly. Now Britt is missing, and I'm going to find her.'

'Not this again,' he says, throwing up his arms. 'Mia, this is ridiculous. First it was Herm, then Jack, now Bryce. This is exactly why you need to go. You're spiralling. Gerry, tell her. She's not well.'

'She doesn't need to go anywhere,' Juniper says, stepping in. 'Bryce does have my sister, and he did kill Lilly. None of this is in Mia's head, and you should be ashamed of yourself for treating her this way. The both of you.'

Gerry peers at me, clearly assessing the situation. 'Mia, if you don't believe you need to go, I'm certainly not going to force you, and if those girls died at the hands of someone, then your friend is right. We need to call the police.'

But Jason isn't having it. 'Gerry, don't let her fool you. She needs help. Just listen to what she's suggesting. It's crazy. The Stantons aren't serial killers.'

'Actually, what I see is a bright young woman who seems quite sure of herself,' Gerry says. 'If there is proof of what you're saying, then removing the one person able to go out and find young Britt seems a very irresponsible thing to do.'

'You've got to be joking.'

'You're sure about this, Mia?' Gerry asks me.

'I am, and we're wasting time. Britt needs our help.'

'Mia, you can't,' Jason objects, stepping forward. 'You can't go out traipsing around in the dark and the snow chasing monsters that don't exist.'

His hands are balled into fists at his sides, and his jaw is tight. This might be the first time my brother has ever been told no, but no matter how hard it is for him to swallow, I'm going to search for Britt.

'The only thing that doesn't exist, Jason, is your ability to concede that maybe, just this once, you're wrong,' I tell him. 'Now get out of my way. Koda and I have a job to do.'

Chapter Forty-One
Juniper

WATCHING Mia stand up to her brother was a revelation. She reclaimed herself. Right there, in that little kitchen with its round wooden table and yellow chequered curtains, she gathered herself the way a storm gathers on the horizon.

When I returned to Wildling, it was without a clue what I would do. I had two options. Save my career or shackle myself to a belief I'd always thought of as liberating – that in Wildling, I was special.

Now there is no doubt in my mind. With Mia's help, I can save my sister, pull her in tight, and stitch together the space that has grown between us. Then I will kick the shit out of this town and everyone in it who thinks they can dictate or destroy other people's lives. I'll ink the names of men who, for too long, have hidden behind sprawling fences and prestigious surnames. Jack, Herm, and Bryce. Daylight will finally shine on the rot they've buried.

'You're incredible,' I tell Mia as she gathers her search-and-rescue gear from a bedroom closet. 'I'd say that it's beyond me why you let the people in this town con-vince you otherwise, but I grew up in Wildling, too, so trust me, I get it.'

'All that matters now is we find Britt,' she says, determi-nation rising in her voice. 'We've already wasted too much time. How long has she been missing?'

I glance at my watch. 'Two hours, but Britt's smart. If anyone can survive this, it's her, and besides, I'd know if something had happened. I'd feel it.'

'If she's out there, Koda and I will find her. You have my word.'

'We will,' I reply in a bid to reassure myself. 'We'll find her.'

Mia stops what she's doing and catches my eye. 'Not *we*, Juniper,' she tells me. 'No offence, but you'll just slow us down out there.'

My chest falls, but I know she's right. The last time I went out into the park, it was Mia who had to save me, but I want to help, and there might be something else I can do. 'Okay, while you search, I'll go to Willow's Crossing,' I tell her. 'Sarah is a good person. She wouldn't want this. I think she'll help us, maybe even get a hold of Bryce and bring him around. She's his mother, after all.'

'You think she'll listen to you?'

'I was almost her daughter-in-law once,' I reply. 'I'd like to think so.'

I watch as Mia spreads everything out across the bed

and points at each item, mentally ticking them off. In my pocket, my mobile phone vibrates, and I see my mother's name on the screen. 'Shit, it's my mum. She and Dad aren't coping very well.'

'They've been through a lot,' Mia says as she places Koda's chew rope into her pack. 'You go take care of your family and speak to Sarah. Koda and I will head to the ranger station. I'll call Daley on the way. He won't like this, but I'm going. You have my word. If Britt's out there, we'll find her. I promise.'

Chapter Forty-Two
Juniper

WHEN I call Mum, she tells me the State Police are at the house going over every detail of Britt's movements before she went missing. That's what they're calling it. *Missing.* Not kidnapped or taken – missing.

Out in front, my headlights devour the dark, and I think about my sister. All the times she must have swallowed Mum's suggestions that she should be more like me. How desperate she must have been for our parents to actually see her, to love her for the incredible girl she is. Maybe if I'd realised sooner, I could have saved Britt from getting caught up in Lilly's drama. I could have told her that she can and should be whoever she wants.

I drive along Wildling Road towards Willow's Crossing. Up ahead, the house is lit up, light spilling from the ground-floor windows. There's no turning back now. After Britt's accusation at dinner the other night, they'll know why I'm here. My stomach twists, and I whisper to myself to stay calm. *They're just people, Juniper,* I remind myself. *Britt is counting on you.*

Relief washes over me when it's Sarah who opens the door instead of Jack.

'Sarah, I need to find Britt,' I blurt, skipping any pleasantries. 'I think Bryce may know something about her disappearance. Can I come in?'

She nods and steps aside. 'Jack isn't home, but let's talk in the library. It's more comfortable.'

I follow her through the entry foyer and notice for the first time how small she looks. Dwarfed by the enormity of the house, Sarah seems fragile as she makes her way down the corridor, moving through a world built for someone much bigger than her – someone like Jack.

When we reach the library, she ushers me in and closes the door. Inside, the room feels different from the rest of the house. Still grand, with soaring mahogany bookshelves and a crackling fire, but there's a warmth to it, a cosiness the other spaces lack. Instead of dark floors and sharp edges, the library is decorated with rugs and cushions. It's softer, feminine – undoubtedly Sarah's place in the house. On the wall hangs a collection of photos of her as a teenager with her sister beside her. Riding horses, running through paddocks, and laughing at a joke no one else could hear.

'Sarah, you of all people must understand how it feels to lose a sister,' I begin, pulling my eyes back to her. 'I've made so many mistakes with Britt. I feel responsible for all of this. I need your help. Please, I need to bring her home safely.'

With a soft sigh, she lowers herself onto the oversized cream couch and twirls her wedding band.

'The police were here.'

'They were?'

'Looking for Jack. Not much happens in Wildling he doesn't know about, so of course this was their first stop.' She leans back against the sofa and stares into the fire. 'He's not here, though, so...'

'Sarah, I found a journal. It belonged to Lilly. It said—'

Before I can finish, Sarah scoffs, catching me off guard. She's always been so polite, so graceful, that the coarse sound feels out of character coming from her.

'That's why you're here?' she asks. 'Well, I'm sorry, Juniper, but I find it difficult to believe that someone like you, an intelligent woman with the tenacity to leave Wildling and move to Sydney to become a journalist, would believe anything a girl like Lilly Daniels wrote in a journal. You know what she was like, and that mother of hers, goodness.' She touches her hand to her chest. 'What happened is unfortunate, of course, but they were hardly upstanding citizens. You must know that.'

'With all due respect, Sarah, that doesn't mean she was a liar.'

Sarah smooths an invisible crease in her linen pants. 'You said Bryce might know where Britt is. Why would you think that? I don't believe he even knows her apart from being your sister, of course.'

I nod, scrambling for what to say next. Of course, she wants to protect her son, but I need to convince her that the best way to do that is by helping me.

'You know how I feel about Bryce. I was going to marry him. You and Jack have felt like family to me my whole life, and I hate that I'm here, Sarah, I hate it, but Britt is my blood.' I pause, then push on. 'The journal said Lilly killed Hazel out in your paddocks. She was jealous of a relationship Hazel had with Bryce. It was an accident of sorts, but you're right about her character. She was blackmailing your son, demanding money not to frame him. Maybe he just wanted it to all go away, to make sure you and Jack didn't find out and think the worst of him. Britt read at least part of the journal. Maybe she confronted him, and he panicked, but we can make this right before it's too late.'

'She was an awful girl.' Sarah stares across the room, her eyes fixed on the photos. 'Just awful.'

'After reading that journal, I couldn't agree more. But we need to focus on Britt. If Bryce has anything to do with what's happened, he could be arrested. You don't want that, do you?' I follow her gaze over to the wall. 'You know what it's like to lose a sister. I can't let that happen.'

Sarah's face hardens, her mouth tightening into a thin line. 'You and Britt are so different. She was never like you, Juniper. It must have been difficult for her, watching you, beloved by the entire town. I imagine she was quite resentful. That's what it's like with sisters.' She turns back, and I notice her eyes have changed. 'Have you ever thought that perhaps Britt concocted this whole gone-missing drama just to punish you?'

'No,' I say, shaking my head. 'She wouldn't do that.'

'Wouldn't she? You'd be surprised how devious younger sisters can be.'

'She wouldn't go this far.'

'When we were young, my sister Missy was a lot like you.'

Frustration knots in my chest. I didn't come here to reminisce about Missy. I need her help to find my sister. 'I'd love to hear more about her someday, Sarah, I really would, but like I said—'

'—and I was a lot like Britt,' she continues, as if I'm not even in the room. 'You wouldn't think so now, of course, but it's true. My father, oh, how he loved Missy. She was just perfect.'

'Sarah—'

'I'm telling you this, Juniper, because I was once the younger sister desperate for attention. Never good enough. Always overlooked. I would have done absolutely anything to be Missy, to feel what it was like. Everyone making a fuss, and saying my name as though I mattered. I'm sure that's just what Britt is doing now. My Bryce wouldn't hurt anyone. He doesn't have it in him. It bothers Jack, you know, how weak he is, but he's always been that way. Even as a boy, he'd never let go of my hand. I loved it, to tell you the truth. There's no love comparable to that between a mother and her son. Especially a boy like Bryce. He always needed me, and that hasn't changed, Juniper. I'm his mother. You need to understand that. So, I'm sorry you came all this way, but I really can't help you.'

Chapter Forty-Three

TWO girls have already been found dead in or near Wildling National Park in the past week. Now that Britt has gone missing, it's only a matter of time before the police call Daley, asking for a canine search and rescue team to go into the park and look for her. This way, we're just being proactive. At least, that's how I plan to spin it. Normally, police make the request. Until then, technically, we can't participate in an investigation, but I'm hoping Daley will understand the gravity of the situation, especially after I explain what Juniper read in Lilly Daniels' journal.

When I pull up outside the station, Daley's truck is parked in the lot, and the light is on inside. It's almost nine o'clock at night. By now everyone else will have gone home, which is probably a good thing.

My boots crunch on the icy ground as I walk around to the back of my vehicle and let Koda out. I grab our gear and head inside, bracing for Daley's reaction. To my surprise, I find him in the control room, leaning over the table and checking off his pack items.

'Daley?'

He stops packing and looks up. 'Thomas, you're here. Good. You and Koda ready?'

'Just like that?' I ask, thrown by how easy it seems.

'Jack called. The police went to Willow's Crossing asking questions. He wants Britt located ASAP and without all the fuss. After Hazel was found on his property, he doesn't want this *turning into another circus.* Quote, unquote. That means it's me and you kid, at least for now.' He clears his throat, and I know there's more. 'He also mentioned you were out with Mimi and the Smith family doing some kind of ritual on his property line yesterday.'

'Right...' I say with a sigh. 'What do you want to hear?'

'What I want to hear, Thomas, is that you weren't out on Willow's Crossing uninvited looking for Hazel's remains, and that it wasn't you doing some kind of hoodoo with your grandmother.'

'Daley...' I trail off because I can't lie to him.

'Goddamn it, Thomas,' he snaps. 'What were you thinking?'

'That Hazel was murdered and left to rot in Jack's paddock, and maybe whoever did it also killed Lilly Daniels.'

'And?'

'I was wrong. Lilly killed Hazel. Then I think Bryce killed Lilly.'

'Care to explain your theory?'

'I will, Daley, but we need to get moving. If I'm right,

every second Britt is alone with Bryce, she's in danger.'

'You really think the Stanton kid has it in him?'

'You don't?'

He tilts his head, thoughtful. 'Honestly? No, the kid's a pussy. Spent half his life hanging off Sarah's skirt in one way or another.'

'It has to be him, Daley. Nothing else makes sense.'

He huffs out a breath and gathers his gear. 'If you say so, Thomas. Either way, let's go find them.'

THE night air is frigid as Daley and I jog beside Koda. Given Bryce's inexperience and likely fragile emotional state, we're banking on the fact he'll try to repeat what worked with Lilly – killing her, then tossing her body into a ravine somewhere nearby.

Starting at the boundary fence between Willow's Crossing and the park, I give Koda a scrap of material from a jacket Britt left in the back of Juniper's car. I hate running him at night. It's dangerous navigating rough terrain in the dark, but waiting until morning could cost Britt her life.

Our headlamps bob along the track as we run deeper into the park. Koda is out in front, bracketing, but not in scent.

'Anything?' Daley huffs, the past few years spent behind a desk catching up to him.

'Not yet. When he picks it up, you'll know.'

Right on cue, Koda stops and lifts his nose. I raise a

hand for Daley to wait. Three sharp barks and Koda pulls forward, but instead of tracking ground scent, his nose is to the air.

'Something's not right,' I call back, as Daley and I chase after him. 'He's not tracking Britt.'

'How can you tell?'

'He's air-scenting. Shit, Daley, this is about to get tricky.'

At low elevations, the national park is full of trees and dense foliage. That means whenever the airflow hits a cluster of trees, it changes direction, forcing Koda to constantly reassess the scent trail.

'Has he picked up Britt's scent?'

'I don't think so,' I shout. 'If they'd come this way on foot, he'd be following ground scent.'

'So, who are we chasing?' Daley calls.

'Not sure, but if I know Koda, we'll find out soon enough.'

As expected, Koda pulls ahead, then slows, nose to the wind. He drifts right, then left, sifting through invisible threads of scent until he finds the one he's looking for.

For the next hour, we crisscross through the park, Koda looping, circling back, then surging forward in a different direction.

'What's... he... doing?' Daley pants, almost spent.

'It's not like in the movies, Daley. He's not Lassie. Sometimes it's messy.'

Suddenly, Koda stiffens, energy surging through the

lead. He's found the scent cone.

'Almost there,' I shout. 'Not much further.'

Branches whip my face as we push forward. Koda's bark is wild and frenzied. Whoever he's tracking is only metres away.

'Catch up!' I yell. 'Now!'

The sound of Daley's laboured breathing grows closer until he's beside me.

'Not bad for an ageing desk jockey,' I manage.

'Can it, Thomas,' he fires back. 'I've got more hours in the field than you've had roast dinners.'

Koda halts, staring into the darkness, barking and pulling so hard against his harness that I struggle to keep my footing. Whoever he's tracking is just beyond the tree line. Daley draws his gun.

'NSW Parks and Wildlife,' he calls. 'Come out slowly. Hands where I can see them.'

My hands tremble with nerves and adrenaline. Whoever emerges could be armed. It could be Bryce with Britt. Anything could be about to happen.

'You've got until the count of three, then we're sending the dog in,' Daley warns.

I snap my head to look at him, but he just shrugs, eyes trained forward. Koda knows the command for attack, but that's something I keep to myself. We've never had cause to use it, but it's important he knows when to protect himself and me should the situation ever arise.

There's movement behind one of the snow gums. Koda growls, straining at his harness.

'Easy, mate,' I tell him. 'Easy.'

'Slowly,' Daley calls. 'No sudden moves. My gun is drawn.'

'Don't shoot,' a nervous voice pleads. 'Please, it's just me, Bryce Stanton.'

'Are you alone?'

'Yes, I'm alone.' He steps out from behind the tree. 'Don't hurt me, please. I didn't do anything.'

Chapter Forty-Four

DALEY steps forward, his gun trained on Bryce. 'Hands where I can see them!'

Bryce freezes, eyes wide, trembling as he slowly raises his arms.

'Where's Britt?' Daley demands, taking a step closer. 'What have you done with her?'

I watch Bryce closely, trying to read him. His lips part, but only a shaky exhale escapes.

'I... I don't know where she is,' he stammers, eyes darting between Daley and me. He shifts his weight, and I catch the faintest trace of mud on his shoes. Even from here, I can see that it matches the terrain we've been searching.

Daley's gun and torch are crossed, both aimed at Bryce. 'Don't make this harder than it has to be, kid.'

'I... I don't know where she is, I swear,' Bryce insists. 'I've been out here looking for her too. She might still be alive.'

My skin prickles. 'What do you mean, *she might still be alive?*'

In the torchlight, Bryce looks like he's about to cry. 'It's all my fault.'

Despite Daley's gun on him, Bryce drops to his knees and begins to sob. Around us, the bush falls silent, holding its breath. Daley lowers his weapon slightly, suspicion and confusion flickering across his face. 'What are you talking about?'

'Mum,' Bryce manages. 'Oh, God. What have I done?'

As his body heaves, my mind races. We thought Bryce picked Lilly up from the station to stop her framing him for Hazel's death, but what if he didn't? What if he'd told his mother what happened, and she was the one who collected Lilly?

'Bryce, tell us what happened,' I try. 'There's still a chance we can find Britt alive.'

He nods, wiping his face with his sleeve. 'It all just happened,' he says. 'Mum and I were heading back from town, and we stopped to fill up. I pumped petrol, and she went in to put it on Dad's account. Next thing I knew, through the window, I saw her and Britt fighting. I ran in, and it was chaos. They were both shouting and screaming. Mum was trying to drag her out of the shop. I finally figured out what was going on. Britt knew I got Lilly pregnant and jumped to the conclusion that I was the one who killed her. Mum said we had to bring her back to Willow's Crossing. Make sure she kept her mouth shut. That's what I thought we were doing.'

'And then?'

He shakes his head, staring out into the darkness. 'Mum made me take her out to the barn. After that, she told me to go back into the house and stay there. I didn't want to because of Lilly, but—'

'Wait. What do you mean because of Lilly?'

Bryce closes his eyes. 'She'd been hassling me. Demanding money or she'd say I killed Hazel. It was a quarter of a million dollars. Mum said she'd fix everything. I thought she meant by paying her off. I didn't know she was going to...'

'Christ, Daley,' I breathe. 'It was Sarah who picked Lilly up from the station that day.'

'But Britt's different,' he continues. 'She was almost family. I went back inside, and when Mum wasn't gone long, I figured she'd just tied her up, you know, to make her sweat it for a while. I waited half an hour, then snuck back down to the barn to let her go. When she wasn't there, I came out here because of where we put Lilly. I was hoping maybe Mum just left here out here or something. That she was still alive.'

'It was you who put Lilly's body in the ravine?'

'I mean, I didn't kill her,' he says with a shrug, 'but she as too heavy for Mum to carry.'

Despite his initial crying, Bryce's reaction when he speaks about Lilly seems detached and emotionless, like she wasn't even a real person.

'Shit,' I mutter, snapping back. 'Juniper went to Willow's Crossing to ask Sarah for help.'

Bryce gasps. 'Junie went to our place? No, no, no...'

I pull out my phone, scroll to Juniper's name, and hit call. After a few rings, it drops out. 'No answer.'

'Call your mother,' Daley snaps at Bryce. 'Now.'

Beside me, Koda whines. 'You're okay, mate,' I soothe, handing him his tug rope as a reward while Bryce dials.

'Put it on speaker,' Daley orders.

The phone rings out, and Bryce shakes his head. 'No answer from Mum either.'

'Shit,' Daley mutters. 'Where's Jack?'

'He wasn't home.'

Daley and I exchange a look. A cold realisation settles in my gut that Britt and Juniper might already be dead.

'Koda didn't pick up Britt's scent out here. Only yours,' I tell Bryce. 'That means she hasn't been anywhere near here. Where else would your mother take her? Maybe Juniper, too?'

He squeezes his eyes shut, shaking his head.

'Think!' Daley shouts. 'Where would she take them?'

'I... I don't know.'

'We can't waste any more time,' I snap. 'Bryce, you have to tell the police everything you just told us.'

'No!' His head jerks up. 'I can't. Mum will go to jail. She was only trying to protect me.'

'Bryce, she killed Lilly and kidnapped Britt. Probably

Juniper now, too.'

Daley tucks his gun and torch away, marches over, and hauls Bryce up by the elbow. 'I've had enough. I'm calling the state police and taking you back to Willow's Crossing.'

'No, you can't!'

In one swift movement, Bryce pulls a pocketknife from his pocket and drives it into Daley's side. He gasps and lets go. Bryce stares at him for a moment, the shock of what he's done obvious in his eyes. Then he turns and bolts into the bush, instantly swallowed up by the dark.

I consider sending Koda after him, but he has a weapon. Instead, I drop to Daley's side.

'Move your arm,' I tell him, pulling out my flashlight. 'Let me see.'

The wound is shallow. Not life threatening.

'Little prick,' Daley growls, pressing a hand to it. 'He's going to pay for that.'

'Call it in,' I tell him. 'I'll put an emergency dressing on this.'

Daley radios the state police while I take a small medical kit out of my pack and press gauze against the wound. 'Britt's not out here,' I say. 'Koda would have picked up her scent.'

'Then she's in one of the buildings at Willow's Crossing.'

'Bryce said he already checked the property.'

'Maybe he did, but not like Koda will.'

'You can't search Jack's property without a police request, Thomas, you'll lose your credentials.'

'I know, but Britt's in trouble and it's time someone stood up to the Stantons.' I meet Daley's eye. 'I'll worry about my credentials tomorrow. Tonight, I'm going to do what someone should have done a long time ago – show the Stantons they don't control this town.'

Chapter Forty-Five
Juniper

SOMETHING isn't right about Sarah. That night in the bar with the gangster Stephano, I knew something was lingering just beneath the surface, something crawling up the back of his throat, just dying to get out. Watching Sarah now, I feel the same way. Just a little push, and perhaps I can get it out of her.

'You might be right, Sarah,' I begin. 'Maybe Britt is just doing this to get back at me. I haven't been a very good sister.' I pause and feign reflection. 'There were so many times I let Mum and Dad act as though I was better than her. Even with Bryce. She never said anything, but I know she always had a crush on him.'

'Missy was the same,' Sarah says, gazing back at the wall. 'Always taking, taking, taking. Everything was always about *her*.'

'That must have been hard on you.'

'Well, like I said before, the thing about younger sisters is that they can be quite conniving.'

'Like Britt.'

'And like me, I suppose.'

'You? I can't imagine that.'

She grins faintly, her eyes dropping. 'Let's just say I wasn't always the pride of Wildling.'

'No, of course not, and I mean... let's be honest, that became my role, didn't it? Being the town's sweetheart. At least that's how it felt to me.'

She glares at me with a look sharp enough to cut. 'Temporarily, perhaps, but you left, Juniper.'

'Well, now that I'm back, I'm thinking of staying. Especially if something's happened to my sister. My parents will need me more than ever.'

'What are you talking about?' She stiffens, shifting to the edge of the couch.

'If something awful has happened to Britt, Mum and Dad will need me here permanently.'

'But your career...'

'... won't matter,' I tell her. 'Family is more important. Maybe I'll stay and be a reporter or write a book about the history of Wildling.'

'You couldn't.' Sarah gasps, her hand flying up to her mouth. 'The history of this town is not something that needs to be splashed about in a book.'

'I'm not sure what choice I'll have. There's not much else for me to do here. Unless...'

'... unless what?'

'Unless you're right about Britt just playing around,' I

say, as if thinking out loud. 'Maybe I could stay, and Bryce and I could work things out. Perhaps he and I could go away together. See the world.'

Immediately, she's up on her feet, wild-eyed. 'You will not take my son away from his home.'

And there it is. The thought of losing her position as the town's darling stung, but the idea of losing Bryce tears her open.

'Is that what you thought Lilly would do?' I ask, standing to meet her gaze. 'You thought her accusations would inevitably take Bryce away from you?'

'Don't be ridiculous.' She moves towards her desk, putting distance between us.

'First with the baby, then by threatening him with the police.'

'I have no idea what you're talking about.'

Her eyes refuse to meet mine, and when I glance down, her hands are trembling.

'It wasn't Bryce who picked Lilly up from the station that day, was it, Sarah? It was you. Did you also take Britt because she thought your son killed Lilly?'

She swings back, eyes blazing. 'How dare you!'

'I'm calling the police,' I say, reaching into my bag. 'You killed Lilly, and you kidnapped my sister.'

Before I can get to my phone, she opens a drawer and pulls out a small handgun.

My breath catches. I step back, hands raised. 'Be calm,

Sarah. We can work this out.'

'You're just like her,' she spits, levelling the gun at me. 'Pretending to be perfect when all the while you're just a bitch.'

'Is Britt all right?'

'Oh, now you care about her,' Sarah sneers. 'She never mattered to you before.'

'Sarah, listen to me. Put the gun down. Take me to Britt.'

'You and Missy,' she mutters. 'You're just the same.'

My mind snaps back to her earlier words. *I was once the younger sister, desperate for attention. Never good enough. Always overlooked. I would have done absolutely anything to be her.*

'Sarah, what happened to your sister?'

'Everyone knows what happened. She drowned herself in the lake behind our farm.'

I study her face. The twitch of her eye. The pinch of her throat as she swallows. 'No,' I whisper as a chill floods the room. 'She didn't.'

Sarah's hand shakes as she raises the gun higher. 'You shut up.'

'Oh my God,' I breathe. 'You killed her. You were sixteen.'

'She was all anyone cared about!' Sarah screams, her voice splintering. 'My father. Even Jack. They all loved Missy. It was as if I didn't even exist.'

'Jack?'

'He's all I've ever loved,' Sarah whispers. 'Even as a young girl, watching him work the fields. He was older, and of course, could never see past Missy, with her long auburn hair and that smile. It was like the sun kissed her the moment she was born. He barely even knew I existed.'

'So, you killed her?'

'I gave myself a fighting chance,' she snaps. 'After she was gone, my father noticed me, and Jack eventually realised I could be more than just Missy's little sister.'

Sarah's confession has my mind reeling. To need love so desperately that you'd kill for it is something I can't imagine. 'Sarah, please. Where's Britt?'

She adjusts her grip on the gun, tucking her hair behind her ear. 'I wanted to kill her, but she reminds me too much of myself.'

'Sarah...'

'You'll see her soon enough. Now turn around and open the door. Don't try anything.'

'I'm doing what you ask,' I say as I reluctantly turn my back to her. 'You have my word. I just want to see my sister.'

'You should know that when the time comes, I won't show you the same mercy I gave Britt,' Sarah hisses, ordering me out of the room. 'You're no better than Missy was, and just like her, you'll get what you deserve.'

Chapter Forty-Six
Britt

WHEN I come to, the first thing I feel is the scratch of splinters against my back. My body aches from the cold floor, and there's barely enough light to see. My heart pounds in my ears, but I remind myself to stay calm. If I want to make it out of this, I have to think.

I feel around, my hands brushing against rough wood and cold metal. I'm in a small underground storage room. Tiny cracks of muted light seep in from the floorboards above, and from the musty smell of hay and mildew, I think I might be under the floor of the barn. I crawl forward on my hands and knees, trying to map out the space.

I carefully get to my feet, reaching up to check how much space there is. My palms brush the boards above, and I'm confident that if stoop just a little, I can stand. I do my best to try and shuffle forward, but my shoulder whacks into something. It topples over with a thud, kicking up a cloud of dust. I cough and wave my hand in front of my face, waiting for the air to clear.

Crates. Nothing that's going to help me get out of here.

This is a nightmare. How was I supposed to know Sarah was a psycho? That she'd fly off the handle and attack me in the shop? I thought she'd be horrified by what her son had done. Getting Lilly pregnant, then killing her to keep her quiet. Instead, she'd caught me unawares, storming around the counter and trying to drag me out. I tried to fight her off, but she was surprisingly strong. When Bryce came in, I knew I was finished. I had no chance against the two of them. When we got back here, Sarah sent Bryce back to the house and then jabbed me with some kind of horse needle. That's the last thing I remember.

Back down on my hands and knees, I feel around the space, hoping for something useful. Finally, my hand closes around a metal rod, maybe a crowbar. I grip it tightly and tap along the walls, listening for any change in sound. If I'm under the floor, there might be space around the outside of the room where I can crawl out.

Tap. Tap. Tap. The sound is dull and solid. I move along the wall, tapping and listening. *Tap. Tap. Clink.* I freeze, my heart skipping a beat. I tap again. The sound is different here – hollow. I feel around until my fingers find a raised edge. It could be the outline of a small hatch or door. My breath catches. There might be a way out. I wedge the bar into the gap and try to pry it open. My teeth clench as I pull with everything I've got, but it's no use. It's jammed shut.

The bar clatters to the floor, the sound ricocheting

through the silence. I bite down hard, forcing back the sob clawing up my throat. *Think, Britt. There has to be a way out.*

Metal grates above me, and I hear the scrape of a key sliding into the lock. Sarah is back.

'Let me out!' I shout at the top of my voice as fresh air and light rush in through the opening hatch. 'Help!'

'Britt!'

'Juniper?'

'Britt, it's me.'

Before I can respond, Juniper tumbles into the tiny room. Above us, Sarah peers down, her face pinched and angry.

'Make the most of your reunion,' she snaps. 'It won't last long.'

The hatch closes with a thud, and a key turns in the lock. I throw myself down beside my sister. 'Juniper, oh my God, I'm so sorry. I told Sarah that Bryce got Lilly pregnant. She must know he killed her to cover up the baby.'

'It wasn't him,' she mumbles, rubbing at the side of her head. 'It was Sarah. She killed Lilly. She also killed her sister back when they were teenagers.'

'What?'

'It's a long story. I read the rest of Lilly's journal.' Juniper takes a moment and then looks at me. 'Britt, Lilly was the one who killed Hazel. Out in the paddock. She saw her with Bryce. She was jealous.'

'No,' I shake my head, refusing to let the words sink in. 'She couldn't have. That's impossible.'

'I know it must be hard to hear, but it's all there in black and white. She tried to pin it on Bryce, so Sarah killed her to protect him. Sarah's a murderer, Britt, and if we don't get out of here, I'm going to be next. Mia is out looking for you, but she's in the park. She won't figure it out in time. We have to find a way out.'

Lilly killed Hazel. I can't wrap my mind around it.

'Britt?'

'What?' I snap back to find my sister staring at me.

'We have to get out of here.'

I push my hair back and try to refocus. 'There's a small door, like a hatch or something, but I can't open it,' I tell her. 'I'm out of ideas.'

'I'm not going to let us die here, Britt.'

Tears burn in my eyes, and I nod as best I can.

'I should have been a better sister to you, Britt. It's my fault we're in this mess. I don't think I've ever said it before, but I'm proud of who you are. You don't take shit from anyone, and I love that about you. In fact, I wish that I was more like you.'

I throw my arms around my sister and pull her in. 'It's funny,' I whisper into her hair, 'because I don't wish I was anything like you.'

She pulls back and searches my face for a moment before

we both break into laughter. 'I love you, Britt.'

'Yeah, yeah, I love you too,' I tell her. 'Now let's get the hell out of here.'

Chapter Forty-Seven

THE night sky hangs low and heavy, clouds smudging out the stars. I draw a breath that tastes of coming snow as images from the last time Koda and I searched Willow's Crossing flash through my mind. Hazel's decomposing body. Her mottled skin and staring eyes.

'Stop it,' I tell myself. 'It won't be like that this time. We'll find them in time.'

Koda glances up at me, and I meet his eye. 'We have to get this right, mate,' I tell him quietly. 'It might be the last search we ever do, but it matters. It's Juniper and Britt, and they need our help.'

He holds my gaze, and as always, I have no doubt he understands every word.

Daley has called in both the state and Winton River police. They'll meet us at Willow's Crossing.

From the boundary line, I stare across at the twinkling lights of the homestead off in the distance. Bryce had a head start. There's every chance the Stantons are already waiting for us, but Britt and Juniper are running out of time.

Koda and I slip onto Jack's property via the northern corner, the closest entry point to the barn where Bryce said he last saw Britt. The snow is getting heavier, settling soft and silent on my shoulders. Beside me, Koda lifts his head, a flake melting on his nose as he tries to lick it away.

As we move deeper into the property, my thoughts race ahead to what comes next. Best case is that we find the girls alive, but there will still be fallout. This will be ruled as an illegal search of a private property. Sarah and Bryce will be arrested. Jack will raise holy hell. My brother's project will lose its backing, and I'll lose my credentials as a canine search and rescue officer. Worst case is something I can't even think about.

After a few minutes, the outline of machinery sheds begins to take shape through the dark. We're still a long way off from the barn or homestead but I stop and take out the piece of Britt's jacket Juniper gave me. Crouching, I press it to Koda's nose. 'This should be a piece of cake for you, mate. All that matters is finding the girls. It's you and me. We've got this.'

I unclip his lead and give the command. 'Koda, search!'

To an outsider, Koda's weaving would look like a dog running loose, but I know better. He is focused. Relentless. He won't stop until he finds the scent source.

'Good job, Koda,' I murmur. 'You're doing great.'

I glance at my watch. Nearly midnight. Five hours since

Britt went missing.

Up ahead, Koda keeps weaving, still searching.

The snow thickens, and the wind turns sharp against my face. Conditions are getting worse. Koda stops and whines as he lifts his nose into the air.

'I know, mate,' I whisper. 'It's freezing.'

At first, I think it's the snow he's sniffing, but then his tail stiffens, and his ears flick forward. He's got something. Not a trail scent, but molecules carried on the wind. The shift in direction has given him what he needs.

'What have you got, Koda?' I whisper.

He barks once, then bolts, sprinting flat-out in the direction of the buildings.

'In scent,' I breathe, a shiver of anticipation running through me as I take off after him.

Snow lashes my face, but I barely feel it. Watching Koda tear through the night, snow catching on his coat, tail high, nose up, is like poetry in motion. He is the most beautiful thing I've ever seen, and for a fleeting second, I know that no matter what happens, whether I lose my credentials, whether Will is gone, or the future is uncertain, everything will be all right – because I have Koda, and together, we are a formidable team.

Chapter Forty-Eight
Juniper

FOR the past half an hour, Britt and I have been trying to lever the side door open. The palms of my hands are blistered, and Britt's fingers are bleeding, but it's no use. It won't budge.

I hear the sound of footsteps overhead, followed by the jingle of keys, and my heart leaps. Maybe Mia found us. Maybe the police are here. Maybe everything is going to be okay.

'Someone's here,' I whisper to Britt. 'Maybe Mia figured it out.'

'I don't hear a dog barking, do you?'

She's right, and my insides shrink. If it were Mia, we'd have heard Koda. 'That doesn't mean it's not her,' I try. 'You never know.'

Air rushes in as the hatch opens, and a ladder clatters down through the hole. 'You two, out, and don't try anything stupid,' Sarah orders. 'Hurry up.'

'So much for the rescue mission,' Britt sighs. 'This is bad.'

My mind flashes back to every true crime podcast I've ever listened to. Being taken to a second location is never a good sign, but I don't want Britt to panic. 'Let's just stay calm,' I tell her. 'Everything will be all right.'

'Wasn't all right for Lilly.'

I hold her gaze and swallow. 'I'm not going to let anything happen to you, Britt. I promise.'

She shoots me a panicked glance before turning and stepping up onto the ladder. Whatever Sarah has planned, it's happening. Desperate to get us out of this, I crouch and take up the crowbar. I keep it down beside me as best I can. It's the only chance we've got.

When Britt pulls herself up and into the barn, I begin climbing the ladder after her. But when I reach the top, a gasp escapes my lips. Bryce is standing next to his mother.

'Bryce, help us,' I gush. 'You can't let this happen. She has to let us go.'

His eyes are red, his face puffy from crying. He looks nothing like the boy I once loved, with his easy smile and irresistible swagger.

'Drop the crowbar, Junie,' he tells me. 'Please, for your own good.'

'Bryce, this isn't who you are,' I press. 'Your mother killed her sister. She's sick and needs help.'

'You shut up!' Sarah snaps, waving the gun in my face. 'Keep your mouth shut! Now drop it!'

She's coming undone. The poised, elegant woman we all

know has vanished. With her wild eyes and jerking movements, Sarah is barely recognisable. I glance at the gun and know I have no chance. The crowbar clatters back down through the hole and my shoulders slump.

'Don't listen to her, son. She's trying to trick you.'

'Bryce, I'm not,' I plead. 'Don't let her do this. At least get Britt out of here.'

For a moment, Bryce looks torn, and my heart surges with hope.

'Hurry up,' Sarah barks. 'We have to move them before that girl and her dog get here.'

Mia and Koda. That's why Sarah's moving us. Britt and I exchange a look, and for the first time, I see a spark of light in her eyes.

'Maybe—'

'Maybe nothing,' Sarah snaps. 'Now open the door. It's time to go.'

Bryce swallows hard, his eyes darting to the gun still gripped in her hand. 'All right, Mum, sorry,' he manages.

Bryce walks over and shoulders the barn door open. Immediately, winter rushes in, covering our faces with snow and sleet. I clench my teeth to try to stop myself from shivering as Sarah orders us outside. The conditions are brutal, but I know it won't hinder Koda. I scan the dark for any sign of him, but the only shapes I see are cows standing silent out in the cold.

'Keep moving!' Sarah's voice cuts through the stillness.

'We don't have all night.'

Bryce walks in front, his movements robotic, as though his body is here but his mind is somewhere else. We'd dreamed of a life together once. I loved him, and he loved me. Now he's an accomplice, chained by loyalty to his mother – something that will alter his life forever.

We trudge through the snow, cold biting through our thin clothes. Behind me, Britt stumbles. I turn, forcing a smile to steady her.

'Keep up,' Sarah snaps as we near the main house.

I trip in the dark, and Bryce reaches out to balance me. His hand brushes mine, and a jolt of memory passes between us. I want to plead with him to stop, but the words won't come.

'Mum, we need to hurry,' he urges, his voice strained. 'They'll be close.'

'We just need to get to the truck.'

He nods, and I catch the flicker in his eyes.

'Where is she taking us?' I ask. 'Where's Jack?'

'Just stay quiet,' he mutters. 'Don't upset her.'

'Bryce, please. Take me but leave Britt. She's just a kid.'

His eyes harden. 'She wasn't just a kid when she told Mum about Lilly.'

'Lilly was her best friend.'

He hesitates, then shakes his head. 'No, Mum's right. I can't go to jail, and neither can she. It can't happen, Juniper. That's not what Dad would do. I'm sorry.'

A few metres from the main homestead, a clutch of large sheds huddle together in the snow. It's where they keep the larger machinery and extra farm vehicles. Once we leave Willow's Crossing in a vehicle, Mia and Koda will never find us.

'Everyone inside,' Sarah orders.

'Where are you taking us?'

'Never mind, just get inside.'

'The police are looking for Britt, and people know I came here. They'll be coming any minute,' I reply.

'All the more reason to hurry,' she snaps. 'Don't worry, we're not going far.'

She bundles us into the back of a farm truck that reeks of hay and mould. Bryce climbs into the passenger seat, and the old leather creaks beneath his weight. 'I think we should find Dad.'

'He's on the way back with Herm,' Sarah replies. 'They'll deal with the police when they arrive.'

'Dad knows?'

'Of course. He wants to protect you as much as I do.'

'I never meant any of this, Mum,' he mutters.

'We'll take care of it. We're family. That's what we do.'

'Just like you took care of Missy?' I ask.

Sarah glares at me in the rear-view mirror. 'It's only because of Missy's sacrifice that I have this family.'

'Missy didn't sacrifice anything. You killed her so you could take what was hers.'

'Mum?' Bryce asks. 'That's not true, is it?'

'Of course not. Don't listen to her.'

'It is true,' I push. 'Don't let her fool you, Bryce. This isn't who you want to be.'

Bryce turns to look at me. He studies my face, then reaches out and takes his mother's hand. 'I believe you, Mum.'

'Good boy. Now put on your seatbelt.'

As he slides the belt across his chest, I glance at Britt, and she mouths *what the hell?* All I can do is shrug, because in this moment, I realise with painful clarity that it's true what people say – you never really know anyone.

Chapter Forty-Nine

WE reach the barn, and Koda dashes inside, bracketing from one side of the building to the other. On each side, horses shift in their stalls, hooves thudding softly against timber, breath puffing in the cold as they sense our movement.

'Britt?' I call out. 'Juniper? Can you hear me?'

I move carefully through the barn, my torch casting a narrow beam of light that picks up dust motes floating in the air. A horse snorts softly in the darkness, another shifts its weight, stall boards creaking.

When there's no answer, I call again but hear only the rustle of straw beneath our feet, the quiet shuffle of hooves, and the occasional drip of melting snow seeping through gaps in the iron roof.

Koda stops suddenly, ears pricked, and tail rigid. He turns in a tight circle, barks, then begins pawing at the ground.

'Whatcha got, mate?' I hurry over. 'What do you have?'

I crouch and shine my torch on a trapdoor in the floor.

A padlock hangs open on its latch.

'Careful, Koda. Stay behind me,' I tell him as I lever the hatch. 'Juniper? Britt?' I call down into the darkness, but only my own voice echoes back.

'They were here, weren't they?' I murmur to Koda. 'But where are they now?'

Suddenly, Koda growls. His energy shifts. The hair along his back rises, and I know there's someone behind me. I slowly reach for my phone and make sure it's in my jeans pocket.

'What do you think you're doing?' Jack barks as I get to my feet.

This is it. The moment I either cower and beg or take a stand. Behind him, Herm steps forward, and I shiver, but not from the cold.

'I believe he asked you a question, Mia,' Herm says. 'You're trespassing, and we've been over this. More than once.'

My heart hammers so hard in my chest that I can hear it echoing in my ears. 'We're searching for Juniper and Britt.'

Jack laughs, and it's a harsh, mocking sound. 'In my barn? You must be out of your mind.'

Herm's eyes bore into me. 'You've got no right to be here without a police request. You're way out of line.'

Koda presses closer, lip curling as he growls at Herm. 'They were here. Sarah must have taken them somewhere, but you both already know that.'

Jack steps in, his hulking frame looming over me. 'Get out. Now.'

Fear twists in my gut, but I stand my ground. 'Your wife killed Lilly. Now she has Juniper and Britt.'

His face darkens and he leans in, finger pointing at me. 'Now you listen to me. I'm giving you until the count of three to take that mongrel and get off my property. And tell your brother he can forget about his drilling project. You just lost him my support.'

I glance at Herm, and he grins. 'You never learn, do you?'

Every word lands like a slap. My hands tremble, not with fear but anger. I curl my fists, nails biting deep into my palms. 'That's where you're wrong, Herm,' I begin, praying my voice will hold. 'I'm sick of you and Jack thinking you run this town and treating everyone in it accordingly. Especially young women.' I turn to Jack. 'You know what he does, and you turn a blind eye. Do you know he did it to me? I was only thirteen years old.'

Jack shifts his weight, avoiding my eye.

'Don't you look away,' I snap, stepping back into his line of sight. 'He's a predator, and you let it happen. He did it to me, he did it to Lilly, and who knows how many other girls in Wildling. You're just as guilty because you've never done a damned thing about it, but that ends now. Lilly kept a journal. Everything Herm did to her is documented, and I'll back it up. I'm done staying quiet.'

But Herm just grins. 'I wouldn't get too cocky there if I were you, Mia. You've got a journal written by an unbalanced teenage girl, who everyone knows was on drugs, and your word, which is questionable at best. And right now, you're trespassing.'

He steps closer, and a shiver creeps along the length of my spine. He's too confident. There must be a reason Jack has protected him all these years. With nothing left to lose, I decide to take a chance.

'Jack, Lilly wrote about your arrangement with Herm in her journal,' I begin. 'He told her everything. What he has on you. How he'll keep using it to make you do whatever he wants.'

Jack glares at Herm, who falters under his gaze.

'That's bullshit. I never said a word about any of it, Jack. I swear.'

Jack snarls. 'Surely you're not that stupid.'

'I've kept my end,' Herm protests. 'She's lying. I never said a word about what happened at the lake.'

...about what happened at the lake.

Everyone knows Sarah's sister Missy drowned herself when they were teenagers. *Or did she?* Back then, Herm was always hanging around, desperate to befriend the rich kids. Could he have witnessed something more sinister? Is that what he's held over them all these years?

'Shut up, you idiot,' Jack growls. 'Stop talking.'

But it's too late. I've heard enough to take the risk. 'Lilly wrote it all down, how Herm uses it to control you. It's all there.'

'You damn idiot,' Jack snaps. 'Why would you tell that Daniels girl about Sarah?'

'Jack, I never said a word,' Herm insists. 'She's lying.'

They both turn on me, but I stand firm.

'Either way, she knows too much,' Jack mutters. 'Daley can speculate all he likes after she's gone, but if you're sure the journal's nonsense, there's no proof.'

'That's where you're wrong,' I counter. 'The journal is very real.'

'Maybe,' Herm concedes. 'But there's nothing in it about Sarah. That much I know, because I never told Lilly a damned thing.'

Together they step forward and Koda growls.

'You'd kill me to keep your secrets?'

'Willow's Crossing is a legacy I swore to protect,' Jack says. 'It's who I am. It's who Bryce will be. His son after him. That matters more than one girl and her dog.'

Before they can come any closer, I pull out my phone. The screen is glowing, Daley's name bright across the front. 'Daley, did you get all that?'

'Loud and clear, Thomas. We're coming in.'

'We'll never be even for what you both did to me,' I say. 'But let's call this a start.'

Behind us, Daley and the Winton River police storm in, guns raised. 'Don't move!' an officer shouts. 'You're both under arrest.'

As Herm and Jack are cuffed, Koda and I step in beside Daley.

'This isn't over,' I tell him. 'We still have to find Sarah and the girls.'

'The state police are on their way. They should be here any minute.'

'Britt was here. Probably Juniper too. Sarah moved them, which means they're still alive.'

Daley eyes me. 'What are you thinking, Thomas?'

I stare out the barn door, into the dark. 'I'm thinking they're still out there, Daley, and I'm going to find them.'

Chapter Fifty

Britt

THIS is all my fault. As we bump along Wildling Road, I close my eyes and silently scream that if this can all just be a dream, I'll go back and keep my mouth shut. I won't try to find out what happened to Lilly. I won't read the journal. I won't tell Sarah that her son is a scumbag.

Since I was a kid, I've spent my whole life doing everything I could to piss off Mum and Dad, to punish them for not loving me as much as they loved Juniper. I didn't care that it meant screwing up my own life, because what did it matter? I didn't matter. I wasn't Juniper.

Now, sitting beside her, I can finally see she isn't perfect. She's not some fairytale princess who has everything handed to her, or a mythical unicorn gliding through life on a rainbow.

All this time, I've been sabotaging myself, and for what? Her life is just as messed up as mine – as everyone's.

Instead of letting the scream escape my lips, I close my eyes and silently promise that if somehow we don't end up dead, I'll stop hating my life and start actually living it. Wildling sucks, but God, I'd give anything to be home right now. *Anything.*

Juniper reaches out and takes my hand. I thread my fingers through hers, and a tear slips over my cheek. 'I don't want to die,' I whisper.

She squeezes my hand so tight it hurts, but in a good way. 'You won't, Britt. I won't let that happen.'

'I'm sorry for being such a pain in the arse.'

She looks at me through the dark and gives me a tight smile. 'I love you, Britt. Everything will be all right.'

'Quiet!' Sarah barks. 'We're almost there.'

The truck turns right and rattles up a long drive.

'This is the access road to Sarah's parents' property,' Juniper whispers. 'What's she doing?'

At first, I have no idea why she's brought us here, but as the truck passes the homestead and continues across the back paddock toward the southern corner, my stomach sinks.

'Oh my God, Juniper...'

My sister turns to me, wide-eyed, as the realisation of Sarah's plan hits her too. She's taking us to the lake where she drowned Missy.

'Sarah, no!' Juniper shouts. 'You can't do this!'

Sarah doesn't answer, and Bryce snaps his head towards his mother. 'Mum, what's going on?'

'They're loose ends.'

'You're going to kill them?'

'We have to.'

He turns around and stares wild-eyed at Juniper. 'Mum, no, you can't.'

'What did you think was going to happen?'

'I... I don't know.'

Bryce turns again and considers us, huddled together in the back seat.

'Please, Bryce,' Juniper cries. 'You can't let her do this.'

'Mum—'

'Quiet!' Sarah snaps. 'You started this, Bryce. Let it be a lesson to you. Everything you do in life has repercussions. One thing affects another, then another, like ripples off a stone skipping across the water. Your bad choices led us here. Now you're going to take responsibility.'

He stares at her through the dark. 'Wait... you want *me* to kill them?'

'That's right.'

Bryce recoils, his back pressing against the door. 'Mum, no. I can't.'

'You need to learn your lesson.'

I steal a glance at Juniper, my heart bashing against my ribs. Her eyes are vacant, staring straight ahead. She's trying to be brave for both of us, but I know she's as terrified as I am.

Out in front, the lake looms dark and inky. I close my eyes and try to remember the last place I felt safe. If this is happening, I need to take myself somewhere else. Anywhere but here.

When the truck moans to a stop, Sarah and Bryce get out. I try the handle, but it's locked and the last of my hope drains away. I want to scream, to fight, but my body won't move. My mind is disconnecting, dragging me to a place where I don't have to be a part of what's about to happen.

'Gag them and bind their hands,' Sarah orders Bryce. 'There's cable ties in the glove box. Old rags too.'

'Mum—'

'Just do it, Bryce. We don't have time.'

'Mum, the police know you have them. This isn't going to work.'

'Herm and your father will deal with the police. They always do.'

'But—'

'Stop arguing and tie their hands. Then get them out and bring them to the edge of the lake.'

Bryce opens the car door and leans close to Juniper. 'I'm going to put these on, but I'll leave them loose,' he whispers. 'I'm sorry.'

'Bryce, don't let her do this, please,' Juniper sobs. 'You can't.'

'Just play along, okay?'

Juniper nods, and Bryce wipes the tears from her face. 'It's going to be okay. Just hold out your hands.'

Outside, the wind has picked up. It blows in through the open car door, picking up our hair and tossing it across our faces. Bryce binds our wrists with the cable ties but leaves them loose enough to slide off. We play along as he leads us down toward the lake, where Sarah is waiting. The snow is so heavy now it's blinding, each breath scraping cold into our lungs.

'Now what?' Bryce shouts to his mother over the wind and snow.

'Now you walk them over to the old jetty and push them in.'

He squares his shoulders, breathes deep, and nods. 'Come on,' he tells us. 'Let's go.'

Juniper kicks and struggles against him. I can't tell if it's real or part of the ruse, but her muffled screams ignite a new wave of panic in me. Sarah's still standing in the headlights, the beams of light illuminating her against the heaving sky.

Underfoot, the jetty is slick with ice. We inch forward as best we can. Juniper stumbles, and Bryce throws an arm out to try to steady her. For a second, I think I see something in his expression. It's hard to tell through the dark and the snow, but it gives me a flicker of hope.

At the end of the jetty, water churned up by the wind slaps against the timbers. Darkness has stitched the lake to the sky, and all I can see is black.

Onshore, Sarah watches us, her gaze fixed. Bryce steps closer, and my chest tightens.

'I'm going to have to push you both in,' he says. 'When

you hit the water, slide your hands out and swim to the other side. If you stay under, she won't see you, not through this snow. It's all I can do. I'm sorry.'

Juniper screams but her gag muffles the sound.

'She has a gun,' Bryce tells her. 'If I let you go now, you won't make it. I hope you'll be okay. You were always a good swimmer, Junie. I never wanted this.'

His flat tone strips away the last of my hope. Bryce is just as broken as his mother. Out here, in the freezing black water of this lake, Juniper and I are going to die.

Chapter Fifty-One

KODA and I step out into the cold. The wind knifes across the rear of Willow's Crossing, sharp enough to sting my eyes. I fumble in my pack for his snow booties, my fingers stiff and clumsy in the cold. Conditions are worsening. By morning, there'll be at least ten centimetres of snow on the ground. Over the coming weeks, even down here in the valley, lakes will freeze, and the trees will turn to skeletons. If Sarah has left the girls outside in an old grain silo or shed, they won't survive the night. If they're anywhere nearby, we have to find them. Tonight.

'All right, Koda. Last search. You ready?' He glances up, then out across the fields. 'We can do this. We've been in worse situations before.'

I hold Britt's fabric under his nose one last time and give the command. Without hesitation, Koda launches himself into the falling snow, unbothered by the harsh conditions. He brackets across the gravel yard outside the barn, nose down, clearly following a trail. Within minutes, he spins, barks, then surges forward. *In scent.*

I run after him, but when he reaches a cluster of sheds, he stops and paws at one of the roller doors. *Could it be this easy?* I wonder.

'Daley, come in,' I say into my radio.

'Daley, over.'

'Koda's got something, a few metres from the barn. Can you come over?'

'On my way.'

Daley arrives and swings open the oversized shed door. Inside is a tractor, a small excavator, a quad bike... and one empty space.

'Shit. She's taken them in a vehicle,' he says. 'You won't find them now, Thomas. Koda's good, but that's impossible.'

Shit!' I curse and march back out, shrugging my pack off and tossing it onto the ground. I rub at the back of my neck and curse again, only this time louder and with more passion.

'You did your best, Thomas. And Christ, you stood up to Herm and Jack,' Daley says, coming to stand beside me. 'You did it, kid. You took on the most powerful men in Wildling and won.'

'But Juniper and Britt are still in danger.'

'The police will handle it. They'll get the rego and track the vehicle. You did your best. Koda can't—'

A gust of wind tears across the field, cutting him off. The air current shifts to the south. I lift my hand to silence him. 'Wait. Look at Koda.'

When we left the barn, Koda had his nose to the ground, trailing Britt's scent from the barn to the shed. Then it was lost. But now, as I watch him lift his head to the wind, nose twitching, my pulse spikes.

'Daley, hand me my pack.'

'What?'

'My pack. Now. Hurry!'

He passes it over, and I sling it onto my shoulders, my eyes locked on Koda. 'Any second now, he's going to run.'

'What?'

Before I can answer, Koda barks. Once, twice, three times, and bolts, vanishing into the dark.

'Get the police and follow my coordinates from the car!' I shout back.

'Mia, what the hell is happening?'

'Air scent!' I yell. 'The wind shifted. He's got them!'

Up ahead, Koda stretches out, bounding across the snowy ground. Nose high. Tail straight. If the wind is right, his nose can catch a scent source from twenty kilometres away. Wherever Sarah has taken the girls, Koda has found the scent cone.

Around us, the storm intensifies. Snow blows in sideways, turning the night into a swirling blur of white. My breath comes in heavy puffs, visible in the cold air as I struggle to keep up with Koda. His brown fur is stark against the snow as he bounds over the rise and fall of the land, never missing a beat.

'Koda, good boy!' I shout, even though my words are immediately swallowed by the wind. We've trained for this but seeing him in action amid a snowstorm is something else entirely. He's a blur of motion as he leaps over a fallen log, never breaking stride.

My flashlight beam cuts through the dark, but it's Koda who leads the way, his instinct taking over. The snow stings my face and my legs burn, but I push on, determined to keep up as best I can. Koda disappears over a rise, and I scramble to follow, boots slipping on the icy slope. At the top, I stop and stare down into the valley. A truck sits parked by the lake at the back of the Gilmore property, headlights blazing against the storm.

'Good job, Koda!' I shout, my voice raw. I fumble for my radio. 'Daley, I've got them! The lake, south corner of the Gilmore property.'

'On our way, Thomas. Do not approach. Do you hear me? She could have a weapon.'

A weapon.

Koda is already too far ahead, and the conditions are too intense for me to call him back. He'll never hear me. Instead, I reach inside myself and find every ounce of energy I have. I need to catch up to him. I have to stop him before he reaches Sarah.

Chapter Fifty-Two
Juniper

I WANT to hurt Bryce. I want to tear at his hair and claw at his face. I want to beg and cry. I want to scream, kick, and lash out until there's nothing left. But out here in the relentless snow and cold, on this icy jetty, there's nothing I can do, nothing that will save us from the freezing black lake below. Even if we managed to run, by the time we reach the start of the jetty, Sarah will be there with her gun. All we can do is get out of our ties as soon as we hit the water and try to swim to the other side of the lake before we die of hypothermia.

In this cold, we'll have about fifteen minutes before our bodies start to shut down. From memory, the opposite shore is about a kilometre away. Maybe we can make it. We can't splash or make noise, but maybe—

Then it hits me. How could I forget? Britt can't swim.

I glance at her, and she stares back. Unblinking, her eyes are wide with fear. I hold her gaze, silently vowing that I won't leave her. If Britt dies, I die. That's just how it is.

I take one last look at Bryce, my eyes pleading with him

to let us go. Then, without hesitation, he pushes me over the edge. The world tilts, and I'm falling, the wind rushing past my ears. My scream is muffled by the gag. The freezing water hits me like a wall of ice, shocking every nerve in my body. The cold is overwhelming, seeping into my bones and stealing my breath. My heavy clothes drag me down, and I sink fast, the darkness swallowing me whole. Eventually, I kick out and break the surface. I struggle out of my ties and swim over to one of the old piers. Gasping for breath, I cling to it as best I can.

Above, I hear the scuffle of Britt's feet on the boards, then a splash as she hits the water and vanishes beneath the surface. Forcing my numb limbs to move, I lunge toward her and catch her just as she bursts up, eyes wide, still bound. I drag her beneath the jetty, yank out her gag, and slip the ties from her wrists. Her skin is already turning blue.

'Hold on to the pier,' I tell her. 'The only chance we have is to stay hidden until they're gone.'

Britt nods, and I wrap my body around hers, desperate to give her any warmth I can. The cold is unbearable. After only a few seconds, my strength begins to wane, but I refuse to give in. 'I won't let you go, Britt,' I promise her through chattering teeth. 'Not now. Not ever.'

Chapter Fifty-Three

'KODA!' I shout as best I can. 'Stop!'

He's too far ahead. Locked onto the scent and running into the wind, I have no chance of calling him back.

Every step is a struggle. The ground has turned into a boggy mix of ice and slush. Through the snow, I can barely see more than a few metres in front of me.

'Koda, stop!' I scream again, but he keeps running. I push harder, ignoring the pain in my legs and the cold seeping into my bones. Every muscle protests, but I force myself to keep moving, to keep following him.

I climb through the fence that separates Willow's Crossing from the Gilmore property. As I draw closer to the lake, I catch sight of him up ahead bounding toward the shape of an old jetty. Sarah's truck sits idling by the water's edge, her shape silhouetted by the glow of its headlights.

'Koda!' Every instinct he has is working against him, carrying him straight toward her.

Over on Wildling Road, I catch the outline of a truck turning onto the Gilmore property. It has no lights on, there's no police car accompanying it, and no sign of Daley. *Why aren't they flying up the road, lights flashing?*

Koda barks, and Sarah whips around at the sound.

'Canine Search and Rescue,' I shout at the top of my voice. 'You have a working dog approaching.'

Sarah's hand rises. I follow the motion and see the shape of a handgun pointed at Koda.

'No!' I scream. 'Put your weapon down!'

Oblivious to the danger, Koda keeps running as a gunshot rings out, splitting the air. My heart lurches, and a knot of terror tightens in my chest.

'Koda!'

I sprint toward the embankment, snow and slush spraying up from my boots. When I reach the shoreline, Sarah lies half sprawled in the water, her hair fanning out around her. The gun is still clutched in her hand and a bloom of red spreads out across out her chest, stark against the snow.

'Mum!' Bryce screams, running toward us and throwing himself down beside her. 'Mum, no, get up!'

I stumble back, and scan the vast sprawl of the Gilmore property for any sign of movement, for anything that will explain how Sarah was shot. The headlights from her idling truck throw light across the lake, cutting through the snow flurries. Beyond that, everything dissolves into shadows.

Nothing makes sense. No muzzle flash, no second figure. Just Sarah's truck idling beside the lake, its engine humming while the storm whips whitecaps across the water's surface.

'Who did this?' Bryce howls, his face twisted with grief. 'Who shot her? Was it you?'

He lunges at me, but I pull back, losing my footing in the mud. Before he gets close enough, his legs buckle and he collapses onto his mother. A low, guttural sound escapes his chest, matching the howl of the wind.

Somewhere in the distance, Koda barks and relief surges through me. Whoever killed Sarah can wait. I need to find him and the girls. I stare out into the darkness, and squint, trying to see through the snow.

Behind me, the wail of sirens grows louder as the police convoy finally closes in. Blue and red lights sweep across the paddock and I turn to see Daley's ranger truck leading the way. Tyres fight for traction on the slushy ground, spitting up snow and gravel as the vehicles tear along the access road, then skid to a halt near the fence line. Doors slam. Officers spill out, radios crackling, their shouts lost to the storm.

Koda barks again, and my head snaps back toward the lake. Finally I see him, further along, spinning in a tight circle as two figures stagger toward the shore. Juniper stumbles forward, dragging Britt along beside her. Their clothes cling to their bodies, ice-crusted hair plastered to their faces. Britt's legs drag limply behind her and my heart lurches.

'Daley, over there!' I call, pointing to the girls. 'Where's the ambulance?'

He spots them and takes off at a run, his torchlight jerking across the dark. 'Enroute! Five minutes out.'

My boots splash in the shallows as I dash after him. As I get closer, Koda bounds toward me, tail high, oblivious to having almost been killed. 'You're all right. You found them,' I whisper, clutching his wet face with both hands. His fur is ice-cold, clumped with snow and mud. 'You did it. You're such a good boy.'

Out in front, Daley wades into the lake. When he reaches Juniper, the water is up to his knees. She instantly collapses against him, never letting go of Britt.

'Juniper, Britt!' I shout as he guides them in. 'Are you all right?'

Juniper looks up and manages a nod. Her hair is plastered to her face, and her skin is grey. Beside her, Britt's teeth chatter so hard she can barely speak, but she's alive.

Together, we hoist the girls up the embankment and toward a fallen log. They ease themselves down and Daley wraps his jacket around Britt's shoulders.

'They'll be okay,' Daley says. 'They're lucky, though. A few more minutes and—' He cuts himself off, shaking his head.

Around us, the flashing lights of emergency vehicles give the property its own uneasy pulse. Down by the lake, a police officer kneels beside Sarah's body while another tries hauling Bryce to his feet. Despite what they did, the pain of it all is hard to watch. As he fights to stay with his mother's body, I turn away and glance back toward the access road. In the dim wash of light, the lone truck I saw first entering the property moves off slowly, fading into the dark.

'Thomas,' Daley says with a nudge, drawing my attention back. 'Ambos are here.'

I tear my gaze away from the disappearing truck and see two ambulances racing toward us, their lights flashing. Relief hits so hard my knees almost buckle.

'Thank God,' I whisper. 'Not a moment too soon.'

Daley and I pull Juniper and Britt up. They stumble more than walk, hanging off our shoulders. Juniper's face is grey, her jaw locked tight. Britt's shaking so hard she can't keep her head up. Her lips are colourless and her face looks hollowed out, as if the cold's scraped the life right out of her.

'The police will have questions,' Daley tells them gently, 'but that can wait. Let's get you warm first.'

The paramedics wrap them in foil blankets. Their voices are brisk but kind, and their hands are steady. When the girls are helped onto stretchers and loaded into the ambulances, I finally feel my body fall slack.

It's over.

Daley and I step aside as the last paramedic climbs in and shuts the doors. The siren blips once, and the ambulance rolls off down the access road, taillights swallowed up by the dark.

'I feel like I could sleep for a week,' I say with a sigh. 'Big night.'

'Huge,' he agrees. 'I'll be on scene for a while. Want me to organise a ride?'

I shake my head. 'Nah. I'm wired. The walk home will do me good.'

He tilts his face to the sky. Dawn is bleeding over the horizon. The snow's stopped, and the wind has eased to a low sigh. I follow his gaze, and for a moment, the timing feels almost deliberate.

'You're sure?'

'I'm okay,' I tell him. 'I need to decompress.'

I hold his gaze for a moment. The weight of the night's events still hanging heavy between us.

'I'm proud of you, Mia,' he says quietly. 'You did real good. Koda too.'

I kick at the ground, and consider hugging him, but change my mind. 'I couldn't have done it without your help,' I say instead. 'You always have my back. I won't forget it.' I pause a moment and take one last look over the property. 'Anyway, I'll see you.'

I turn, and Koda falls in beside me as we head out along the Gilmore access road.

At the front gate, I step out onto Wildling Road and then stop. Instead of turning left toward home we go right, headed for Mimi's. When we get there, she's already on the porch, a curl of steam rising from her cup of tea.

'You're awake early,' I say.

She nods, warming her hands around the cup. 'Sounded like a bit of trouble over at the Gilmore place. Woke me up. Looks like you've had a night, kiddo.'

I glance back toward the farm. 'You could say that. Sarah Stanton is dead. Jack and Herm are in custody.'

Mimi tilts her head. 'That so?'

'Sarah kidnapped Juniper and Britt Davis. She tried to kill Koda.'

'You don't say?'

I study my grandmother. There's something different in her eyes. 'Any chance of a lift back to town? I was going to walk but I'm more tired than I thought.'

She sets her cup down gently. 'I'd love to, kiddo, but you know I'm not allowed to take my old truck off Wildling Road.'

I nod slowly. 'You've got a good view of the lake from up there, Mimi.'

She peers across. 'Not so bad.'

'It was you, wasn't it? That shotgun you keep in the truck. You saved Koda.'

'You finally outed Herm?' she asks, ignoring my question. 'He'll pay for what he did?'

'Looks that way.'

'Jack's in custody?'

I nod.

'And Sarah's dead.'

'She is.'

'Then it don't matter who did what,' Mimi says with a knowing look. 'The three debts have been repaid.'

'Three?' I ask. 'Lilly and Hazel. Who's the third?'

Mimi stares out toward the Gilmore farm. 'I always liked young Missy. She had sass. Never did believe she was the sort to take her own life.'

I stare at Mimi in surprise. 'How could you know?'

But in usual Mimi fashion, she just nods and sips her tea. 'You have a safe walk home now, kiddo.'

Chapter Fifty-Four
Three Months Later

WILDLING is blanketed in white. Most winters, I welcome the snow. I take comfort in the way it transforms the world, creating a stillness that erases the imperfections of the past. But this year, no amount of snow will ever cover the things I've seen, the pain I've felt, or the secrets I've uncovered.

Everything is different now.

I'm different.

The Sweetie's firepit crackles beside us, warm and welcoming, as Koda presses in against my leg.

'Hey, sorry we're late,' Juniper says as she and Britt sit down. 'There was a bit of debate over who would drive.'

'Still navigating sisterhood, then?' I ask with a grin.

'Something like that.' Juniper and Britt share a smile, and the warmth between them is clear.

After they recovered from almost being killed on the Gilmores' lake, Juniper wrote a story that ran on the front page of nearly every newspaper in the country. She's since been offered a book deal and her own podcast. The *Sydney*

Daily begged her to come back, but so far, she's still here in Wildling.

'Anyway, thanks for coming to meet me,' she says. 'I have news.'

I lean in, eager to hear it. Over the past three months, she and I have grown close. Juniper is probably the first real friend I've ever had, and I secretly hope her news is that she's staying for good.

'Wildling used to have a newspaper. Do you remember?'

'Sure,' I say. 'The *Wildling Gazette*.'

'Well, I was thinking of bringing it back to life.'

'Juniper, that's amazing,' I gush. 'Does that mean you're staying?'

She nods, and beside her, Britt beams. Last week, Britt enrolled to start back at school next semester. Whether she'll stay in Wildling after graduation is anyone's guess, but at least now she has options. Whatever she chooses, I know she'll make her mark.

'I'm so happy to hear that,' I tell Juniper. 'If there's anything I can do to help...'

'Well, you can be my source for everything that happens in the national park for starters.'

We share a smile as Amelia approaches the table, pen and pad in hand.

'Okay, you three,' she says. 'What'll it be?'

Juniper and Britt give her their orders, and I scan the menu. As soon as I see it, I grin.

'You know what?' I tell Amelia when she looks at me. 'I'm going to have the eggs benedict.'

Epilogue

KODA and I take our time walking home. He sniffs as I stroll thinking about Juniper and Britt and what incredible women they are. Wildling really does feel different these days – lighter, as if spring might come early this year.

My phone buzzes in my pocket, and I take it out. Daley's name lights up the screen.

'Thomas.'

'It's happened again,' he says, urgency sharp in his voice. 'And we've got souls unaccounted for. You and Koda need to get in here. Now.'

'Where this time?'

'Where do you think?'

'Shit,' I mutter. 'I'll grab our things and be right there.'

Despite Jack's fall from grace, two months ago Jason's geothermal drilling project was given the green light by the State Government. His company wasted no time setting up the rig in the western corner of the park and firing up the operation.

Since the drilling began, there have been three landslides. Small ones, but serious enough to leave their mark. The first buried two hikers under snow and rubble. Koda and I found them, but it took the SES hours to dig them out.

And that was just the beginning.

The second destroyed a stretch of trail used every spring by families wanting to see the wildflowers. The third wiped out part of a fence at Sam Cassidy's brumby sanctuary.

It's hard to believe the timing is a coincidence. Jason's rig churns day and night, a giant metal mosquito drilling into the earth's veins, and the mountain seems to be bleeding because of it.

But each time, Jason swears it's nothing to do with the drill.

'It's not the rig, Mia,' he said last week, his tone equal parts exhaustion and exasperation. 'You're overthinking it.'

Maybe I am. Or maybe I'm not.

Jason's reaction to my involvement in solving the murder of Lilly Daniels and Hazel Smith hurt me. He didn't trust me. He thought the worst and put his career first. But he's my brother, and we're trying to move past it.

I haven't told him how much the landslides scare me. How I hold my breath every time I hear the faint rumble of the rig in the distance. It feels like a betrayal, doubting him, and I know better than anyone how much that can hurt. But with every landslide, my doubts grow.

'Thomas, there's something else,' Daley says, his voice dropping. 'And it won't be easy to hear.'

The line falls silent. I stop walking and hold my breath. 'Daley, what is it?'

'It's your brother, Mia. He's been reported missing.'

DEADMAN'S HOLLOW

BOOK TWO

WILDLING K9 MYSTERY SERIES

Chapter One

The snow comes in whispers.

Tiny flecks of ice drift through the early morning light like ash, dissolving as soon as they touch my face. Koda moves ahead of me, nose low, tail straight out in a tight, purposeful line. Around us, the world is blanketed in a silence stitched together by ghost gums and frost-glazed rock.

'You've got this,' I whisper to Koda. 'Keep going.'

The missing campers have been out here for four nights. Long enough for dehydration, exposure, and panic to have set in. Long enough for the mountain to have swallowed them whole.

Koda threads through snowgrass and low scrub, nose twitching. His breath clouds white against the grey morning, ears flicking like tuning forks. He pauses at the edge of the creek and noses the surface. I kneel beside him, my gloved fingers skimming the ground.

'Whatcha got, Koda?' I ask. 'Hey? Whatcha got?'

The pattern is shallow, softened by fresh snowfall, but

there's no mistaking it – the sole of a hiking boot.

'Good job, buddy,' I tell him. 'Not much further now.'

Koda pushes ahead, nose to the ground, while snow drifts sideways across the ridgeline. It's mid-September, technically spring, but up here the seasons don't listen to calendars. Snow still clings to the ridges, iced hard in the mornings and melting to slush by midday. Even at fourteen hundred metres, the air is cold enough to numb my fingers. The wind swings through without warning, stealing warmth and throwing flurries into my eyes. One minute you can see forever. The next, the park disappears.

The campers, a group of environmental researchers from Sydney, lodged a Trip Intention Form with NSW Parks that should have seen them out two days ago. When their nominated contact, the sister of Rajesh Patel, raised the alarm, police requested that Koda and I lead the search. We're one of two canine teams. There's at least twenty other searchers out here, more to be brought in tomorrow if we come up empty-handed.

Up ahead, a granite formation the locals call Razorback Ridge looms into view – pale, time-scoured boulders jutting from the slope like vertebrae. Above us, a helicopter beats its way across the sky, low enough to rattle the air in my chest.

This is the first time we've searched this corner of the park since Jason went missing four months ago. It's too rocky for skiers, even in heavy snowfall, and tricky to access.

Koda halts and stares at a patch of broken snowgrass up ahead.

'What is it?' I ask, crouching to his level. 'What do you see?'

He glances back at me and pulls against his harness. Overhead, storm clouds hunch over the western range and the air shifts – subtle and unmistakable.

The rest of the search team is spread across the lower country behind us – police, SES, community volunteers, and the other canine unit, working the marked trails to the east. Drones picked up nothing on thermals. Radio chatter has been quiet for the last hour. No sightings. No objects. No leads. If Koda's right, whatever went wrong happened up here, where the land is higher, rougher, and already slipping into weather that's turning mean.

I pull the radio from my shoulder and press the button. 'Daley, it's Thomas. Come in.'

Static, then my boss's gruff voice booms onto the line. 'Daley.'

'They're up here. We're at approximately fourteen hundred metres. Koda's getting close, but—' I glance west. Clouds are thickening over the ridgeline, dark, low, moving faster than they should. Classic pre-front behaviour '—the weather's about to turn.'

'Then head back,' he says. 'I'm not risking losing my best team up there.'

'Rain will rewrite the ground,' I say, more to myself than Daley. 'Wash out the scent trail.'

'Did you hear me, Thomas? Get back down here. Now. That's an order.'

I snap my gaze across the range. At fourteen hundred metres, the country sits in an uneasy middle ground – too high for shelter, too low for clean snowpack. Snow gums stoop against the slope, white trunks twisted and scarred by wind. Beyond them, the mountains roll out in dull-blue waves, ridge after ridge fading into cloud as the weather closes in.

'Roger that,' I say. 'Wind's picking up. Heading back now.'

I replace the radio and breathe in. Damp earth. Granite. Rain, closing in fast.

Snow dusts the chocolate fur along Koda's spine, clinging to the feathering around his legs and tail. His ears are pricked into the wind. He reads the weather better than I ever will.

'We should head back,' I tell him. 'It's the smart thing to do.'

He barks and prances on the spot, eyes darting from me to the trail ahead and back again.

'You think we're close, don't you?' I glance over my shoulder at the track back to base. Even now, it's a solid two-hour trip.

If we turn back now, whatever trail Koda's found will

be gone. We could return later and switch to air-scent, but we're already close. I can feel it.

'Looks like a rain front. We've survived worse,' I tell him. 'I'm brave if you are.'

Koda barks and pulls against the harness. I'll keep him on the long line. Bad weather isn't the time to risk losing sight of him up here, which means I need to keep up and not end up on my arse in these slippery conditions.

I unclip the radio. 'It's Thomas, come in.'

'You'd better be on your way down.'

'Yeah, about that—'

'God damn it. What did I say?'

'We're too close. Once the rain hits, we're done. We'll have to start from scratch. You know that.'

'What I know is that you're a pain in my arse.'

'I care about you too,' I say, unable to stop the edge of a smirk. 'We'll get them. Keep the medivac chopper on alert. Won't be long now.'

I replace the radio and centre myself. This might be a mistake, but if someone was out here looking for my brother, I'd want them to keep going. Whoever these campers are, they have people who love them. People sitting hunched on couches right now, hands clenched, eyes red from crying. If we're their only chance, we can't turn back. I trust my dog. And if he says they're close, then they're close. Koda is never wrong.

About the Author

Nikki Lee Taylor is an Australian author. In 2024, she was awarded the Sisters in Crime Scarlet Stiletto Award for Crime Fiction. Her latest title, Wildling Road, also won the 2025 Hawkeye Manuscript Development Award.
Nikki has written three independent titles, including International Bestseller *The Secrets We Keep, The Truth We Tell*, and *The Alibi.*
Nikki is a former news journalist, coffee addict, dog trainer, and competes in canine scent work trials with her dog Saxon. She lives in Newcastle, NSW.

Let's Stay In Touch

I love to hear from my readers and endeavor to answer all emails personally.

You can reach me at **nikki@nikkileetaylor.com**

- Website: nikkileetaylor.com

- Substack: nikkileetaylor.substack.com

- Insta: nikkileetaylor_author

- FB: Nikki Lee Taylor

- Goodreads: Nikki Lee Taylor